CALL ME BY **MY NAME**

CALL ME BY MY NAME

John Ed Bradley

Atheneum Books for Young Readers
NEW YORK LONDON TORONTO SYDNEY NEW DELHI

ATHENEUM BOOKS FOR YOUNG READERS
An imprint of Simon & Schuster Children's Publishing Division
1230 Avenue of the Americas, New York, New York 10020

Jacket design by Russell Gordon
Book design by Bob Steimle
The text for this book is set in Adobe Caslon Pro.
Manufactured in the United States of America
First Edition
2 4 6 8 10 9 7 5 3 1
Library of Congress Cataloging-in-Publication Data
Bradley, John Ed.
Call me by my name / John Ed Bradley.—First edition.
p. cm
Summary: "Growing up in Louisiana in the late 1960s, Tater Henry, has experienced a lot of prejudice. Despite the town's sensibilities, Rodney Boulett and his twin sister Angie befriend Tater, and as their friendship grows stronger, Tater and Rodney become an unstoppable force on the football field. Rodney's world is turned upside down when he sees Tater and Angie growing closer. Teammates, best friends—all of it is threatened by hate Rodney did not know was inside of him. As the town learns to accept notions like a black quarterback, some changes are too difficult to accept"—Provided by publisher.
ISBN 978-1-4424-9793-1 (hardcover : alk. paper)
ISBN 978-1-4424-9795-5 (eBook)
[1. Race relations—Fiction. 2. Prejudices—Fiction. 3. Friendship—Fiction. 4. Football—Fiction.
5. African Americans—Fiction. 6. Louisiana—History—20th century—Fiction.] I. Title.
PZ7.B72466Cal 2014
[Fic]—dc23
2013031133

For Kim and Hannah

★

CHAPTER ONE

★

The distance was to blame. It made him hard to categorize. "Is that one of them Redbones?" Curly Trussell asked, reaching for a bat just in case.

I lowered my mitt and strained for a better look. The kid was about a hundred yards away, moving past the pool and the pool house and the snowball stand, where "She Loves You" was playing over speakers attached to the roof. Then he crossed Market Street and entered the old shell road that ran between the tennis courts and the civic center. He was heading straight for us now, arms pumping, steps keeping time to the music. The way he carried himself, you had to wonder if he thought he was welcome. A splash of sunlight fell from the trees and caught him just right, and I could hear gasps from some of the guys. We'd all seen maids in South City Park before, and a few old trusties from the jailhouse pushing mowers and pulling weeds, but except for them, black people weren't permitted. They couldn't ride bikes or drive their cars through the park, let alone play ball there. The town had a place for them.

It was May of 1965, and school had just let out for the summer.

There were hundreds of us scattered over three fields waiting for tryouts to begin. Until this moment I'd been loosening up with the other Pony League kids—playing catch, swinging a bat with a doughnut on the barrel, and running sprints in the weeds.

"Look at him, Curly!" Freddie Sanders yelled. "Look close. That's a full-blown colored if I ever saw one."

Then a bunch of them ran to the road and grabbed shell to throw.

I couldn't see how the kid posed much of a threat. He was on the lean side, with an overall construction so rickety you wondered if he even *ate*. Give him a different skin color and he could've been one of us—just another kid with dreams of glory in his head. His striped tube socks climbed up to his kneecaps and his black All-Stars had holes punched in the fabric. A short-fingered infielders glove hung from his belt and shone with a fresh coat of linseed oil, and the rest of his clothes—the gray T-shirt tucked into jean shorts, the faded feed-store cap—might've come from my own closet.

He was showing no fear that I could make out, and maybe that added to why they had such a problem with him. "Let's get him!" Curly shouted. "Let's make him pay." And now the shell started to fly.

It couldn't have hurt much because it was mostly powdery chips and pieces, but it was enough to drop him to the ground. He curled up in a defensive posture, arms wrapped around his head, legs wheeling, as if he were riding a bike. Everybody laughed at how scared he looked, including some of the adults. These were the players' fathers who'd volunteered to coach the teams.

"Hey, boy, nobody wants you here," one man called out.

"What is wrong with you, little brother?" said another. "You wake up this morning hankering for a beating?"

Then Curly let out a war cry and went hauling off in the kid's direction. He stood over him with the bat held high above his head, hands wrapped around the handle. He looked like somebody with an ax about to chop some wood, only today the wood was the kid's head. I figured he was probably just trying to scare him, but I also knew that it wasn't wise to take chances with a person like Curly, and so I decided to do something. I ran up to him and caught him square in the back first with a shoulder and then with a forearm. Both Curly and the bat went sailing in the weeds.

The shell kept falling and the kid kept bawling. And finally I covered his body with mine.

He was scrawny in my arms, like sticks in a sack, and his breath smelled of toothpaste, the cinnamon kind. That he was a skeleton who brushed his teeth made me feel even sorrier for him. "Don't you know the rules?" I asked him.

"What rules?"

"You're in the wrong park. They don't let Negroes in here."

"Who doesn't?"

I couldn't answer that so I let it pass without trying to.

We waited until the shell stopped coming. I got up and brushed myself off, then I lifted him to his feet and dusted him off too. I put his cap back on. Then I pointed to where we should go and started walking with him there. We went past the pool and down a path in the woods that wound to the bayou that formed the park's western border.

"You'll be fine once you make it to Railroad Avenue," I told him.

A pedestrian bridge crossed the bayou to the other side. He got about halfway across and turned around. "I just wanted to play some ball," he said.

"Not here you can't," I said. And already I was trying to understand what I'd done, the risk I'd taken. I'd have to explain myself when I got back to the Pony League field. I'd have to argue that I still was as white as everybody else.

And what would I tell Pops if he found out?

The kid stopped again on the other side of the bridge, and this time he cupped his mouth with his hands. "My name is Tater Henry," he said.

"Rodney Boulet," I answered, saying it the old French way: *Boo-lay*.

I watched him take a dirt trail that cut between large ranch-style houses. These were houses where white people lived, which meant the trail was for whites only.

Tater was up near the street when a man appeared and stood in his yard yelling. He was yelling the usual things you heard when a black person turned up where he wasn't supposed to be and you had to put him in his place.

Tater lifted an arm and waved as if he and the man were old friends, then he kept on his way.

I was with Angie when I saw him again a few weeks later. He was raking out clumps of grass clippings in front of one of the old mansions on Court Street. I could hear a mower coming from the back lawn. The side gate in the iron fence was open and you could see a black man through it, his bald head shining with sweat as he cut rows running parallel with the fence and the street.

Angie and I were on our bikes heading toward downtown and J. W. Low to pick up something for Mama. I slowed and wheeled back around. "How you been, Tater?"

He kept working. He didn't say anything.

"Did you go out for baseball at the black park?" I asked him.

He shook his head.

"How come?"

"You can't see? I got me this job instead."

I watched him a while. He had his cap turned around on his head, and his long socks had fallen down to his ankles. He looked to be about my age, which was ten going on eleven. He might've had the skinniest calves I'd ever seen. His skin was darker than I remembered. "Is your name really Tater?"

"Tatum."

"Ta*tum*? So Tater's your nickname?"

He nodded and picked up the pace with his rake. After a minute he turned his back to me. "I'm sorry, but I need to work." And he glanced over at the gate.

"See you."

"See you too, Rodney."

I caught up with Angie at the dime store. She was in the sewing-needs section, digging around for a certain kind of ribbon that Mama wanted. "He's the only black person you've ever talked to, isn't he?" she said.

I didn't have to think long. "Yes, he is."

"Did it make you feel tingly all over?"

"What is that supposed to mean?"

"Nothing," she said and then laughed.

"Have you ever talked to a black person?" I asked.

"All the time."

"Where?"

"Everywhere. I ain't scared."

I knew it was a lie. "Pops would kill you," I said.

"Not if he didn't find out," she said, which was true, of course. He couldn't kill her as long as it remained a secret.

Then that winter we ran into Tater again. The lawnmower repairman also bought pecans, and Pops took Angie and me there to sell the ones we'd picked at our grandparents' farm. Tater was inside the small metal building with a sack of his own. He didn't have many. He'd wheeled them over in a toy wagon with rust-eaten holes in the bed and in the words RADIO FLYER on the sides.

He looked at me, and then he looked at Angie, but he seemed to know better than to look at Pops. I would've talked to him had Angie and I been alone. In a minute he was gone, the empty wagon clattering behind him.

"You pay the blacks the same amount per pound you pay the whites?" Pops asked the man who was doing the weighing.

"Same price."

"Now that ain't right," Pops said.

The man shrugged. "A pecan is a pecan."

"The hell it is," Pops told him.

Pops was like that—ornery, and always wondering why he had to be the one to come up short when everybody else was getting more. Now the man was telling him that black pecans were no different than white pecans. I could see Pops's face flame red and the veins in his neck puff up. "We'll just have to agree to disagree," he said.

The man didn't have to ask him about what. Instead he reached into Tater's pile and came out with a single pecan, then he removed a second pecan from our bag laying on the scales. He held his hand out, one pecan next to the other in his palm. They looked identical to me.

"That one's ours," Pops said.

The man was slow to smile. "Be reasonable," he said.

"I'm telling you, that's the white pecan."

The man tossed the pecan Pops had chosen into Tater's pile, and then he dropped the other one into ours. The man hadn't paid Pops our money yet, but that didn't stop Pops from lunging at him. A table stood between them, and Pops nearly knocked it over trying to get at him. Pecans spilled to the floor and puddled at our feet.

"Get out," the man said.

"Six bucks," Pops said, and stuck his hand out.

The man removed a wad of cash from his pocket and threw a couple of bills at Pops. "Get out," he said again.

On the drive home we sat side by side in the cab of his truck, an old Chevy Cameo. In our haste to leave, our usual seating arrangement had been confused, and now I was stuck between him and Angie. I could feel the heat coming off his body, see the sweat like dew drops in the hair of his forearms.

"I don't like the way the wind is blowing," he said when we were halfway home. I leaned forward and looked off at the trees even though I knew he was talking about Tater's pecans.

The next time we saw Tater was at the Delta, the movie house in town. He was waiting in line at the colored entrance. He was wearing nice clothes—church clothes, probably—and there was a lady with him. She kept her hands on his shoulders.

Then again in somebody else's yard, weeding a flower garden. Then standing at the colored window at the Shrimp Boat, waiting for a dinner order. Then out in front of the Coke plant, watching a white man on a forklift load crates on a truck.

Time went by, years went by, and I kept seeing him everywhere—this kid I'd never noticed before; the kind I wouldn't let myself notice until that day he showed up in our park. How does somebody go from being invisible to being everywhere you look? How is he suddenly there when he didn't exist before?

He wasn't a friend yet, but he was familiar and we always acknowledged each other. Most times he just touched the bill of his cap, but on occasion he'd wave. Then he started calling out my name and I started calling out his. And eventually he even felt safe enough to call out Angie's.

He waited four years before coming back out for baseball. It was 1969 now, and he came up the same route as before, walking past the pool and the pool house and the snowball stand, crossing Market Street, and then entering the old shell road half-dancing to whatever music was playing. My age group had graduated to the Babe Ruth League, and once again we were waiting for tryouts to start. Unlike before, nobody threw shell at him. Instead they all stood together and stared, and they really let him have it with their mouths.

"Hey, boy, you get lost on your way to the projects?" one of the coaches yelled.

"What's wrong, my man?" another of the dads shouted. "Haven't you heard what happened to that preacher in Memphis?" That was Martin Luther King Jr., murdered the year before.

Tater just kept coming. When he got closer and it started to look like Curly might go at him again, I stepped out a ways to make sure there weren't any problems. Puberty had found me the year before, and I was already six-foot-two and two hundred and thirty-five pounds. I was what Mama called "husky," and when we shopped for my clothes we had to drive an hour to Baton Rouge to find a specialty store for the big and tall. The one good thing about being so large was that nobody messed with me—*ever*.

"Good to see you, Tater," I told him.

"You too, Rodney."

I walked with him through the guys staring wild-eyed and the men chewing toothpicks, and we set up off to the side and started playing catch. He had a good arm and his throws popped in my mitt, making everyone turn for a look.

"They hate me and they don't even know me," he said between throws. It wasn't that he felt sorry for himself. It was more like he suddenly needed to say something that was true.

"Don't let it bother you," I told him.

Then he threw the ball so hard I thought for sure he'd broken a bone in my hand.

Tater dazzled us all during the tryout, or at least those of us who bothered to pay attention to him. He still had that little oil-wet glove, and even though it was no bigger than his hand, nothing got past him. During drills, one of the coaches hit fly balls in the outfield, and we took turns catching them, and when one came off his bat too hard and sailed high over our heads and past us, it was Tater who broke from the group and chased it down, catching it at a full gallop with his back to the hitter, like Willie Mays. He could throw the ball on a rope from the outfield fence to home plate, and he was fastest on the base paths.

The coach of the Redbirds, Junior Doucet, won a coin toss and made me the first pick of the draft, and all those boys later he made Tater the last pick. Tater had outperformed the other kids and me, but he'd come to us black, and for that he had to wait. That the park allowed him to play at all was the biggest surprise, although I learned later that some of the coaches thought the federal government had sent Tater to test town leaders who'd been resisting integration.

One day that summer I got up the nerve to ask Tater why he was there.

"South City Park is closer to where I live," he said. "It's less than a mile away. North City Park is more like three miles."

"We thought maybe you were sent to infiltrate the white culture and gather information for rabble-rousers bent on toppling our way of life."

"Who told you that?"

I didn't want to admit that it was Pops so I said, "I just heard it around."

Tater shook his head. "It's two miles difference, Rodney. I don't own a bike."

Mama worked at home as a seamstress. Pops worked as a night watchman at the plant in town where they made cooking oil.

He punched in at 11:00 p.m. and punched out at 7:00 a.m., five days a week. Even though he had to get his sleep during the day, he still never missed any of my games, including those with early afternoon starts. I'd always look for him on the other side of the fence down on the first base line, standing by himself in his blue clothes, the leather strings on his steel-toe boots hanging loose. He never cheered or said anything when I got a hit or picked off a base runner trying to steal. He kept quiet even when we won close ones. My teammates said he looked "hard to know." I explained that he'd served in Korea and just wasn't one for any nonsense.

I inherited my size from Mama's people. She actually stood two inches taller and weighed about fifty pounds more than Pops. She called her business Unique Boutique, and she specialized in evening gowns. Ladies were always coming to the house to get measured, and there were always bal masque outfits draped over the furniture. You'd have to sit on the floor to watch TV so as not to rumple the pretty things she was making.

Mama suffered from lupus and didn't feel well outside in the hot sunlight, and this kept her from attending many of my games. Over supper I'd have to tell her how they went, and whenever I described something sensational like a grand-slam home run or a triple play, she'd turn to Angie and say "Is your brother lying again?"

Angie was on the South City Park swim team and sometimes had to practice when I was playing, but she made most of my games and sat in the bleachers behind the backstop. She showed up with a sketchbook and a paint box full of colored pencils, and she made pictures of whatever caught her fancy: a player sliding into home, the pitcher coming out of his windup, dragonflies lighting on top of a batting helmet. Most people never guessed that we were twins—Angie was a green-eyed blonde and trim, while I was a brown-eyed monster who could make little kids cry if I looked at them too long—but Angie herself always said we were "one and the same and nobody without each other."

I believed this to be true, although we probably weren't much different from most twins. We shared a room and slept in beds pushed up next to each other until a year ago when she got her first period and Pops decided it was time to turn the sleeping porch into a bedroom. I liked having my own space, but some nights I felt so lonely I couldn't stand it. I'd return to Angie's room, clear out a place on the floor next to her bed, and sleep there on a pallet of pillows.

Today she was wearing a tank top and short shorts. You could see the tan lines on her shoulders left by her bathing suit, and she had a tied-off leather string hanging from around her neck with a key at the end of it.

The key opened the lock on the rear gate of the park's pool yard. Angie wore it like jewelry, she once explained to me, because it was good luck and a source of pride and something no other swim team member had, not even Craig Fink, the boys' captain and a state champion in the breaststroke. The key meant she could let herself in anytime she wanted, and she often did so, bicycling to the park at 5:00 a.m. to get some laps in before the pool house opened at seven. Angie was oblivious to the reaction she brought out in guys our age, but that didn't stop them from saying things.

"God, she's fine," I heard Randy Billedeaux say at the start of batting practice.

"Knock it off. That's his sister," Tater said before I could speak up.

He and I were waiting for our turns at the plate. Five cuts were all you got before games, and things moved fast.

"We're what's called fraternal twins," I told him, for some reason thinking he should know. "Mama might've carried us at the same time, but somehow we came out different. I was born before she was, but I never knew if that's why I'm so much bigger."

"I had me a twin once," he said.

"What do you mean you had one?"

"It was a girl too. Rosalie. She came out already deceased. That's what my auntie told me, anyway." He pronounced it *ahn-tee*. "My great aunt, I should say. She's my mom's mother's sister. I live with her."

"Why don't you live with your parents?"

"I just don't."

"But why don't you?"

"Because I don't, all right?"

I couldn't imagine life without my parents, but life without Angie would be even worse. "All right," I told him.

By the bottom of the fifth inning the score was 9–0. We were winning again, and the game must've been boring to watch because the bleachers were quiet and even Angie had stopped cheering. The league had a ten-run rule, which meant we needed only one more run for the umps to call the game. Tater was the first batter up, and I was right behind him in the lineup.

"Which one of you is going to end this thing and let us go home?" Angie called from her seat.

I was in the on-deck circle. I lowered my bat and lifted my gloved left hand over my head. Tater stepped out of the batter's box and signaled for a time-out. Now he raised a hand too.

"Do it for me, Tater," Angie said.

He shook off a laugh and seemed to have trouble regaining his concentration, but he still managed to crush the first pitch that came at him. The ball flew high over the left field fence for a home run, and the game was over. Tater ran around the bases at a slow jog. He crossed home plate and fell into my arms and those of our teammates. Then he casually walked over to the backstop. Angie was standing and applauding along with everybody else. Tater pointed at her. "You asked for it," he said.

But the old lady standing in front of Angie thought Tater was talking to her. "I did?" She tapped a wrinkled hand against her chest. "Why, thank you, boy."

I guess that taught him. Tater would hit more home runs that summer, but he never again was quite so proud of himself afterward.

★ ★ ★

We lived about a mile from the park on Helen Street, and even after Pops converted the porch, the house still had only about a thousand square feet of living space. There was one bathroom for the four of us, and it was barely large enough to hold a sink, a toilet, and a tub. The house had a TV antenna on the roof and striped metal awnings over the windows. We thought the asbestos siding was pretty, especially during a rainstorm when the material repelled water and shone with a pearl's iridescence.

Pops wasn't a complicated man, but I still didn't understand him. His happiest moments seemed to come when he was by himself—out fishing at Bayou Courtableau or tending to his vegetable garden behind the house. He grew some pretty tomatoes, along with cucumbers, squash, snap beans, and eggplant. He'd put the vegetables in brown A&P bags and drive in the Cameo from house to house, knocking on doors and taking his hat off when somebody answered. "We're about drowning in them," he'd say as he handed over each bag. It was strange seeing him be all generous with the neighbors, especially when you compared him to the Pops we got at home. Angie always said that the only time we saw flowers in the house was on days after Pops had a moody spell and needed to make up with Mama.

We couldn't afford to have a black lady come in and clean the house like others on the south end could. These neighbors weren't well off either, but their jobs as bank tellers and schoolteachers and auto mechanics earned them enough to hire full-time maids and yardmen. I couldn't imagine how little a maid and a yardman were earning if they depended on the guy from Lalonde's Cajun Plumbing for their livings.

That first summer with Tater was just starting when one of the guys on our team, Marco Miller, pulled me aside during practice and told me he had a secret. He looked around to make sure we were alone. "Tater's auntie, the lady he lives with . . . ? She's our maid. She cleans our house."

"Yeah?"

"Her name is Miss Nettie. Last night I rode with my mother when she took her home. I knew Miss Nettie had somebody she was raising, but I didn't know it was Tater until we got there. It was starting to drizzle, and he came outside with an umbrella. I don't think he saw me, but they live in a shack. It's so small, it looked more like a doghouse than a house where people live."

Tater was in the outfield shagging flies. We both looked at him.

"So that's your secret?" I said.

"Mom told me Tater's father shot his mother, then shot himself. Tater was just a baby in the house in a crib, but that's how he wound up with Miss Nettie. Miss Nettie is *old*. She didn't want to take him, but there wasn't nobody else."

Something jumped in me, sort of like the way it did that day they threw shell at him. I'd known Marco Miller since Little League and never had a problem with him. But right then I felt like laying him out. It was his tone I didn't appreciate, the satisfaction he took in letting me know that Tater was a kid nobody wanted.

Making me feel almost as bad was knowing that Tater had kept this information from me. I'd thought we were better friends than that. "Don't tell this to anybody else," I said to Marco.

"How come?"

"Because it's nobody's business. And don't let him know that you know."

"Don't let who know?"

"*Tater*. Come on, man. Who else?"

Along with the size, I had a death stare that I liked to use to instill fear in my opponents. I gave Marco Miller one now.

"I hear you," he said, and walked off.

I didn't go straight home after practice. Instead I rode my bike a distance behind Tater and followed him up Bertheaud Avenue to where it crossed Railroad Avenue and the train tracks to Burleigh's corner grocery. He went into the store and came out a few minutes later with some ropes of licorice and a bottle of red pop, then he walked up Washington Street a couple of blocks to Park Avenue and took a left. The neighborhood changed now from white to black. I'd heard stories about white kids who'd had their bikes stolen out from under them when they drifted into this part of town. But it worried me more that Tater would catch me tagging behind him.

He walked up a ways under the shade of some gnarly old cedar trees and hung a right on Abe Lincoln Street. The house he went into wasn't much, but it wasn't as bad as Marco had described. A yellow porch light was burning and a single kitchenette chair stood on the front porch. Fig and kumquat trees grew in the side yard. The back had a wire fence keeping some chickens in, along with a small coop made of rusty wire and gray boards.

We were still inside the city limits, but the place looked like it belonged in the country alongside a road nobody drove down anymore.

I rode up closer and halfway hid behind a tree. A car drove past—either a Firebird or a Camaro, I couldn't tell which—and I could hear music even though the windows were up.

As well as I thought I knew the town, and as much as I'd roamed it, this place was like finding a door in your home that you'd never noticed before and opening it to a room that you hadn't known was there. It occurred to me that there was a world I knew nothing about, and this was the world of colored people. God or somebody or something had made things in two parts—the white part and the colored part, and here was that other one. They must've had college-educated professional people like doctors and lawyers and teachers. They must've had priests and preachers and morticians and accountants and insurance agents. But I had never seen those kinds among them. I'd only seen the ones who worked in the service trade. In other words, the ones who served the whites.

I was getting ready to head home when Tater poked his head out from the screen door, then bounded off the porch and came running toward me.

"Hey, Rodney," he said. "My auntie wants to know if you'd like to have supper with us."

"No, thank you, Tater."

"She's frying pork chops."

"That's okay."

"Did you hear me, man? I said pork chops. You're going to take a pass on pork chops? What is wrong with you, brother?"

I left him and started pedaling as fast as I could down Railroad Avenue. I wasn't far along when I heard him call out, "Okay, be that way then," and finally, "Bye to you too."

Railroad ended and became Parkview Drive, and now the houses got bigger and some were brick. I shouldn't have raced off, but the prospect of dinner with him and his aunt had made me nervous. Pops could barely tolerate seeing Tater and me play ball together, and I knew how he'd act if he ever learned that I'd gone so far as to share food with him, too.

As I rode home, I kept wondering about the differences between the world where Tater lived and the one I came from. Four years ago Pops had been able to tell a black pecan from a white one, and that was only a starting point. I'd also heard him call dogs that belonged to black people "black dogs," even though their fur was white or brown or some other color. A dog could be purebred with papers, but if it belonged to a Negro, it was a black dog and nowhere near the equal of the lowest mutt that belonged to a white person. Cars were "black cars" when black people owned them, and it didn't matter if their paint jobs were actually white or green or some other. There were black stores, too, and black clothes and black music and black food. And to Pops the color always meant not as good. Even when applied to a human being like Tater.

I got home and could smell Mama's cooking out in the carport. It was fried pork chops, and I figured there must've been a sale today at the A&P for the white shoppers as well as the black ones. Angie was setting the table as I came through the door, and

Mama was at the sink mashing some potatoes. It got hot inside whenever they used the stove, which was a big Chambers installed in the 1940s when the house was built. Pops was sitting over by the window unit, reading the paper and trying to keep cool. He had the Astros game on the radio, and he was already dressed for work, his hair swept straight back and showing comb marks. He hadn't put on his boots yet, and you could see his white ribbed socks folded over at the ankle.

Maybe because I still had the story about Tater's parents in my head, but I glanced over at Pops's Chiang Kai-shek rifle hanging on a rack on the wall. He'd taken it off a dead enemy soldier and displayed it now as a trophy for all to see. Right below it and covered with a frilly dress half-made was Mama's sewing machine.

"Rodney, where you been, son?" Pops said, and lowered the volume on the radio.

I propped my bat with my mitt hanging from the barrel against where the pie safe met the wall.

"Practice, and then I followed Tater Henry home."

"You followed him home? Why would you do that?"

"Just curious, I guess."

"I don't understand," he said. "What could there possibly be about a colored boy that makes anybody curious?"

It was the kind of question that really was a statement, so I figured he didn't require an answer. I sat in my chair.

Angie's freckles came out whenever she got too much sun, and they were out now on her cheeks and the crown of her nose. Even though the house smelled of fried food, I could smell chlorine when she sat next to me.

Pops came over and joined us at the table. "Rodney," he said, meaning he'd selected me to say grace. I made the sign of the cross and said the prayer in what felt like slow motion, knowing that if I went too fast, he'd only have me say it over again. I finished and reached for the potatoes.

"Tater invited me to supper," I said.

"Supper, did he?" Pops said. "Imagine that—supper with the brothers and the sisters."

"I told him I couldn't."

"They prefer to be called Negroes or coloreds," Angie said.

"Were you polite?" Mama asked. "Did you thank him?"

"Thank him?" Pops said.

"It wouldn't have been the first time I ate black food," I said. "I spent the night at T-Boy Bertrand's once, and his maid cooked supper. It was fried chicken, turnip greens, smothered black-eyed peas, and cornbread."

"Was it good?" Mama asked.

"It was delicious."

"Mama's cooked all those things before," Angie said. "What made what you ate at T-Boy's black food?"

"Because the maid cooked it?" I answered in the form of a question, which let her know how ignorant she was.

Then we looked at her, all three of us, in a way that must've had her wondering if we'd ever really noticed her before.

★★★

More and more people started turning out for our games. Nobody said it was because there was a black guy playing in the white park, but I couldn't think of another reason to explain it. Where in years before, you'd get one parent for every player on a team; now both parents showed up, along with siblings and grandparents, and even cousins and friends from the neighborhood. The younger people in the crowds probably came to see a special talent play, but I agreed with Pops and his theory about why so many older folks were showing up—they wanted to be there in case the Black Panthers marched on the park and the white youth needed protecting.

The bleachers filled up early, and people ringed the field with lawn chairs. They brought metal ice coolers stamped with beer logos, and they popped their cans and drank. Their feet were propped up on the wire fence.

We won all our games that month. Tater played center field and hit third; I was the catcher and cleanup hitter. If any of the guys on the other teams were ugly to him, I never saw it. However, I did hear that a gang of potheads jumped him one day when he was walking home. They'd been hiding behind a large brick barbecue pit in the picnic area, and Tater had to fend them off with a stick.

"Wasn't nothing," Tater said when I asked him about it.

"Did they hit you?"

"Yeah, they hit me. But I hit them back."

Over the July Fourth weekend we faced the Steers. We were both undefeated and dominating all the other teams, and the winner would claim first place and the fast track to the town's Babe Ruth League title. Curly Trussell was the Steers' best player, and he'd already pitched a no-hitter against the league's third-best team, mainly by throwing curveballs, sliders, and other junk of such quality that he had everybody rocking back on their heels and whiffing.

Half an hour before our scheduled 5:00 p.m. start, the field was packed four deep along the base lines. We were taking batting practice when I heard the first heckler. Tater was at the plate. On the other side of the fence was a man with a can of Old Milwaukee in his hand. He leaned heavily against the dented chicken wire and belched.

"Hey, batter batter," he said. "Hey, batter batter . . ."

I'd heard the chant before, but then the man substituted the word "batter" with something else, and Coach Doucet immediately came running over and yelled at the man to watch his mouth.

"How you do that, Junior?" the man said. "Watch my mouth?" Now he crossed his eyes and looked down his nose. "Show me how you do that."

Coach Doucet didn't have an answer, but at least he'd distracted the man, and Tater was able to finish his swings.

"What a bunch of garbage," I said as Tater walked past me.

He leaned his bat against the fence and walked into the dugout for his glove. "Let it go, Rodney."

"You didn't hear the name that dude was calling you?"

He shook his head. "Let it go," he said again.

Coach Doucet and the coach for the Steers met with the umpires at home plate and exchanged lineup cards, and I drifted out past first base, looking for Pops. He wasn't in his usual spot, and I couldn't locate him on the other side of the field either. "Here, Rodney," I finally heard him call out. And I spotted him with Angie and Mama in the bleachers behind the backstop.

It really did something to me, seeing my family there, Mama especially. She was wearing a straw hat and big, square-frame sunglasses, and she'd brought a fan to help with the heat. The lupus alone should've kept her home and out of the sun, but I also knew she was ashamed of her weight and dreaded bumping into people who might remind her that she was a beauty in high school and the first runner-up in the 1949 Yambilee Queen pageant.

I had Curly to worry about, so I didn't let myself dwell on Mama for long. He was only about half my size, but he was so intense that kids in the park said he belonged in Pineville, a town in the central part of the state where there was a big hospital for mental patients. His father ran a bar on the parish line, and nobody but her customers ever saw his mother anymore. Curly might've been white trash, but he could really make you look stupid, and I looked extra stupid my first two times at bat when I didn't even get the bat off my shoulder and watched one fastball after another run past me.

Tater didn't do any better. He popped up to the first baseman and struck out, his first strikeout of the year, and now he was coming up again in the bottom of the last inning with two outs and the Steers leading 4–3. With the win so close at hand, Curly was throwing even harder than he had to start the game, and his junk pitches were working better than ever too. Tater swung and missed at two curveballs, and then Curly followed up with three errant fastballs, all of them high and away, making the count full. The next pitch was identical to the first two, and Tater did a surprising thing. Just as the ball was leaving Curly's hand, he stepped up to the front of the batter's box and squared off to bunt. The ball met his bat and dribbled toward third, and he outran the throw to first.

I was next. I walked out to booing and stood outside the batter's box and looked over to where Mama and Pops and Angie were sitting.

"You can do it, Rodney," I heard Tater call out, his voice clear to me even though hundreds of other people were yelling for me to fail.

I set up deep in the box, choked up high on the bat's handle, and shifted my weight to my back foot. I'd decided to forgo any titanic roundhouse swings this time and to simply try to make contact with the ball. Tater took a three-step lead, and Curly looked him back one, and now the ball was coming toward me. As soon as it left Curly's hand, I picked up the rotation, or lack of one. It was a knuckleball, widely advertised as the toughest pitch there was to hit. But this one didn't move or bounce around much, and the reason was probably because it was the first knuckler Curly had thrown all day. From where I stood, the ball looked as big as a dinner plate, and without being conscious of what I was doing I strode forward and met the pitch the moment it crossed the plate. It didn't feel like I'd hit it hard, and I thought I'd just lost the game with a pop-up to the infield.

But then I saw Tater leap in the air as he broke for second, and I looked up and located the ball in flight. It had already climbed higher than all the other blasts I'd hit that summer, and it was still climbing when it connected with a light tower on the other side of the fence. I heard a report like a rifle shot, and then the ball ricocheted back into the field.

All Tater and I had to do now was touch each base and home plate and the game was over, but as he cleared third I saw something flying toward him from the direction of the pitcher's mound. It was Curly's glove. Tater stopped to avoid being hit, but then Curly charged and knocked him to the ground. The two of them tumbled in the grass between the field and our dugout. I left the base path and ran over to help, even though by now Coach Doucet had grabbed Curly and pulled him away.

Curly was kicking his legs and swinging his arms and making sounds like an animal in a fight with another animal when it understands that to lose is to die. I helped Tater to his feet and saw a trail of blood at his nose. Then Curly's father moved past us in a blur of ear hoops and jailhouse tattoos. I thought he'd come to defend his son, but instead he reared back with one of his biker boots and nailed Curly in the stomach, knocking him on his back. Until now I'd always thought I had it bad with Pops. He'd beaten me before with belts from his closet and switches from the ligustrum hedge, but I couldn't recall ever taking a boot in the gut.

"Can Rodney and me cross home plate now?" Tater asked.

"Go on," Coach Doucet said, then waved us on like a traffic cop.

We made it across, but the thrill of what we'd done was gone. Most of our teammates, afraid to get close to Curly's father, had already returned to the dugout, and a different excitement had come over the field. The umpires were meeting on the mound with parents of some of the Steers, and then Coach Doucet joined them. If I was hearing right, he was arguing for justice, a word I'd never heard mentioned at a baseball game before. Finally the ump broke from the group and walked over to where Tater was sitting.

"You're suspended for the rest of the summer for fighting," he said.

"That was Curly fighting," Tater said.

"You're telling me you weren't fighting?"

"That wasn't fighting. I was trying to get him off of me."

"You also showboated on your way to second. They might abide that kind of behavior on the north end but not here. Get your things together and go home. That's an order."

Tater turned to Coach Doucet. "But I just jumped a little when Rodney hit it."

"Let's go," the ump said.

"For the rest of the summer?"

"One other thing. You never brought a release from your parents when you signed up to play. Without that release you don't qualify." The ump worked himself out of his chest protector and removed his shin guards. Clouds of sweat soaked his black shirt, and you could smell his body odor from ten feet away. "We got rules on this side of town, and if you expect to participate, you have got to respect them," he said. "I should've sent you packing weeks ago." And now he pointed to what must've been an imaginary door out of the park.

"What about Curly Trussell?" came a voice from the other side of the backstop. I didn't have to look to know it was Mama.

"Curly was provoked," the ump said.

"He was not provoked. He started it."

"He's suspended for one game, and if he curses or throws his glove again, he's done, just like this one."

"Well, you should be ashamed," Angie said in the loudest voice yet.

"I didn't make the rules," the ump said, "I just enforce them." And with that he gathered up his equipment and left the field.

The ump's other job was working the register at a convenience store called the Fill-A-Sack, and I told myself it would be a long time before I ever went there again.

"She Loves You" wasn't playing over the park speakers, but you might've thought it was to see Tater on his way out. I figured he was trying to give the appearance that everything was fine. Still, I was sick for him. I thought about running after him, but then Angie jumped down from the bleachers and took off in his direction. I waited with Mama and Pops until she came back.

"I invited him to my swim meet Friday," she said.

"You did what, Angela?" Pops said.

Angie didn't answer. She knew he'd heard her the first time.

"They won't let a colored boy anywhere near that pool," Mama said. "Rodney, ride your bike on up ahead and tell him politely that your sister made a mistake."

"Why me, Mama? Make Angie do it."

"Just go tell him, please. That poor young man doesn't need another situation, and I certainly don't need the whole town talking about the colored boy who watched my daughter gallivant around half-naked at the pool."

"I don't do that," Angie said. "It's a swim meet, Mama. I swim."

"Rodney, go on, boy," Pops said.

I rode through trees and past the picnic grounds crowded with barbecue pits to where Tater was crossing the pedestrian bridge over the bayou. I tried to figure out what to say to him, and I didn't know what that might be until I finally said it. "Hey, Tater, they don't have swim meets on the north end?"

His expression let me know the question wasn't one he'd expected, especially from me. "What are you trying to say, Rodney?"

"They'll just treat you bad again. It'll be worse than today."

"If I let things like that worry me, I'd never leave the house." He was standing in the middle of the bridge, and he leaned against the railing now and spat at the water below. "Was it Angie who sent you?"

I shook my head.

"Your mama's a nice person, Rodney. I heard her yelling at that ump. But it was Angie who asked me to come see her swim, and unless Angie takes the invitation back, I plan on being there."

He spat one more time before leaving.

A tall hurricane fence surrounded the pool yard, with three strands of barbed wire running along the top. About ten feet from the fence were two stands of bleachers that were close enough to some oak trees to get shade, which made it tolerable for Mama, even on the worst summer days. Whenever Angie had a meet, we tried to arrive about an hour early to claim seats up on the top bench for the best shade and the best view. We arrived earlier than usual today, with more than an hour to spare, and Tater was already there waiting.

He was wearing a white button-down shirt with long sleeves, navy dress pants, and penny loafers with soles barely scuffed. He also had on a new cowboy belt, carved with his name, TATER HENRY, in the brown leather.

"I wish I could get you to dress like that," Mama said, and cut me a look. It was July and hot, and I had on cutoffs, a T-shirt, and flip-flops—what I always wore on days like this one.

Pops was quiet. He couldn't have been happy seeing Tater, and he'd had only about three hours of sleep all day. His feet banged against the board planks as he led us up to our spot. To protect against splinters, he'd brought a pair of foam seat cushions, and he set one down for Mama, then used the other for himself.

"Tater, how are you, son?" Mama asked, and looked over.

"Doing pretty good, Mrs. Boulet. How are you?"

"Will you tell your auntie something for me? Will you tell her I said you shine like a brand-new copper penny today?"

"I appreciate that, Mrs. Boulet. She's the one that bought me this outfit. I hope it isn't too much."

"Of course it isn't. Would you like to come sit with us?"

Pops started gnashing his teeth, the muscles in his jaw working. Then he pulled at the crotch of his pants, as if he'd just now noticed how tight they were.

"Come sit," Mama said to Tater.

"Yes, ma'am," and he tried to suppress a smile. I could smell him—equal parts hair oil and Aqua Velva—even before he slid over.

For a few minutes all you could hear was the noise from the pool. Then Tater said, "Why aren't you on the swim team with Angie, Rodney?"

"I have baseball. I couldn't do both."

"You can swim, though, right?"

"Yeah, I can swim. Can't you?"

"No. I've never even been in a pool."

"Not ever?"

He shook his head.

"Not even a baby pool?"

"I tried to take lessons. I heard somebody talking about it at Redbirds' practice, then I saw a paper on the pool-house door when I was walking home one day. I came and got in line with my dollar fifty—that's what it cost to take them for the summer—and when I got to the desk, that old lady, Miss Daigle, said I needed to leave because they didn't want any darkies in the water."

"She called you that?"

"Not exactly. She said they didn't want darkies, then she said she was going to call the police if I didn't leave that minute."

It was hard to hear, and I was relieved when Angie and her teammates came out to loosen up and swim practice laps. I gave a sharp whistle to let her know where we were sitting, and she answered with a wave.

The sun had combined with chlorine to streak her hair with gold strands. Bands of muscle and sinew stood out on her long limbs. Every time she came out of the pool dripping with water, I wondered how we could be related, let alone twins.

"Is he with you?" I heard somebody say. It was a park employee, standing behind the bleachers.

"Yes, he is," my mother said.

"That colored person there?"

"That's right, George," Mama answered when Pops wouldn't. "This is Tater Henry, my son's teammate on the Redbirds."

George Fontenot was older, maybe sixty. Dressed all in khaki, he usually handled maintenance at the park. "Yeah, all right," he said. "He's the one got kicked out for picking a fight with the Trussell boy."

Tater had come wearing all new clothes and a belt with his name on it, and even they weren't going to be enough to spare him today.

"George, your pool looks lovely," Mama said.

"Kind of you, thanks. Every morning at seven o'clock sharp, when I skim the surface, I wish they'd built it somewhere else on account of them trees. You can get the leaves easy enough, but it's the moss that gives you fits. Who builds a pool next to trees?"

"Only somebody with a man like you, George," Mama said.

You could see what her words did to him. He no longer was worried about Tater. Instead he hitched up his pants and went back to spearing trash with a nail at the end of a stick.

The meet featured only three teams, ours and two others from nearby towns. Angie easily ranked as her team's strongest individual female competitor, and she also anchored the girls' relays. There was no limit to the number of events a single swimmer could participate in, and by the last race Angie had already won four medals, three of them gold and one silver. Tater and I stood tall and cheered like crazy people without a thought to how it might be taken by the visitors from out of town.

As Angie was stretching before her last event, a man looked back at us from his seat at the bottom of the bleachers and spoke to my father. "Is all that really necessary?" he asked.

Pops didn't answer, and the man got up and walked over to the fence. He stood leaning against it, but I could tell he wasn't done yet. Right before the swimmers stepped on their starting blocks, he returned to the bleachers and sat in his old place.

"Please ignore us," my mother said. Then she brought a finger up to her lips and gestured for Tater and me to keep quiet.

It must've been the man's daughter who swam the second leg of her team's last race, a freestyle relay. When the girl in that spot hit the water, he started yelling, "Kick, kick, kick," but actually saying, "Keek, keek, keek." She was a strong swimmer and built a two-stroke lead, which the next girl was able to maintain for the team's anchor. The bleachers were shaking as people pounded their feet on the boards. I whistled again right before Angie dove into the water for her team's last leg. By the time she reached the other side, she'd already caught up to the leader. She passed the girl after coming out of her turn.

Both Tater and I had forgotten Mama's warning to keep quiet, and we were making more noise than anyone else in the bleachers when

Angie thrust ahead by half a dozen strokes to end the race. Next came the medal ceremony, and we might've escaped without incident had Tater not thought to add one final cheer.

"Keek, keek, keek!" he shouted.

Pushing between spectators, the man climbed the bleachers and grabbed Tater by the throat before any of us could react. Pops reached for the guy, but lost his balance and fell sideways against the boards. I landed a right to the side of the man's face and whipped his head back, but somehow he held on to Tater. It was Mama who stopped him. She gripped his earlobe and pulled it, as if she'd lost one of hers and needed a replacement. Tater broke free and fell over coughing and spitting out ropes. Then Mama let the man go.

"What is wrong with you?" she said.

It was a while before the man could answer. "You know what's wrong," he muttered.

It was time to leave. "You're not walking home alone," Mama said to Tater. "Let's go. You and Rodney climb in back."

We sat on the bed with our backs against the bulkhead. The wind felt good after the moist heat under the trees, and I had a moment to think about what had just happened. I seemed to understand that for as long as we were friends and he was black and I was white, there would be apologies to be made—if not for my own words and actions against him, then for the words and actions of others.

On Abe Lincoln, Pops pulled up to the curb, and Tater jumped out even before we'd come to a stop. It was my first good look at him, and I saw the smudges on his shirt and the rips to his pants. His neck was red and there were four round marks, each about the size of a dime, left by the points of the man's fingers.

Pops had his window rolled down and his arm poking out, the elbow bleeding from a scratch he'd suffered in the melee. Splinters stood out in the meat of his forearm.

"Please tell Angie I said it was great she won all them races," Tater said.

Pops seemed to be trying to decide whether it was too big a request. Eventually Mama said, "We'll do that, Tater."

"Mrs. Boulet, I'm grateful to you for helping me out the way you did."

"Not everybody is so full of contempt for his fellow man as that fool," she said, although by the look on her face I wondered if she believed it.

"I'm sorry if I caused any trouble."

"No, baby," Mama said. "We're the ones who are sorry. The world has a lot of growing up to do. You go on inside now and tell Miss Nettie to call me if she has any questions about today."

Tater climbed up on the porch and stood at the door, straightening out his clothes. They might've been new, but they were also ruined. He tucked his shirttail back in and brushed dirt off his pants, and he made sure his belt was in place, with his name facing out from the rear to anybody who might be curious about who he was.

Mama was too upset to cook supper that night, so Angie and I ate fried bologna sandwiches on TV trays in the living room. Pops left for the plant after the news, and it was midnight before we went to bed. Even then nobody slept much.

I lay awake in the dark, trying to make sense of things I'd probably never understand. Finally I got up and moved to Angie's room. "Poor Tater," I heard her mumble, even though she looked to be sleeping.

Toward dawn I sat up on the pallet on the floor and glanced over at her. Angie was a person people automatically liked just because of how she looked. But what about those who brought out hatred in others for the same reason? I wondered what it would be like to have people want to choke your neck before they even knew you, and it all made me wish that I lived in another time—not in the past when things might've been worse, but in the future when all the madness had been worked out.

Tater stayed clear of South City Park the rest of the summer. He didn't see us lose the Babe Ruth League title by dropping two straight to the Steers in the season's last game and tiebreaker playoff, and he missed the awards banquet at the barbecue pits, where, in his absence, I won the trophy for the Redbirds' most valuable player. Mama asked me if I saw him around anymore. I told her no, why would I? And that was the truth, even though it was also the truth that I'd spent a lot of time looking for him.

I rode my bike down past the barbecue pits to the bayou and whiled away many an hour on the pedestrian bridge. I spat at the water until I had cottonmouth. I stared off at the trail, trying to will him to materialize. One day I was hanging around by the snowball stand, listening to music when The Beatles came on. They were singing "She

Loves You" again. It made me feel so bad I got on my bike and rode out of the park as fast as I could.

I wanted my reuniting with Tater to seem accidental, but I knew he was done with us, and the only certain way to see him again was to show up at his house.

It was the first week of August, and the park was starting to quiet down, with the baseball and swim programs finished until next year. I rode to Abe Lincoln and stopped on the corner and had a look around. I wasn't there long, maybe five minutes, when I heard music coming from down the street. I recognized the car. It was the one from three months ago, the black sports model with white racing stripes running from end to end on the hood. It moved faster now and fishtailed around the corner. Then after another few minutes I heard it approaching again, only now it was coming right at me.

I don't know why I didn't try to get out of the way. The only defense I put up was to wave my arms, and then the driver's door flew open, slamming into me and the bike and sending us sprawling against the curb. It happened so fast I didn't have time to brace myself. I hit the ground hard, and one of the bike's pedals dug into my shinbone just below the knee.

I didn't get a good look at the driver, and he was long gone by the time I got my wind back and stood up again. I could feel blood from my knee running down into my sock. My shorts had split open along the seam that ran from the waist to the crotch. My right shoulder and ribcage were throbbing.

What had I ever done to that dude? I wondered.

I limped over to Tater's and banged on the front door. It took only seconds for him to pull it open, and he immediately started calling for his aunt. I would learn later that the kind of house they lived in was a shotgun, with a total of four small rooms leading from one to the next, all the way to the back. Tater put my arm over his shoulder and led me through a living room and bedroom. Next up was a bathroom, and past it I could see a kitchen. His aunt Nettie, appearing by my side all of a sudden, was not quite as ancient as I'd imagined. She seemed familiar, and then I remembered the lady with Tater at the movies four years ago. She wasn't wearing a domestic's uniform but a stylish outfit with a lot of color and open-toe shoes that showed her painted nails.

I roughed out a description of the incident, and she shook her head. "Lord, that boy," she said.

"You know him?" I asked.

She didn't answer. Instead she guided me to the bathroom and turned on the water in the tub. It was an ancient claw-foot job with a metal hoop above it holding a shower curtain. She removed my shoe and sock and put my leg under the water. It didn't burn for long, and then the water went from cold to warm, and I could feel the pain go away and my body begin to relax. I felt like a little kid, the way she handled me. She rubbed the tips of her fingers over the cut and puckered her lips and blew on it. "Shh, shh," she kept saying. The pain in my ribs and shoulder was still there, but I'd been hurt worse, and the truth was I worried more about the rip in my shorts than the injury. The rip had left me exposed, my underwear showing.

"You're going to be fine, Rodney," Miss Nettie said in a reassuring voice.

"You sure I don't need stitches?"

She shook her head. "You got a cut, nothing terrible. But it's more a brush burn—you must've scraped it on the cement." She said it this way: *see*-ment. "Some air will do you good, so let's not cover it just yet. When you get home put some Mercurochrome on it. Will you make sure to do that?"

"Yes, ma'am."

She dried me off with a bath towel, then used a small pair of scissors to trim the skin around the wound. Her hair was done in a long braid pulled in front of her shoulder, and it hung down almost as far as my leg.

"Now, Rodney," she said, "you'll need to give me those shorts. I'll sew the seat back together and make them as good as new."

"Thank you, but I don't think so."

"You're going to need to ride your bike home later on, right?" She laughed now. "You're a big guy. The police might come and arrest you if you go out like that. We'll put this towel around you and you go sit in the room with Tater and relax yourself. I'll have the shorts ready in no time."

Old rose-colored paper with a flower pattern covered the walls. A small lamp with a canvas shade was burning on a table in a corner. A double bed with a plain spread took up most of the room, but there was a second bed, a single with a wrought-iron headboard, standing against the wall. Over that bed there was a black-and-white photograph of Bart Starr, quarterback of the Green Bay Packers. The photo showed him wearing a dark number 15 jersey and pitching the ball at the camera. The picture was signed in ballpoint ink and housed in a metal drugstore frame.

"Nice, huh?" Tater said, standing behind me.

"Better than that," I answered.

The room was so tiny that only a narrow space about a foot wide separated one bed from the other. "Sit over here," Tater said. He nodded toward the smaller bed, then sat on the edge of the larger one. "Come on, Rodney. Take a load off, man. You can look at Bart Starr."

And so I did that, taking in the quarterback in his black cleats, the ball pitched at a perfect spiral. I wondered why a guy Tater's age would be sharing a bedroom with his aunt. I also wondered why Tater would hang a picture of a white player above his bed when there were plenty of black heroes he could've displayed: Gale Sayers, the running back; Muhammad Ali, the boxer; Oscar Robertson, the basketball player; Hank Aaron, the baseball star. The room was finished with a painted chest of drawers, an old wooden chair with Tater's penny loafers under it, and, hanging by the door, a faded picture of Jesus.

"In case you were wondering," he said, "I mostly sleep on the couch in the front room."

"I wasn't wondering. How'd you get it?" I didn't have to tell him I was talking about the photograph.

"Bart Starr sent it to me."

"And why would he do that?"

"Because I wrote him a letter."

"That's all it took?"

"I told him he was my favorite player and that I was going to play quarterback for the Packers one day. Next thing you know that picture's in my mailbox."

A Negro playing quarterback in the pros? I knew it would never happen, but I didn't want to hurt his feelings by saying so.

"Was the car a black Camaro," he asked, "with stripes and a big antenna coming up out of the trunk?"

I didn't remember the antenna. "Big white stripes took up the whole hood?"

"That's it." He walked over to the chest and opened the bottom drawer. He dug under some clothes and found a pocketknife, which he unfolded to reveal a well-worn blade. "Nobody does that to one of mine and gets away with it. I'll fix him."

"How're you planning to do that, Tater?"

"The less you know the better."

"You're not going to stick him with that knife, are you?"

He snorted a laugh that let me know what he thought of the question. "He's a no-account hoodlum always looking for trouble. Everybody calls him Smooth because he's just so cool, you know? He can't stand seeing people get anywhere, can't even tolerate a nice guy like me having a white friend. You'd be surprised how many other black folks feel that way. It's not just the whites not wanting us to mix. I'll wait a few weeks until he won't think to make the connection, then I'll pop one of his tires." He closed the blade and returned the knife to the drawer. "How come you crossed the tracks today, Rodney?"

"No reason."

"I can't believe y'all couldn't beat the Steers again."

"I know." And now it was my turn to show him something. I reached down the front of my shirt and pulled out Angie's key hanging from around my neck. "It's for the lock on the gate to the pool yard. Miss Daigle gave it to Angie so she could go early in the morning and get some laps in before they opened up for the day. Angie's season is over, and Miss Daigle must've forgotten to ask for the key back. I've been planning this since the swim meet when you told me you'd never been in a pool before. We have almost three weeks before school starts."

"Get out of here, Rodney."

"I already got permission from Mama. Pops doesn't have to know."

"You would do that, man?"

"She wasn't easy. I had to work it hard. I told her it was a gift we'd be giving you. She finally broke down and said it was fine as long as Pops didn't find out and we went well enough before Mr. Fontenot reported to clean the pool. There was one other thing. You'd have to get the green light from your auntie. Think she'd let you?"

Miss Nettie must've been standing outside the door the whole time. She leaned in and tossed my shorts at me.

"Yes," Tater said, reading the look on her face. "I think she would."

The night before his first lesson I put a bath towel over my alarm clock to make sure the sound was muted when it went off at 4:00 a.m.

Mama had left some cold bacon and biscuits for me on a plate on the stove, and I ate them standing at the sink. I'd worn my swim trunks to bed, and now all I had to put on were a T-shirt and flip-flops. The key to the pool yard hung from my neck. I'd had less than six hours of sleep, but I wasn't tired at all. I kept working through a checklist in my head of the different exercises I planned to teach him once we got in the water. It was a quarter after four when I heard someone shuffling toward me from down the hall. I was preparing to apologize to Mama for waking her when Angie appeared. She, too, had gone to bed in her swimsuit, although I hadn't known this until now.

"What do you think you're doing?" I asked.

"I'm going with you," she said. "I'm the one with experience teaching kids how to swim. You can barely tread water." There was a biscuit left on the stove. She sat at the table and ate it. "We have two and a half weeks, Rodney—enough time for me to teach him, but not nearly enough for you. Sorry, baby."

We set out on our bikes a few minutes later, pedaling at the same speed and moving through clouds of bugs that swarmed under the streetlights. The only person we encountered was a newspaper deliveryman making his rounds in a pickup truck. He motored past us, holding the steering wheel with one hand and flinging rolled-up papers from his open window with the other.

We reached the pool and deposited our bikes under one of the bleachers and only about ten feet away from where Tater had been hiding in wait behind a tree. He stepped out and said, "What are you doing here?" It startled us both.

Angie shushed him. "I came to help. I'm the swimmer in the family, remember?"

"If only you knew how much this means to me, Angie."

"I'm glad," she answered. "But don't you think you should lower your voice a little? All three of us could end up in jail for this."

"There's not a soul in this park but us," Tater said, still using his normal tone. "I got here thirty minutes ago, and I still haven't seen a single car pass by."

"We have an hour and a half," I said, whispering despite his confidence. "I checked the news last night, and it said daybreak is at seven, which is also the time Mr. Fontenot comes to clean the pool. We need to be out of here by six thirty at the latest. That'll put Angie and me at home before Pops gets back from work."

There was a security light at either end of the pool house, cutting the dark with a yellow-green glow. Angie led us through the gate to the lifeguard station. She and I needed only seconds to strip down to our suits, but Tater's baggy trunks were under a layer of everyday clothing—long pants and a shirt with buttons, and brogans that needed to be untied. His shorts were new—so new, in fact, that the price tag was still on them. Not wanting to embarrass him in front of Angie, I walked over to him and pulled it off.

"Thanks," he said. "I kept it on because I thought you might not show. I was ready to return them in case you changed your mind."

Angie swam a couple of laps to warm up, and when she finished, she came over to where Tater and I were standing at the shallow end. "Are you nervous?" she asked him. "You don't look nervous."

"I'm excited. I've never been in water this deep."

"You'll experience two things when we go out a little deeper. You're going to be concerned about touching bottom, and the weight of the water against your chest might scare you a little. See those numbers along the side of the pool?" She pointed to them. "That tells you how deep you are. Three is three feet. Four is four feet." She moved closer to him. "Okay. So the first thing you need to learn is how to hold your breath under water."

"I can do that already."

"Then show me."

"I learned in the tub when I was little."

She nodded. "Show me."

And so he did. He went under and stayed down for about thirty seconds. "Good," she said. "Now I want you to watch closely and do what I'm doing."

She held on to the ledge and extended her body out behind her, and then she started to kick her legs. Her kicking was so smooth it barely roiled the surface. I imitated the exercise and after studying us a while Tater positioned himself between Angie and me and began to kick.

"Excellent," she said. "Now give me your hands. I want you to keep kicking, and I'm going to guide you from one side to the other. We won't go deep. Keep your head out of the water and breathe normally. Stop when you get tired."

She waited at a short distance with her arms extended out in front of her and her hands turned palms up on the surface. It was sharing the water with him that people would've objected to. And their hands touching. Their hands touching would've had more men wanting to strangle him. He started to kick and to propel himself forward, and they came together easily enough, and she was moving backward now and guiding him to the other side. They went round and round in this manner, and I lay on my back on the rippled surface and gazed off at the stars in the sky.

"I had me a twin once," Tater said when they stopped for a break.

She nodded. "Rodney told me."

"They gave her a name even though she came out already deceased."

"I'm sorry," Angie said.

"It was Rosalie."

"Rosalie," she repeated.

"I sometimes wonder what she would be like—what kind of person, you know? I never knew her, but I always knew she was missing. I could feel it." He waited until Angie looked at him. "You could've taught her to swim too."

Even in the strange light from the pool house I could sense a stillness coming over Angie. She went down under water, then immediately came back up, in a move to clear her head, I supposed. "Ready now for the next challenge?" she asked.

"Ready when you are."

She held his hand and led him out into deeper water until the surface reached halfway up his upper torso, and she showed him how to stroke his arms. He held his hands open as she did—flat but slightly cupped, thumbs tucked—and they walked back and forth from one side of the pool to the other making roundhouse motions against the surface. "You're a natural-born swimmer," I heard her say. "Like a Labrador."

"Like a who?" And then came Tater's laughter, too loud for comfort, really, as it echoed in the trees toward the barbecue pits. "Better watch out," he said. "I'll be racing you before you know it, Angie Boulet."

"Yes, you will. And beating me."

And his laughter came again.

I'd left my wristwatch on top of my shirt, and now I climbed out of the water and padded over to the lifeguard station to check the time. We still had ten minutes left and he was already close to swimming. I leaned forward to put the watch back, and in that instant something shot past me on the other side of the fence. It was a jogger, running at a labored pace only about ten feet away. He was wearing heavy gray sweats with the hood of the sweater covering his head. He navigated the sidewalk, then cut over past the bleachers to a path that took him into the trees toward the picnic grounds. When he didn't slow down, I figured he hadn't noticed us. I checked my watch again—it was 6:23. If he lived nearby, we could probably expect to see him each morning at about the same time. Most joggers I knew kept to a strict routine.

And this was how it happened. The jogger returned every morning at the same time, a man as routine in his habits as the sun itself. Only the color of his sweats seemed to change as he alternated between gray, royal blue, and navy. We ended each lesson as soon as he ran past us and turned for the trees.

★★★

Baseball had brought Tater and me together, but it was those mornings in the pool when we really got close. "I can't believe how cool he is," I told Angie as we were riding our bikes home after the first week of lessons.

"Me neither," she said.

"Sometimes I forget he's black. It's like he's anybody else."

"Imagine that," she answered.

As Tater's swimming skills improved, Angie came up with exercises to push him harder. One morning she removed the leather string from the pool key and tossed the key into deep water, and then she ordered Tater to dive for it. Because it was darker on the bottom than on the surface, he had to feel around for the key and test both his capacity for holding his breath and his ability to remain under. Angie used my watch to time each dive, and she challenged him to better his mark every time he went in.

"God, you're slow," I'd say to him when he popped up for air. "Is that the best you can do?"

When he'd heard enough, he said, "Can you do better?"

I'd been swimming since I was five years old, but I still couldn't match his best time. Not pleased with losing to a novice, I challenged him to dive with me for the key at the same time.

"You mean both of us going for it at once?" he asked.

"Yes. And just to be clear, there are no rules prohibiting interference once we're in the water."

"Interference?"

I was making it up as I went along. "Uh-huh. In other words, if I want to push or pull you away from the key, I can do it. And you can do the same to me."

"What if I punch you in the mouth?"

"Sure. That too. It's anything goes down there."

We stood a few feet apart from each other at the deep end. Angie climbed to the top of the lifeguard station and lobbed the key in the water, then she called out, "Ready . . . set . . . *go*," and Tater and I dove in together.

He beat me nine out of ten times, but I roughed him up enough under water to keep the competition close. "What about you?" he said to Angie, after he must've grown bored with winning so easily. "Think you can take me?"

Now it was my turn to throw the key from the lifeguard station, and I did so with what I thought was theatrical flair. Rather than simply drop the key in the water, I posed like a ballerina dancing *en pointe*, then I segued into a baseball pitcher's motion as he comes with heat from the top of the mound. The key met the surface with a *pa-lunk*, and I waited until it had time to reach the bottom before letting them start.

Tater made it interesting, but Angie still dominated. The whole time I watched from high above, their bodies driving through the water side by side: his a dark spear probing the cloudy blue; hers a lighter one.

The winner resurfaced holding the key above her head. The loser pretended to be devastated.

★ ★ ★

I hated for those days to end, but the new school year was about to start, and it was time to give up the pool and summer.

At home Pops sat by the air conditioner with his paper and complained in a loud voice about "the blacks taking over." What riled him was desegregation, a story that inspired bold headlines and had white parents scared for their children's future. While the rest of the country's public schools had integrated years before, ours were just now getting around to it, and only because the federal courts were forcing us. The situation was more than a lot of white families could accept. Over the summer two private schools had opened for those who refused to let their kids share classrooms with blacks. Rebel flags had started appearing in the back windows of cars and pickup trucks, along with bumper stickers showing the flag and the words "Keep It Flying." Even Pops had put a sticker on the Cameo. But Mama and Angie had removed it one afternoon while he slept, peeling it off in ragged pieces with butter knives from the kitchen.

Despite his feelings about integration, there never was any discussion about where Angie and I were going to school. We'd turned fifteen on August 12, and we were set to be sophomores at the public high school—old enough to fend for ourselves. Pops might've railed against integration, but the truth was he and Mama didn't make enough money to send us anywhere else.

"Is it true we're all going to be going to the same school now?" Tater asked one morning in the pool.

"Yes," Angie replied. "And we'll also be classmates. I just hope we have homeroom together. Wouldn't that be cool?"

Tater seemed to find such a scenario hard to believe. "I can remember, when I was little, we would have to step off the sidewalk if a white man was coming toward us. That man could be an unemployed drunk who spent most nights in the jailhouse. If he was white, you had to give him room."

Our daily adventure in the pool suddenly didn't seem as daring as it had been when we started. Angie must've been thinking the same thing. "If the schools are integrating," she said, "it's only a matter of time before the parks do too. And once South City Park opens to black people, so will the pool."

"Incredible," Tater said.

Angie looked up at a sky moving from night to day. "I can almost see a time when we eat in the same restaurants and attend the same churches," she said.

Tater's last lesson was on a Friday. I heard a soft rain ticking against the house when my alarm went off, making it almost impossible to get up and drag my sleep-deprived body to the kitchen. Angie was already at the table. The rind of a tangerine lay in pieces on an open napkin in front of her. Next to it stood an empty glass with cranberry juice darkening the bottom. No cold biscuits for me today. But I did find a stale honey bun in a paper bag on top of the refrigerator. It must've been two weeks old. I bit into it and felt my molars sting in protest.

Tater was quieter than usual when we reached the pool, and I wondered if he, like me, was contemplating the end of our dark, dreamy hours together. He wore a raincoat draped over his shoulders, the bill of his cap poking out from under the hood. He followed us into the yard and we stripped at the foot of the lifeguard station, and then he dove into the deep end, the first of us in. We watched him swim under water all the way to the other end, from twelve to three feet, and he didn't come up for air once. He touched the wall, then swam back again. I marveled at his athleticism.

Angie had always worn a one-piece suit, but today she was in a bikini, a flowery number that left little to the imagination. She'd bought it only the week before, and when she'd tried it on at home and walked into the living room Pops had told her it was pretty, but sorry, he couldn't let her leave the house with it on.

"Go cover yourself," I told her now.

"I am covered."

"That ain't covered."

She looked down at the suit. "But it's cute."

We didn't say much else that morning. Tater and Angie swam laps and dove for the key, but I mostly floated on my back in the shallow end. Tater by now was probably my best friend, but I wasn't sure about all the other blacks I was going to have to go to school with. It bothered me that Angie and I were part of the generation that was being pushed together with blacks. Why do it now? Why not wait another few years, until Angie and I had graduated and were in college?

I was still floating on my back when I heard the jogger making his approach. He was earlier than usual, but he came up on his regular route, and I lifted my head off the surface and watched him as he ran the length of the fence. He wasn't running as fast today, and I felt my heart begin to punch against my ribs when he stopped and faced us. He stared out first at me, then at Angie and Tater. We'd made it this far. What were the odds that somebody would catch us on our last day?

He pulled the hood back, and I saw a familiar face. It was Junior Doucet, our baseball coach that summer. I climbed out of the pool and walked over to where he was standing. "So you knew we were here all along?" I asked.

He needed a moment to figure out the best way to answer. "I ran into your mother at the A&P a few weeks ago. She knew I jogged in the park each morning, and she asked me to keep an eye out, since she couldn't."

Angie and Tater got out of the pool and came walking over. "It's Coach Doucet," I told them, and then Tater repeated his name.

I felt pretty foolish at this moment. We'd thought we were being so daring, when we'd had a chaperone all along. "So you timed your run to let us know when we needed to head home?" I asked, even though I knew the answer.

He was facing Tater. "I'm sorry I didn't do a better job fighting for you earlier in the summer," he said. "I hope this makes things right between us."

"It wasn't your fault, Coach," Tater said.

Coach Doucet shook his head, as if to say he knew better. "One day I suspect we'll remember this time and understand just how silly it was."

And with that he pulled the hood back over his head and took off running down the trail through the trees.

That Sunday under the pecan tree, Pops cleaned a clutter of sacalait on an old cypress worktable. A lone stray calico watched from the shade of the ligustrums nearby. He was using an electric knife to fillet the fish—the same knife he used to carve the turkey at holiday meals. Inside, Mama and Angie made homemade ice cream with fresh cream and chunks of Ruston peaches we'd picked up after church at a roadside stand. I was sitting in the living room, pretending to work on a crossword puzzle. In actual fact I was trying to avoid being noticed because I was feeling especially lazy today and didn't want them to ask me to turn the handle on the ice-cream bucket. I was using the power of my mind to make myself invisible. So far I'd been successful.

"By the way," Angie said, her breath thin for all the effort she was putting out, "Julie's maid told her last night that they would prefer not to be called colored or Negro anymore. She says they want to be called black now."

"Is that true?" Mama asked. She was chopping a block of ice in the sink with a wood-handled pick. "Who makes these decisions for them? Do they all want to be called black? You're talking about millions of people. Was there a vote?"

"Julie heard her say it. So remember that at school tomorrow, will you, Rodney?"

My shield of invisibility had been penetrated.

"Rodney? Will you remember that?"

"I'll remember," I said. "Whenever I see one, I'll walk up and say 'Hi, I understand you're not a colored or a Negro anymore, but a black.' I'm sure they'll appreciate my sensitivity."

"Rodney, come on, son," Mama said. "Your turn to crank."

I was giving it my all—and shaking the whole house—when Pops came in with water dripping from his arms. He'd rinsed the fish scales off outside with the hose but had forgotten to have a towel handy. He held his arms up like a surgeon who'd just finished scrubbing before surgery and was ready now for his nurse to help him get his gloves on.

"You're going to mess up my floor," Mama said.

"It's water."

"I know it's water, Dr. Kildare, but you've got fish mixed with it, and you'll leave little dots where you drip."

I wondered if there'd be fights in the halls. I wondered if anybody was going to bring knives or guns or brass knuckles. There'd been rumors. One of our neighbors was keeping his daughter home just to be safe, as were a lot of other white parents. I didn't believe any of the stories, but Pops did. He had me doing curls with a pair of dumbbells to make sure my biceps broadcast a certain message.

Pops had caught the fish that morning, and we had them along with hush puppies, cucumber and tomato slices, and iced tea. We also had the ice cream for dessert and ate it from cereal bowls while watching TV. The news from Vietnam came to us in grainy black and white. My uncle Bay-Bay was there, fighting with the Marines. Pops liked to pretend his baby brother was still working on a crawfish farm in Evangeline Parish, rather than rooting Viet Cong out of tunnels.

He got up and changed the channel. "Ed Sullivan's still an hour away," Mama said.

"In that case how about something we can digest by?" he said.

There was a hi-fi console standing along the wall, as big as a coffin. He put a Ferrante & Teicher record on the turntable with the volume turned low, and we ate our ice cream to the whisper of golden pianos.

"Pops, guess what?" Angie said. She didn't wait for him. "Julie's maid said they want to be called black from now on."

I'd hoped we were done with it. She'd caught Pops as he was about to put another spoonful in his mouth. "They do? Who does?"

"Colored people," she said. "Negroes."

"They want to be called blacks now?"

"That's what Julie said."

"Then we'll have to make sure to call them something else," he said.

I kept looking at her. She didn't acknowledge me.

"When I was a child," Mama said, "I had an uncle who used to say with utmost sincerity that he had no problem with the opposite race. Isn't that the most amazing thing? The opposite race . . . I mean, yes, he confused the expression, but don't you think he was really revealing his true feelings about colored—" She stopped herself. "I'm sorry, I mean black people. In any case, it stuck in my head and here I am mentioning it all these years later."

"Like there were only two races," Angie said, "the white one and the black one."

"Exactly."

"Most I know around here aren't even black to start with, like Simmons at the plant," Pops said. "They've got something else mixed in—what you call cream in the coffee. In New Orleans they call that café au lait. When I was a kid we called that high yellow, but I understand it's not polite to say that now." He ate some more and added as an afterthought: "You hardly see any *black* blacks anymore, the way you would have in the olden days, when they first got off the boats."

"The boats?" Mama asked. "You make them sound so primitive. But they weren't the only ones who got here in boats. How do you think we got here? In jumbo airplanes? In air-conditioned buses?"

Angie: "You ever look closely at Tater Henry? He's a lot like Mr. Simmons—a palette of many colors, all blended together. You even have yellow ochre and umber in the mix. Best of all, there's vermilion, which I think makes all the difference. True black doesn't reflect light, anyway, and that young man is positively radiant, so what does that make him?"

"Yellow okra," I told her. "What the heck is yellow okra?"

Pops got up and turned off the music. "Mark my words," he said. "This experiment won't work—this black-and-white thing? I could blame the federal judge that's forced it on us, but I still say it's Abra-damn Lincoln who got this ball rolling."

We knew when to stand up to him and when to let his declarations pass. If he looked overly tired, we let him get away with almost anything, and this day his eyelids were drooping and he slurred his words.

Angie and I finished our ice cream and brought our bowls to the sink. "It's like he forgets what year it is," I whispered to her as Pops kept on.

"Not only the year, but the century," she said.

★

CHAPTER TWO

★

The high school had moved to its new location only about five years before we got there. It was a large, rectangular-shaped pile of brown bricks that most people in town hated. It looked like an airplane terminal, some complained. Pops said it better resembled a mausoleum.

When the big day finally arrived, the sight of black students on campus didn't shock me much, nor was I traumatized by having to share the halls with them. A lone police cruiser remained parked all day near the front entrance, its red emergency light rotating on the roof, as if to warn against mischief. On my way to fifth-hour English class, I looked out the main doors and spotted a cop slumped behind the wheel. He was using his window as a pillow and sleeping the afternoon away.

"Shucks," Curly Trussell said. "There wasn't a single stabbing all day. What fun is that?"

Integration, I quickly learned, was an elusive concept and easy to avoid despite government mandates. We might've attended a school with as many blacks as whites, but Angie and I had classes with few black students, and all of our teachers were white. Administrators had divided the student body into groups, ostensibly according to past academic performance, and Angie and I landed in the top group. Like me, Tater had been a solid B student the year before, but he was assigned to the second group, which better reflected the school's racial makeup. The third group, also known as the last group, was all black except for a couple of hardcore delinquents who probably belonged in a reformatory.

In rural towns like ours, people tended to judge the quality of any given year on how well the crops grew and the prices farmers got for them. But we measured our value on how many games the football team won. In a move that blacks opposed as much as whites, the local school board waited until classes started to let Coach Hollis Cadet assemble his team and commence practice. By forgoing two-a-days at the end of August, the board had only delayed the inevitable and guaranteed that we'd be unprepared and probably lousy once the season started. The board also canceled the Jamboree, the exhibition game that always opened the season. The decision incited such an uproar that a petition circulated calling for the heads of the board members, not a few of whom walked out one morning to find the trees on their front lawns draped with toilet paper. The local paper said the board was concerned about crowd control. How blacks and whites interacted after being thrust together at a large public event was an unknown that it didn't want to face.

"The board got something right for a change," Pops said at dinner one night. "I say better safe than sorry." He shoveled more corn in his mouth. "Nothing some people like more than an excuse to riot."

Everybody knew my size made me a good prospect for football.

The year before I'd started at left tackle on the freshman team, earning the award for Most Outstanding Offensive Lineman at season's end. I'd been planning to go out for the varsity as soon as practice started, if ever it started.

At the close of our first day of classes, Coach Cadet and his assistants stood outside the main entrance handing out bulletins inviting boys to try out. As I left the building he grabbed me by a shirtsleeve and led me off to the side. "Can I count on you, Rodney?" he asked.

His tone was almost confidential, even though we'd never had an actual conversation before. "To do what, Coach?"

"To make this school a winner again. We need team players like you, Rodney."

Tater left the building moments later, but Coach let him walk right on by. Head bowed, hands nervously jiggling the coins in his pockets, Tater was waiting in line for a bus ride home when I caught up to him. "You going out for football?" I asked.

"I'd planned on it until a minute ago. Did you see that, Rodney? He looked right through me, like I was invisible."

"He can't be expected to know the black guys yet. Cut him a break, will you?" I grabbed his arm and pulled him out of line. "Come with me," I said.

He followed me back to the front of the school where the coaches were hitting up more prospects, all of them white.

"This is Tater Henry, Coach Cadet," I said.

The way he looked at him, Coach might've just been introduced to a female tryout. "Your name is Tater, as in *po*-tater?"

"My real name's Tatum, Coach Cadet. But I couldn't pronounce it very well when I was little and the mispronunciation stuck."

Coach seemed to find the explanation less interesting than I did. He glanced at his watch and checked the doors again to see who was coming out. "You play ball, son?"

"Yes, sir."

"What position?"

"Quarterback."

"You said quarterback or cornerback?"

"Quarterback."

Coach Cadet smiled at the absurdity. "You don't want to be a quarterback," he said. "Our playbook is eighteen pages long."

They stood looking at each other: Tater silent; Coach Cadet smacking gum. "However I can contribute, Coach," Tater finally said.

"That's what I want to hear," Coach answered.

About seventy guys turned out the next day. We sat in the bleachers in the gym, and Coach Cadet and his staff looked out at white players grouped together on the left and black players huddled on the right. At the center of this arrangement was a divide a few feet wide, with only Tater and me sitting next to each other about halfway up.

For twenty minutes Coach harangued us about the differences between team players and turds. He'd played guard at Texas Christian many years ago, before helmets came equipped with face masks, and the tip of his nose was a cauliflower mass, the bridge a lumpy knot. Because his skin sunburned easily, he covered himself with cold cream to soothe the pain and protect from blistering. Today he was wearing so much of the stuff he looked like a Kabuki dancer, with a bright pink undertone peeking through. A whistle hung by an orange-and-black cord from around his neck.

Turds had no place in football, he said now in closing, and he vowed to run any off. "Are you a turd?" he asked one guy, pointing. Then he confronted another: "What about you, Nestor? You look like a turd to me."

We all had to deny it. "Not me, Coach," I said when it was my turn.

"I ain't no turd," Tater nearly shouted when Coach Cadet came to him.

"Turds have been the ruination of many a fine football team," Coach said in summation. "I'd rather have a bunch of team players without much talent than a bunch of turds with all the talent in the world."

Next, Coach had his assistants form a half circle behind him, and he instructed the junior and senior players to come down from the bleachers and stand behind the coaches according to their positions. That left thirty sophomores, and now Coach had each of us stand for an eyeball test. He assessed our overall appearance and assigned us our positions without bothering to ask where we wanted to play. As expected, he sent me to stand behind the offensive line coach, and he had Tater join the defensive backs coach. Our entire future in football depended on a once-over that lasted no longer than five seconds, and after a while I noticed a pattern. White kids got the marquee jobs, such as quarterback, running back, split end, safety, and middle linebacker. The black guys got the less glamorous positions. Coach Cadet didn't explain why particular positions were the domain of whites only, but it was understood that blacks weren't suited for them. They ended up standing behind the assistants who coached the defensive line and secondary—positions, it occurred to me, that didn't require you to be very smart.

One black player, Rubin Lazarus, hesitated when Coach told him he was a defensive lineman. "But can I go out for linebacker?" he asked. "Middle linebacker?"

Coach Cadet laughed and glanced back at his assistants, all but one of them white. "The middle linebacker is captain of the defense," he said. "He has to make quick reads and call out schemes, and this means he has to think on his feet. Can you do that?" Before Rubin could answer, Coach said, "I didn't think so."

They made Curly Trussell a quarterback. Before the meeting started, Curly had knelt at one end of the basketball court and thrown spirals with a football to the other end. His passes were pretty to watch, and he'd demonstrated his accuracy by ricocheting them off a wall and landing them in a trashcan. The guys had erupted with cheers after each one found its mark, and Curly had danced around flexing his right bicep. Even the coaches had clapped for him.

"The opportunity will come," I said to a dejected Tater, hoping to give him a lift. "And when it does, you'll make the most of it."

"I'd rather not talk about opportunities," he replied. That was the closest he'd ever come to complaining.

After the meeting, we were issued helmets, pads, and practice uniforms, and then we were ushered out onto the field and put through drills until dusk fell at around eight o'clock. The coaches pushed so hard that guys were falling out from exhaustion everywhere you looked. I puked once myself, a real gully washer that strangely left me feeling better when I was finished.

"Get it all out, Rodney?" Coach Cadet asked when it looked like I was done.

"I think so, Coach."

"Good. Now get back out there and show me how bad you want it."

Practices were compartmentalized by position, which meant I spent most of the day with the offensive linemen, or Bigfeet, as we'd taken to calling ourselves. Casting around for a name to illustrate who we were as a unit, we'd tried the Sasquatches for a while but found the word hard to say. Eventually we'd settled on Bigfeet, the plural of Bigfoot, the hirsute giant that was half man and half ape and so shy he rarely left the woods. I saw Tater only at the end of the day when it was time for team drills, and even then we had little contact. We closed out each workout with sprints, and he was the kind of guy who had to win each one, while I was the kind who was happy just to finish them at all. Coach Cadet had us huddle around him for one last speech, and then we headed to the locker room. Or at least we were free to go there. Tater always went to the weight room instead and lifted for another half hour. If I hadn't collapsed yet, he made sure I joined him.

Our bodies had changed dramatically since the start of that summer—Tater's more than mine. While I seemed to have added mostly girth, Tater had packed on muscle. He wouldn't be fifteen until November, but the thin kid who'd been all kneecaps and elbows was now so well put together you wondered how it had happened.

"Man, what does Miss Nettie feed you?" I asked him.

"Not enough," he said, taking the question seriously. "She works late and most nights doesn't get home until I've already gone to bed."

"So what do you eat?"

"I'll fry me some eggs or warm a can of beans. Sometimes it's cereal and milk. Whatever I can find in the house, I guess."

One night after practice I was pumping out reps on the bench press while he spotted me. It suddenly became impossible to do another one, and Tater started grunting like a hog to push me on. "It's the fourth quarter," he said. "Come on, Rodney. Do it for Regina." Regina Perrault was a classmate, and I'd let Tater know what I thought about her. "Regina," he said now. "Regina . . . Regina . . . *Regina* . . ."

And somehow I was able to get the barbell off my chest, extend my arms, and complete a final rep.

It was his turn next. He'd pressed a hundred and eighty-five pounds nine times, but he wanted more, and I was yelling him on: "It's all on you, brother. You've got to get it done. Come on, Tater. Do it for Miss Nettie—for *Miss Nettie*, Tater."

He paused with the barbell fully extended, and his face went slack. A smile sputtered across his lips, and he gave his head a quick shake. "You get Regina and I get my auntie? Now that ain't right." Then he started to laugh.

I went to grab the bar, but he quickly lowered the weight to his chest and pushed it out one last time.

★★★

With the Jamboree scratched from the schedule, Coach Cadet filled the open date with an intrasquad scrimmage at school. We'd been banging on one another at practice for almost two weeks, and now we had a chance to bang on one another in a game setting. He and the other coaches divided the squad into two teams, the Orange and the Black, our school colors. They wanted a full-blown dress rehearsal under the lights, and they found a crew of referees to work it. The game was supposed to be a reward for the sacrifices we'd been making, and the coaches thought it would be good for morale to have our parents see us in uniform, so they had wooden bleachers installed along one side of the practice field with enough seating to accommodate a few hundred people. Coach gave us permission to invite immediate family only.

"Keep it to a minimum," he said. "Make sure it's people you know who aren't going to cause trouble."

All the black guys looked at one another. "Not to be racial about it," Coach Cadet said, "but I just don't feel like getting hauled in by the school board, you understand?"

Tater and I were both on the Orange squad, and that Friday after classes the equipment manager issued game uniforms, which seemed little better than the ones we'd been wearing at practice. They dated back a few years, judging from the patches that covered holes and tears in the fabric and the tattered condition of the numbers and striping. We had three hours to burn before kickoff, and most of us whiled away the time in the gym watching the cheerleaders and pep squad rehearse their routines.

"She's something, huh?" Tater said.

I looked at where he was looking, and that was the cheerleaders. Angie had made the squad, and so had Patrice Jolivette, a junior with curves galore. One day I'd caught Tater staring at Patrice in the lunchroom, but everybody stared at her, including white boys like me. "Yeah, man, she does that to me too," I said.

The school had selected an equal number of black and white cheerleaders, and Patrice had been named cocaptain of the squad, an honor she shared with Beverly Charleville, the white senior chosen to assure racial parity. Today, Patrice was wearing a maroon sweatshirt over her uniform with the face of a snarling, floppy-eared bulldog on the front. She'd been a cheerleader last year for the town's black school, J. S. Clark High, and the shirt was a faded souvenir of her time there.

"Just think," I said to Tater. "If we hadn't been forced to desegregate, you'd be a Bulldog now instead of a Tiger. Whatever happened to that old school, anyway?"

"What do you mean what happened to it? It's gone. They closed it. And they turned the building into a crummy junior high." The outrage in his voice surprised me, and he wasn't finished. "Clark was a great school," he said. "And it had great sports teams. There were some cabinets when you walked in that were full of trophies won by all the championship teams."

I'd spent some time looking at the trophies in the cabinets at our own school, but I hadn't seen any won by Clark's athletes. "Where is all that stuff—you know, the trophies from those years before integration?"

"Left behind," he said. "Just left behind like none of it mattered. What's that tell you, Rodney?"

At home Pops had been using the word "militant" to describe angry blacks who made the news roaring for civil rights, and I might've tried the word out on Tater now had I not wanted to hear his answer.

"All those seasons at Clark?" he went on. "The pictures of former players? Their medals and ribbons? It's like it never happened. I like seeing progress, Rodney. I like this school a lot, and I'm proud to be a Tiger. But if you ask me, Clark deserved better."

We were out on the field an hour later. Everybody wore the same white helmets with orange-and-black stripes, but our side wore orange jerseys and white pants, while the other squad had on black jerseys and black pants. The Black looked more intimidating than we did, and one of the coaches acknowledged as much when he stood laughing at us during stretches and yelled out, "Dang if you don't look like a pumpkin patch, the way you're lined up in rows just now."

Coach Cadet had also arranged for the school band to perform, but it was proficient with only "Hold That Tiger," an old ragtime tune that was our fight song. The band played it over and over, and we were already sick of it by the time we were done with warm-ups and waiting for the game to start.

I'd dominated every defensive lineman on the team except for Rubin Lazarus, who was every bit as strong as I was, even though I outweighed him by thirty pounds. Rubin added to an appearance of menace with eye black that ran down his face in streaks. The eye black seemed an odd addition, considering we were playing at night, but the overall effect was undeniable: Here was a very intense and likely deranged person you didn't want to trifle with.

Rubin was so good that I quickly forgot there were other players sharing the field. We became the center of the universe, with a spotlight shining down on us from a hole in the heavens. As the game went on, I despised every large and small piece of him, and I despised his mother and father for siring such an animal, and the mothers and fathers who sired them. There were yet more generations to despise, especially after he knocked me to my knees and stepped on my tender vegetation en route to sacking the quarterback.

We went at it hard, and it occurred to me, even as we were pounding on each other, that the intimacy involved in blocking a guy is a personal act that brings you closer to another human being than any other activity but one. Your skin rubs against his skin. You smell his breath and feel his weight when the play is done and he's lying on top of you in the pile. You stare into his eyes from inches away and search for signs of surrender.

By the end of the first quarter I'd already sweated enough to fill bathtubs, and my uniform had absorbed much of what he'd lost. And what I'd lost had gone into his. Everybody else was playing a game. I was playing for my life.

"You got me that time, Rodney," Rubin told me late in the fourth quarter, after I'd driven him ten yards off the line and dumped him on his back.

"I got lucky," I said.

"Yeah? Heck, man, you get lucky a lot."

★★★

We had scored in the last minute to beat them, 27–23, on a Hail Mary pass from Curly to wideout Louie Boudreaux. Louie ran a go route up the sideline and caught the ball in the end zone when the cornerback assigned to cover him, Joey Pierre, lost his footing and fell to the ground. Louie held the ball up to show that he'd made the catch, and the referees blew their whistles to signal it was over.

As I was removing my pads on the sideline I heard a ruckus in the stands. Several men were fighting. I automatically assumed it was between blacks and whites and the race-based brawl we'd all been dreading. But I looked more closely and saw only black men involved. Because it was the first extracurricular event bringing blacks and whites together, the school had hired a police detail to handle just such a scenario, and now cops climbed into the stands and broke up the scrum. I'd seen enough to understand what had happened. Somebody had said something to Joey Pierre's father, who'd said something in reply. And then the brawl had started. Joey's dad had blood running down his face. The other guy's shirt had been ripped off his body. Five or six other men also were tending to injuries or torn clothes.

"You ain't nothing but a beast, Rodney Boulet," I heard somebody say behind me. I spun around and there stood Rubin, his eye black so badly smudged that it covered his whole face. "I'm just glad we can go back to being on the same team again."

"Me too," I told him. "Thanks for the competition, brother."

We started walking toward the locker room, and I spotted my

parents in the parking lot between the practice field and the school. They'd left the stands before the fight started, I was glad to see. Pops was standing off to the side smoking a cigarette, and Mama had joined other parents and the cheerleaders to form a gauntlet for us to walk through on our way to the showers. We strode the gauntlet in single file, lugging our helmets and shoulder pads and exchanging hugs and high fives with anyone who wanted them. Tater was walking right in front of me, and when he approached Angie, she came up on her toes and kissed the side of his face. I gave her a look that immediately put her on the defensive. "He's like my other twin brother," she said, and then she went to kiss me on the cheek too.

I pushed past her.

"Come on, Rodney. It's nothing."

I turned back once I reached the door to the locker room, and she was still standing there, her mouth fixed in a pout. Was what passed between her and Tater really that big a deal? I decided it wasn't, and I also decided I'd have felt the same had she kissed one of my white teammates. In fact, had she kissed Curly Trussell, I probably would've put my helmet and shoulder pads back on and gone after him. To further calibrate my feelings, I reminded myself that I'd just spent three hours in ferocious physical contact with Rubin Lazarus, the two of us swapping bodily fluids as my big warm bulk pressed up against his. I was wrong and I knew it, so I puckered my lips and blew her a kiss with the flat of my hand held up to my face. Just like Angie, she leaped up as if to catch it, then she brought the kiss down to her chest and held it with both hands against the place over her heart.

★★★

Tater had started at cornerback and on special teams, and from what I could tell he'd played well, shutting down the receivers he was assigned to cover and forcing a fumble on a kickoff that we turned into six points. But he was quiet in the locker room and slow to dress. He seemed lost in the throes of trying to sort out some small torment. I knew something was wrong, and I worried that he'd witnessed my scene with Angie and taken exception. When I finished dressing I walked over to his locker.

"What's wrong now?" I asked.

"It's about what happened after the game."

I couldn't blame him for being unhappy with me, and I was about to apologize when he said, "If you're black, you can't even be human and make a mistake. Your daddy gets beat up for it afterward." He sprayed some deodorant under his arms and I stepped back to escape the cloud. "I don't like Joey Pierre, you understand? He's got a motor mouth, and he plays dirty. But that touchdown at the end? Louie beat him because Joey lost his footing and fell down. That could happen to anybody. But the fight after the game? Come on, man. What does that tell you?"

What does that tell you? It was becoming his mantra. And while I didn't have an answer, he probably didn't have one either. For some reason I flashed to that day last summer when he vowed to exact revenge on that hoodlum Smooth for knocking me off my bike. "Blacks not only have to put up with what white people do to them," he said. "They have to put up with what black people do. It ain't fair any way you look at it."

"All right, Tater. I'll grant you that. But maybe the fight was over something else. Maybe Joey's dad owed the guy some money."

"Yeah?"

"Yeah. Or maybe they had a fender bender in the parking lot before the game. Joey getting burned was just an excuse for them to settle things."

I could tell he wasn't buying it. The muscles in his jaw kept bunching up in knots, and he fought with his socks like they were the cause of his irritation.

"I'm just saying you should consider the possibility that they might've fought even if Louie had been black," I said. "It could've been over something else, without the . . ."

He was smiling at me. "Without the what?"

"Without the broader racial implications," I said.

The broader racial implications? The words sounded strange to me too, and I wasn't sure where they'd come from, but at least I'd succeeded in getting him to lighten up. He began to laugh. "You're a sophomore in high school, Rodney. Who taught you how to talk like that? You sound like Dead Eye Dud." Dead Eye Dud—Mr. Dudley to everybody else—was a biology teacher at school.

"It just came out," I said. "When you're smart like me, smart things just pour out of your mouth even when you're not trying."

"No wonder you're in the top group," he answered.

Some seasons you want to put in a shoe box and hide in the closet, up high on a shelf where even an extension ladder can't reach. If the closet has a burned-out bulb in the light socket, so much the better. We lost every game that year, the one to New Iberia by sixty-three points, another to Franklin by forty-two. Tater and I played enough to letter, but neither of us could beat out the guys ahead of us on the depth chart.

After the last game Coach Cadet met privately with each of his returning players. That came to almost fifty meetings, spread out over two weeks. In his office a large panel of florescent lights was humming overhead. I sat in a plastic form chair in front of his desk.

"You were our best offensive lineman by far, Rodney," he said, "and I regret not sitting Tommy." He meant Tom Smith, the senior who'd started every game ahead of me.

"I like Tom, Coach. I voted for him for team captain. And I'm not sure I was any better than he was."

"Yes, you are too sure," he said. "And so was everybody else. But the kid was a good leader and a positive influence, and I couldn't break his heart by putting him on the bench when it was his last year here and you have two more to play."

"I understand, Coach."

"We learned some hard truths this year, didn't we, Rodney? Losing humbles the proud, and I needed humbling. I can tell you I won't have much of a future at this school if we continue to operate the way we have. We can't win if I'm playing favorites and not starting my best people. And we can't win if I'm playing them out of position."

I wondered if he was saying he planned to move me to a different spot on the line. But then he said, "Take Rubin Lazarus. Why didn't

I let him play middle linebacker? Lord knows he's got all the tools for the position. And what about your boy Tater? He said he was a quarterback, but I didn't give him a chance to prove it. That was wrong. Don't tell him anything just yet, but come spring I'm going to let him have a try. I'll catch hell for it, playing a black boy at quarterback, but I'm a fifty-three-year-old man. I can take it." He leaned forward and his whistle clanked against his metal desk. "No matter what people say—and I'm talking about white people now—blacks are the exact same as we are, Rodney. That's the main thing I learned from this god-awful year. When you look at yourself in the mirror in the morning and start asking if you're a racist, that's when you know you are one."

I was a little uncomfortable hearing him talk like that. He wasn't my teammate or classmate or friend. He was my coach. "I never took you as having it against the blacks, Coach. And I don't think any of the black guys on the team did either."

"We might lose next year, but it won't be because I beat us. It'll be because the team on the other side of the ball beat us."

"Yes, sir."

"What do you get when you pour Jell-O into a Jell-O mold, Rodney? You get Jell-O, don't you? Then what do you get when you pour hate?"

"Hate?"

"That's right. And that's what they poured into me."

I thought I knew what he was talking about, and a picture of Pops popped in my head. He was sitting by the air conditioner with his paper, socks folded over and black wiry hair standing out against the white of his ankles.

"Things will be different from here on out, son. If I expect to be a better coach I have got to be a better man. That's all for now, Rodney. Here, shake my hand. It's been a pleasure."

I always loved how sports gave you the chance to start all over again with each new season. Baseball ended and football began. Football ended and basketball took its place. Basketball dovetailed into track and track into baseball. You recovered from the loss of one by moving forward to the beginning of another.

That winter Tater and I played basketball, then we ran track, or he ran track while I threw the shot and discus. In March baseball started, and we both went out for the team. There was one day when we had a baseball game on the same day that we had a track meet, both at our home fields behind the school. Tater and I changed out of our baseball uniforms in the dugout and ran over to the track stadium in time to win medals and score points. We played these sports trying always to win, but none meant as much to us as football. Football was everything.

When the baseball season ended, Coach Cadet conducted two weeks of spring practice for his football team before school let out for the summer. Most of the workouts featured man-on-man drills that let the coaches evaluate talent and make roster decisions for the upcoming year. It was the time when players won jobs, and it was when they lost them. It was also the time when guys you'd never paid much attention to suddenly announced their potential, and it was when some you thought you could count on faded into the shadows.

Our first workout hadn't even started when Curly Trussell let everybody know he had the strongest arm on the team. He did this by kneeling on the goal line and chucking passes deep. By now he was able to cover about forty yards, a distance that many a high school quarterback would've been proud to claim even from an upright position. After each pass Curly hopped to his feet, did an obnoxious dance in the end zone, then pointed to his flexed right bicep to show what a stud he was.

A few other players tried throwing from a knee, but none got the ball far downfield. I even took a turn and managed only twenty yards, my pass wobbling off course and prompting some of the guys to flap around like ducks that had just taken bellies full of buckshot. Then Tater gave it a try. Right knee planted in the sod, he pointed to T-Boy Bertrand and said, "Go long." T-Boy took off sprinting hard and glanced back for the ball after about thirty yards. "Longer," Tater said, then waited until T-Boy had crossed the 40-yard-line before letting the pass go. His motion and delivery were perfect, the way he brought the ball up high at the point of his shoulder and released it from the top of his throwing arc. The ball sailed in a clean spiral that T-Boy caught over his shoulder without breaking stride. It had traveled fifty-one yards.

We all knew Tater oozed athleticism, but I was as shocked by his arm strength as everyone else. Rather than maul him as the other guys were doing, I ran over to Curly, made a muscle with my arm, and pointed to it. Had anybody else mocked him this way I'm sure there'd have been a problem ("Yeah, like blood spilled," Tater said later, when I told him what I'd done), but Curly knew better than to challenge me. I now stood six-foot-five and weighed two hundred and seventy pounds, and I could drive the five-man blocking sled from one side of the field to the other all by myself.

The throw gave Coach Cadet a chance to redeem himself for how he'd treated Tater last season. It also gave him a chance to make history, at least in our small part of the world. "You know something?" he said. "You really are a quarterback."

Everybody went silent for a moment, and then a chorus of cheers came up. Coach waited until things quieted down to call over the equipment manger. He instructed him to swap Tater's jersey with the number 28 for one with the number 11. "We still need you on defense," Coach said, "but I want you to get some work at quarterback, too."

You could see Tater's Adam's apple rise and fall in his neck. "Yes, sir."

"So you're a quarterback now."

"Yes, sir."

"Say it, son. Say it to me and to your teammates. Let us hear it."

"I'm a quarterback."

"You're a quarterback."

"I'm a quarterback!" Tater shouted.

Curly might've had the arm, but he struggled with the playbook and out on the field he couldn't tell zone from man coverage. At the start of two-a-days that August he reported to the locker room in the morning with his clothes reeking of cigarette smoke, and one day he showed up stinking of marijuana. Coach Cadet called a team meeting and lectured us again about the differences between team players and turds, and all the while he stared at Curly, who sat slumped forward in his chair fighting off sleep and his eyes half closed. We all knew that Curly came from a rough home. Still, that was no excuse. He was one of us now, and we expected better.

Coach named senior Orville Jagneaux the starter, and he slotted Curly, the better talent by a mile, at number two. Tater was third team. "You've got to start somewhere," I told him as we stood at the equipment cage, inspecting the depth chart.

I was wrong to think he needed encouragement. "See that person? See him?" He pointed to his name next to the number 3. "It won't be long before he's here." And now he tapped the top spot on the chart. "It's meant to be, Rodney."

Later that day, during the break between the morning and afternoon practices, I went to a sporting goods store in town and ordered T-shirts for every player on the offensive line. I had the store add the word "Bigfoot" in bold letters across the front of each shirt. The season was about to start, and I thought the shirts might help bring us closer together. The order was ready in a couple of days, and I paid for it with money I'd saved from selling pecans. I handed out the shirts before our noon position meetings. One of the guys had quit that morning, so there was a shirt left over. I gave it to Tater. "You're no Sasquatch," I told him, "but you're definitely one of us."

Tater wore it under his shoulder pads that day, and he would wear it at every practice and game for the rest of his career at the school. On those days when it got dirty or soaked with sweat, he washed it in a sink in the big bathroom where we showered. Using a small wire hand brush and a bar of Lava soap, he scrubbed it clean, then let it dry on a wire hanger at his locker.

Despite the T-shirts, and despite our honest effort to reverse a culture of losing at the school, the new season didn't start out well. Tater and I were juniors now, but it looked like a repeat of the year before. It's hard to say exactly why our team was so bad, but we never seemed to enter a game expecting to win, an attitude that our opponents made sure to exploit week after week.

Tater played cornerback and special teams, and each day at practice Coach had him quarterback the scout squad against the first-team defense. He showed potential running the option, but he was prone to mental errors that came from lack of experience. He was best when he tucked the ball and ran with it, and he could make all the throws, but everything about his game had an impromptu feel, like an actor making up dialogue when he forgot his lines. He looked confused and impatient as he set up in the pocket and let the ball fly, often to players for the wrong side.

I once asked our offensive coordinator, Bubba Valentine, why he and Coach Cadet never let Tater play quarterback in games. We were losing every week and what harm could be done?

"He needs to learn the offense better," Coach Valentine said. "And we need to be careful not to throw him to the wolves too soon. Some people will want to see him fail for the obvious reason. We can't let that happen."

"But he might not fail, Coach."

"Right. And that could also be a problem."

We played our games on Friday night, which made our Thursday practice the lightest of the week. After classes let out at three o'clock Coach Cadet convened a brief team meeting in the locker room, then we went out to the practice field for a walk-through. This amounted to both the offense and defense, dressed in gym clothes and helmets, stepping through assignments in preparation for the game the next day. I'd been starting since the Jamboree, and every Thursday without fail Coach Cadet called me into his office and handed over a film projector and spools of game tape for me to take home and watch overnight. The film showed our next opponent's game from the week before, and I studied it with a particular focus on the players I'd be facing, with the aim of learning their strengths and weaknesses and finding a way to get the better of them. Tired of his blunders at practice, Tater asked me if he could attend my home film sessions, and I went to Mama for permission.

"It's perfectly fine with me," she said. "Your friends are always welcome, you know that. But you should clear it with your father first, just to make sure there are no misunderstandings."

I caught him outside in the garden, after he'd had a rare good day of sleep. The tomato season was past, and he was chopping down the plants and folding rabbit manure into the soil.

"Don't you have any white teammates you could invite over?" he asked.

"It's Tater, Pops."

"I know who it is. But he's still a black, ain't he?"

"You can't possibly know how you sound."

He dropped more pellets onto the ground. "The neighbors won't like it, and it's not the example I want to be setting for you and your sister. But yeah, Rodney, he can come. He can even come in through the front door."

He seemed to be waiting for me to say something, but all I did was stare at him.

"Your old man," he said at last, "he's not so bad, now, is he?"

We set up the projector in my bedroom and played the film on an old bedsheet I'd hung from the wall with thumbtacks. We kept the door closed and the lights off and took turns with the clicker, watching plays over and over again. All the while we communicated with each other in the peculiar language of football:

"Look at Willie, Tater. See how far off the ball he is. He wants you to think he's going to drop back in protection, but he's really got Three Gap. Now check out Mike. Mike's going to fill the hole as soon as the center blocks down. Okay, now where is Sam? Tell me."

"Sam's head-up on the tight end."

"And what's the coverage?"

"Man."

"And what should work here?"

"Play action? Maybe a draw, depending on down and distance."

"What else?"

"Send the split end deep and pull Willie with him, then quick-pitch to the weak side. Or fake the pitch and tuck it and run."

Willie, Sam, and Mike weren't the names of players on the defense. They were the three linebacker positions. The first letters of their names represented how they lined up against our offensive formation—weak side, strong side, and middle.

After a couple of hours Mama came to the door and shoved it open a crack. "Halftime," she said, and the smell of supper pushed in and found us like a hammer blow. Behind her Angie was holding a tray loaded with food. One night it was shrimp étouffée; another it was overstuffed catfish and oyster po'boys and sweet potato fries. We didn't eat at the kitchen table because Pops wouldn't let us, but I was willing to give him that much as long as he didn't stop Tater's visits.

Tater and I lunged for the food before Angie could put the tray down. Some days Angie and Mama stood at the door, watching us with equal parts awe and admiration.

"We cook for hours, and then it's gone in minutes," Mama said.

"Minutes? Seconds, more like," Angie said.

"You should open a restaurant, Mrs. Boulet," Tater told her after every meal.

Then Mama had her chance to say: "Thank you, sweetheart. Make sure you take a plate home to Miss Nettie, you hear?"

It never occurred to Tater and me that we should've been eating lighter meals on nights before games. We cared only about filling our guts with what tasted good, and we weren't discriminating in this pursuit.

The night before we played Morgan City, Angie brought in a

ceramic vase along with supper, and sticking up from it were hand-painted cutouts of flowers. She'd made them with construction paper and decorated them with beads and baubles from old Mardi Gras throws. She'd then manipulated the flowers into forms that gave them a three-dimensional effect.

"Are these peonies?" Tater asked.

"Yes, they are peonies. One bunch is for you, Tater, and the other is for Rodney."

"How do you know about peonies?" I asked him.

The question seemed to embarrass him. "I guess from paying attention."

A guy who knew the names of flowers? I couldn't fathom it.

Later that night, after I'd given Tater a ride home in the Cameo and I was winding down before bed, I picked up a flowery scent that I hadn't noticed before. Tater had taken his bunch with him, and mine alone stood now in Angie's little ceramic vase. I brought my face down and inhaled. Sure enough, she'd sprayed perfume on the construction paper and made it smell like something from the garden.

Peonies, I supposed.

That was Angie for you.

At night, when he was tired and in a bad mood, Pops would ask Angie and me how the experiment was going. His cynicism didn't merit an answer, but we gave him a couple, anyway.

"Great," Angie said.

"Very well," I replied.

But the truth was quite a bit different. Most of the white students hadn't let themselves get to know the black kids, and the same could be said of many of the black kids—they had few white friends.

I'd hoped that white students at the new private schools in town would be returning in droves after reconsidering their decisions to break from the public system, but this wasn't happening. Instead whites continued to transfer out of our school. And now there were more black students than white ones; the 50–50 split had become a 60–40 split. When you walked down the halls between classes, you understood which group was the true minority.

"They're everywhere," I heard Freddie Sanders complain one day. "You can't even have lunch without one of them coming over and trying to sit at your table."

"Shut up," I told him.

My priority was the football team, so I mourned the siphoning of talent. Add players from the other schools in town and we likely would've had a dominant football program. Instead we had the smallest enrollment in our district. We also were its biggest loser.

One night after practice I returned home and found Pops sitting at the kitchen table with the local paper spread out in front of him. He pointed. "Read this first, then you can eat," he said. "Mama, get Rodney a glass of water."

It was a story about a lawsuit filed against the school board by one of our assistant basketball coaches, Joshua Dupre, a black man. His complaint said that the basketball team counted sixteen players, all but four of them black, and yet it had a white head coach, Robbie Brown, who'd unfairly been named to the position by the board. Furthermore, Coach Dupre said he'd been a successful head coach at J. S. Clark for nearly twenty years, while his twenty-five-year-old boss had only four years of coaching experience.

The year before, I'd played for these coaches and thought they liked each other. At practice and in games, Coach Dupre had seemed dedicated to Coach Brown and content in his subordinate role. But all along, I understood now, Coach Dupre had believed he deserved to be in charge and would've been if not for his race.

After I finished reading the story, Pops rapped his knuckles against the table. "It took us two hundred and fifty some-odd years to get to this point and now they want it all overnight," he said.

"But you can understand why, can't you?" I told him. "Wouldn't you want it overnight if you had to wait that long?"

He shook his head. "Good lord, boy, whose side are you on?"

At school our classes were now called advanced instead of top group, and they still were mostly white, even though they included more college-bound black kids. Beginning with homeroom, Tater had the same schedule as Angie and me. We always sat on the last row of desks on the right side of the room—Angie first then Tater and me behind her, in that order. Patrice Jolivette, peeking her head in the door one day, laughed and said we looked like an "ass-backward Oreo cookie."

The legend of Tater Henry began when we played New Iberia at Donald Gardner Stadium before a crowd of a few hundred, mostly visiting fans.

It was cold that Halloween Eve night, and we were 1–7 on the year, the second worst team in the district and only one win better than Lafayette Northside, which we'd needed an overtime miracle to beat.

Our team colors were the colors of the season, and Angie and Patrice and the other cheerleaders decorated the stadium with plastic jack-o'-lanterns, Spanish moss from nearby trees, fake spiderwebs made with yarn, and large cardboard cutouts showing spooked cats with spines raised. Hand-painted posters and banners rimmed the playing field: SENIOR GIRLS SAY GEAUX TIGERS, BOO TO THE YELLOW JACKETS, and my favorite, GOD BLESS THE BIGFEET.

The game had not been going well when Orville Jagneaux, setting up to pass on our 30-yard-line, went down late in the second quarter with a knee injury. Curly Trussell should've entered the game as Orville's replacement, but Coach Cadet had suspended him from the team the day before when a hall monitor caught him lighting up in a men's room. "Number 11!" I heard Coach shouting from where I stood out on the field, keeping vigil over Orville. "Get your hat on, number 11. It's your turn, son. Let's go."

The crowd was oblivious to the moment, but I knew what it meant. Unless you were looking for him, it would've been hard to tell that our new quarterback was black. Tater barely showed a patch of skin under the white socks that met his pants at the knee and the bands and pads that covered his arms. Orville went off the field on a stretcher, as Tater entered it at a hard sprint, helmet on, chin strap buckled tight.

"As metaphors go," Angie would tell me later that night, "this was one for the ages."

New Iberia, loaded with future college talent, was already three touchdowns ahead. At this rate they were going to beat us 42–0, but I'd have taken that; we were playing so poorly. I kept checking the scoreboard and wishing the clock would speed up. When Tater stepped into the huddle, I wondered how he'd been spending his time. He'd been out with the defense and special teams, but he couldn't have been paying attention to other aspects of the game. Otherwise he'd have known that the offense hadn't been able to move the ball past midfield.

"We're going to win this thing, okay?" he said in a calm voice, showing not a trace of doubt. "Twenty-one points ain't jack."

Our senior players should've laughed him off the field, but Tater spoke with the kind of conviction that didn't allow for doubt.

"Wayland, Glynn, Eugene. Lemuel. Rodney. Give me the best you've got, and I swear to God we'll beat these suckers."

His first play behind center, signaled in by Coach Valentine from the sideline, was a simple rollout to the right, or strong side, where T-Boy Bertrand was lined up. T-Boy was the rare tight end who was as adept as a blocker at the point of attack as he was as a receiver running complicated routes. His assignment now was to shed the defensive end and to run a down-and-out, or sideline pattern, which meant he was expected to sprint ten yards down the field before breaking hard to his right for the sideline. T-Boy was Tater's primary receiver. His secondary receiver was Louie Boudreaux, the split end whose job was to run straight up the field and pull the coverage with him, giving T-Boy more space to get open. But of course New Iberia was all over it, as they'd been all over everything else we'd tried tonight.

Tater took the snap and moved to his right parallel to the line of scrimmage and about three yards deep. New Iberia's defensive end chipped T-Boy with a forearm and knocked him off balance, then its Sam linebacker closed in fast, nullifying T-Boy as an option. At the same time their best cornerback was running stride for stride with Louie, removing him as a possible target as well. Nobody was open, so Tater's only choice now was to run the ball. In the same situation Orville would've been lucky to get back to the line of scrimmage, and Curly would've thrown the ball away. But Tater put a move on the end that left him grabbing air, then he hurdled over the Mike linebacker, who'd come charging hard with his head down. Tater stumbled forward for a few yards before dropping a hand to the ground to right himself, then he found a seam that led him along a diagonal path to the end zone.

The play developed so quickly that I was still blocking when the crowd noise reached me.

Watching the game film with the team the next day, Coach Cadet used the clock on the locker room wall to time how long it took Tater to score from the instant he abandoned the pass and started to run. Even with the moves he made, he'd covered a distance of seventy yards in nine seconds.

"That's movin', boys," Coach Cadet said to applause, even as Tater sat expressionless in the middle of us.

The run ended and he crossed the goal line and dropped to a knee, ball still gripped in his arm as a silent prayer issued from his lips. Miss Nettie had raised Tater a devout Baptist, and he kissed his clenched fist and pointed to the sky before hopping back to his feet and tossing the ball to the nearest official.

There was bedlam in the stadium. I spotted Angie running up the sideline, chasing after Tater along with Patrice and the other cheerleaders. Then I located Mama and Pops high in the seats. She was standing and cheering with all the other home fans—all of them but Pops, I should say. He was sitting with his chin in his hand, like someone who'd just been awakened from a nap and didn't appreciate it.

Tater scored three more touchdowns in the second half—one with his legs, the other two with his arm—but our defense still couldn't stop them and we lost despite his heroics. The stadium usually cleared out quickly, with only a few sympathetic parents waiting for us outside the dressing room, but tonight several dozen people were there, all of them anxious to see Tater out of uniform.

I was walking directly in front of him, and I felt their weight as they closed in. He reached a hand out and grabbed my shoulder, and the commotion grew louder as we pressed forward. We eventually made it past the ticket gate and reached the place where Mama and Pops were waiting by the bus that would take the team back to school. It's a peculiar thing to hear people cheer for you after you've lost, but it had been that kind of night. I noticed a clutch of New Iberia's fans, dressed in yellow and black. They'd stuck around for their own look at Tater with his helmet off.

Pops wasn't impressed to see us, but Mama hugged us both even though our jerseys were soaked with sweat.

"Where's Miss Nettie tonight?" she asked Tater.

"She had to work."

"On Friday night?"

"She babysits when Mr. and Mrs. Miller have to go somewhere."

"But we sat not far from the Millers in the stadium tonight."

Tater didn't answer. The Millers had the pleasure of watching their no-talent son Marco sit on his helmet on the sideline the entire evening, while the sole guardian of the game's star player was assigned to caring for the rest of their snotty-nosed kids.

We'd almost reached the bus when Angie arrived. She wrapped her arms around me first and had to wait for Patrice to untangle herself from Tater before she could congratulate him. Black girls had never registered with me until I was forced to go to school with them, but now whenever I saw Patrice and she cast her big green eyes upon me, I lapsed into silence and nervous trembling. She was "*black* black," as Pops would say, and yet she spoke with the heavy local patois, which would suggest she came up in a Cajun home. Cajuns were white people, and this was another revelation about attending school with Louisiana's black kids that I never could've anticipated: Many of them had accents as stubbornly French as my own.

I might've found Patrice bewitching, but there was no way, even without Tater in the picture, that I could ever have asked her out. And there was no way she could've accepted, had I been able to. The integration of public schools might've been old news by now, but the line drawn between us was still as wide and as deep as a wartime trench, and there were consequences if you tried to cross it. I knew of no interracial couples at school, and I definitely wasn't man enough to partner in the first one.

The coaches let the cheerleaders ride with us on the bus back to campus, and Patrice, pretending to be unable to find a place to sit, perched herself on Tater's padded knee. Angie stood in the aisle. "Baby, you did so good," Patrice kept saying.

"Got to give credit where credit is due," Tater said.

"Is that you, Rodney?" Patrice asked.

"Big Rod blew me some holes open tonight," Tater said. "Holes as wide across as this bus."

"Way to go, Rodney," Patrice said. We looked at each other, though not for long.

Friday was by far the best night of the week, especially when we played at home. In the locker room at school we showered and changed back into street clothes, then we piled into cars and pickups and drove as a herd to the Little Chef on West Landry Street. Angie and the other girls pumped coins into the jukebox outside on the covered patio, and we listened to the Kinks and Mungo Jerry and had Cokes and pizzaburgers, the house specialty. The white players did these things, anyway. Until New Iberia, when Tater accepted an invitation from one of the senior white players to join us, none of my black teammates had ever made an appearance at our postgame party.

Tater sat on the tailgate of Wayland Broussard's pickup truck and ate a basket of fried chicken fingers, compliments of T-Boy Bertrand. When Tater finished the chicken, somebody else gave him a jumbo hot dog buried under a mound of shredded cheese. He ate that, and then they brought him a paper boat holding corn chips with stewed ground meat and yet more cheese on top. I'd gone to the Little Chef after every game and I'd never been given free food.

"You keep playing like you did tonight," I told him, "and they're going to make you fat as a walrus."

"Then I won't be running past anybody, will I?"

"No, you won't."

"Then I should stop this minute." And he stuffed more food in his mouth.

The crowd started to thin. We hung around watching Angie dance with some of her girlfriends.

On other Fridays after games, she had sought me out and asked me to join her, and I'd always politely declined. But she didn't come looking for me tonight.

I wondered if it was because she didn't want to feel compelled to ask Tater to dance once I turned her down. She would've been sensitive to his feelings, and I was sure she wouldn't have wanted to hurt her reputation, besides.

The party ended at midnight when the restaurant stopped serving, then the stragglers headed home. Mama usually had food waiting for Angie and me on the stove, but as a rule she didn't come out of her room unless we knocked on the door and asked for her. She understood that it was the only time during the week that Angie and I had alone together, and she knew how important those hours were to us. After cleaning the dishes, Angie and I moved to the living room where we could talk louder and more freely without fear of waking Mama. Still wearing her cheerleader uniform, Angie played records on the hi-fi with the volume turned down low, and we listened in the darkness while sprawled out on our backs on the oval-shaped rug that covered the floor. Angie was partial to R & B and singers like Al Green and Marvin Gaye, and I would have to commandeer the needle to hear any of my favorites, which tended to be bands like the Bee Gees, Rare Earth, and Three Dog Night.

We stayed up as late as our bodies let us, then fell asleep on the floor. Pops returned home at seven thirty, reeking of sweat and bean oil, his eyes red from the long night at the plant. He was carrying a bag of doughnuts and a copy of a Baton Rouge newspaper. He sat at the kitchen table and turned to the sports section. A STAR IS BORN, read a headline prominently placed above the fold. BLACK QB EXCITES IN DEFEAT.

It wasn't every day you saw a picture of a black amateur on the section's front page, but this one showed Tater making a move on some hapless defender on his way to the end zone.

"I can't believe this," Pops said, flicking a finger against the photo. "I mean the picture itself—a colored boy, and he's not even from Baton Rouge. You never saw this when I was growing up. Everybody would've canceled their subscriptions."

"Can we show it to him?" Angie asked.

"Tater?"

She nodded. "He couldn't have done it without Rodney and his offensive line—I heard him say it."

"I tell you right now, that boy would be nothing without Rodney."

"It's true. But we're still proud of him, Pops. And Miss Nettie's such a nice person. They deserve this. Don't you think so?"

He poured a cup of coffee and stood drinking it at the sink. He looked at us suddenly. "That part of town is dangerous, especially for a white girl."

"No place is dangerous if I'm with Rodney," Angie said.

"How're y'all planning to get there? Ride your bikes again?"

It was a while before Angie or I said anything. "In the Cameo if you'll give us the keys," I whispered.

They made a loud clap when they hit the table, and both Angie and I jumped. "Rodney, don't be long, son. And remember to keep your head on a swivel."

Ten minutes later we were parked in front of Tater's house. I walked to the door with the paper while Angie waited at the curb with the windows rolled down even though it was close to freezing out. I knocked against the old board siding next to the door, and Tater answered, holding his game cleats. He'd been polishing them and shiny black tar stained his hands.

"Thought you'd like to know what people are saying about you," I said, and slapped the folded paper against his chest.

He stepped out onto the porch and gave Angie a wave, then he put the shoes down and had a look at the story. He didn't read past the headline. "Just think what they'll write when a Chinese quarterback has a big game," he said.

I didn't understand.

"Not that I ever met one," he said, "but they're supposed to be yellow, right? Chinese people?"

He walked past me and stood on the steps where there was more sun. "Yellow quarterback excites in defeat? You think they'll say that? Or what if it's an Indian? Now that would sell papers: Red quarterback excites in defeat. I'd even go out and buy me a copy of that one."

"You should be grateful," I said. "Instead you're sounding like a militant."

He turned back around and made sure I was paying attention. "Would it have been so hard to have the headline say, 'QB Henry Excites in Defeat'? Come on, Rodney. Don't just see what color some dude is. Call him by his name." He hopped down from the steps and jogged to the truck, still holding the paper.

"Everybody's talking about somebody by the name of Tater Henry," Angie said.

He looked at her for half a minute. "Hey," he said.

"Hey," she answered.

"That was nice of y'all to bring the paper, Angie. I'll make sure to show my auntie when she gets home from work tonight."

I got back into the truck and started the engine.

"I wonder if Coach will let Curly play next week," Tater said. He leaned in the passenger-side window and brought his face up close to Angie's.

"As long as you're healthy, Curly will never get in another game," I said. "Do you understand what you did last night, Tater? You rushed for a hundred and fifty-seven yards. You threw for nearly three hundred more. And you did it against one of the best defenses in the state in less than three quarters of football."

From the look on his face I could tell he still didn't believe he'd supplanted Curly on the depth chart. Coach Cadet had put him in against New Iberia only because Orville was hurt, Curly was suspended, and there was no one else. To Tater's way of thinking, earning the position by playing well still wasn't enough.

"I know what you're thinking," I said, "but it can't be about that anymore."

"White quarterback excites in defeat," he said. "How come they never say that?" Then he walked back to the house and disappeared inside.

We traveled to away games in a yellow school bus, two men to a bench seat. Tater and I always sat next to each other. We made the trips already dressed in our uniforms, shoulder pads and helmets riding on wire luggage racks above our heads.

The state had three distinct regions: New Orleans, North Louisiana, and Acadiana, the twenty-two parish southern area where we lived. Lafayette High had the best team among Acadiana schools, and the Lions had been destroying everybody, including other highly ranked programs from our district. If they could beat us tonight, they would finish the regular season undefeated and enter the playoffs as a favorite to win the Class AAAA state title. One sports columnist had predicted that we would lose by forty-eight points. He said we would lose by more if for some reason Tater Henry didn't play.

"Lord have mercy," I heard Coach Valentine say as we pulled up to their stadium.

It was twice as big as ours, and their fans were already tailgating in the parking lot. I saw what looked like hundreds of honey-haired women in green outfits, every last one of them watching us with a smirk on her face. "How dare you?" they seemed to be saying. "How dare you come here in your yellow school bus and pretend to be good enough to share the air we breathe." The men, too, were all preppy types, and all attitude, dressed today in the same obnoxious green.

In the bus we sat enveloped in silence and took in the carnival past our windows—the pewter flasks, the Chinet plates piled high with ham and potato salad, the furry lion mascot waving the knot at the end of its tail. HEY, TIGERS, GO CRY IN YOUR GUMBO read a hand-painted sign on the side of an Airstream travel trailer.

Lafayette High was the largest, richest, and whitest school in our district, and its fans were the snottiest. "Get ready, Tater Henry!" one of them shouted. "We're going to bury you, boy."

This prompted Rubin to rock his head back and roar, "Yeah? You and what army?" which prompted cheers from the rest of us.

Tater and I had watched enough film the night before to understand what we were facing. Their defense hadn't been scored on in three weeks, and their offense mowed people down.

Blue-chip players destined for college careers populated their roster, and one of them, running back Levi Woodworth, the best of only three black starters on the squad, had set a state record in the one-hundred-yard-dash last spring. Earlier in the season recruiters from

Michigan and Ohio State had made trips to Lafayette to see him play, but word was he favored Notre Dame.

Most of the Lafayette players were sons of privilege and wealth. Their fathers were petroleum engineers, oil industry executives, offshore helicopter pilots, doctors, lawyers, and university professors. Ours were yam-kiln operators, tractor mechanics, soybean and chicken farmers, grocery clerks, bricklayers, and night watchmen. Our blue-collar pedigree should've produced stouter athletes, but as a team they were bigger, stronger, and faster than we were. I wondered why this was: Did they eat better than we did? More likely they were superior specimens because their school had a much larger male population. Their coaches had more athletes to choose from, while ours had to take what they got.

We were wearing our away uniforms—black pants, orange jerseys, and white helmets. As we left the bus and marched single file toward the field, I heard one of their fans shout: "Hey, somebody tell them Halloween's over!"

A hard rain soaked the field as we were warming up, but the wet turf didn't slow them down any. They scored touchdowns on three of their first five possessions and hit on a field goal late in the second quarter. For all their success, we had our share as well, and it was Tater again who provided it, outgaining Levi Woodworth on the ground, and throwing for more yards than Ronny Rome, their all-state quarterback. At half, the score was 24–14, and I believed we had a shot if only our defense could play better and stop them.

I was trading strides with Tater on the way to the locker room when he stopped suddenly and looked off down the sideline toward a corner of the end zone. There on the track that encircled the field stood Miss Nettie, dressed tonight in a purple pantsuit that flapped against her in the wet wind. She was holding a striped golf umbrella over someone in a wheelchair, but for the distance I couldn't make out who the other person was. Tater waved. Miss Nettie hollered out something in reply, while the figure in the chair—man or woman, I couldn't tell—sat without moving.

"Who's that with her?" I asked him.

"Tell you later."

"The Millers let her come to the game?"

"Later," he said, then ran on ahead.

Tater was sixteen years old. He was six-one and a hundred and seventy pounds. Until the spring he had never even taken a practice snap at quarterback, and only two weeks before he was still running scout squad. But in the second half he did it the way all the great ones do it, and that primarily was by equal parts talent and force of will. He refused to make a bad read or throw a bad ball, and he refused to be tackled, even when they came at him three and four at a time.

We scored three touchdowns in the third quarter, all of them through the air. Louie had two, T-Boy the other. After each touchdown Tater came off the field, took a knee down the sideline where he had an unobstructed view, then stared past the end zone at Miss Nettie and her charge in the wheelchair.

"Who is it?" I asked him again as the fourth quarter was starting.

"Not now, Rodney."

"Tell me. It's driving me crazy."

He shook his head. "No."

Rubin, playing middle linebacker, also dominated in the second half. He ended one of Lafayette's possessions with a diving interception that gave us good field position, and he tackled Ronny Rome for a safety the next time the Lions got the ball. Rubin also made Levi Woodworth look quite ordinary. The state's best running back gained only forty-seven rushing yards, his lowest total on the year.

Not that it mattered much, but I wasn't so bad either. I owned their all-American defensive end, Saul Ernestine, driving him around the field as if his cleats had popped off. And once in pass protection, I hit him so hard his knees gave out and he dropped to the ground like an old quilt falling off the bed.

Our last touchdown came with less than a minute on the clock, and this time Tater did it with his legs. After faking the dive to Jasper Bacquet, he cleared scrimmage and found himself on a clear path to the end zone on the right side of the field. Instead he ran to the left where Lafayette's defenders were in pursuit. He had to beat at least six of them, and he did so with moves I'd never seen from a high school kid before. He hurdled the last of them and came down on his feet, and rather than kneel and pray and toss the ball to the official, as was his way, he ran straight out of the end zone and handed the ball to the person in the wheelchair.

I realized now why he'd run left through a minefield when to run right would've been the easier way to go: He wanted to finish the play in front of Miss Nettie and her companion.

The refs flagged him for delay of game, but the touchdown counted and the game was ours. Lafayette would go on to win state that year, but we'd beaten them by ten points, mainly because of Tater.

We mobbed him in the corner of the end zone, and I saw now that the person in the chair was a woman—a black woman—who appeared to be physically disabled. She hid her face behind a dark curtain of lace hanging from her wide-brimmed hat, but you could see scarring and what looked like pebbles standing out on the surface of her face. One of the refs ran up to her and asked for the ball. She held it out to him, a task that required such effort you'd have thought it was a fifty-pound dumbbell.

Tater left her and jogged to the sideline to wait out the last seconds of the game, and fans on our side started chanting his name.

"*Tay*," the right half of the bleachers called out.

"Ter," answered the left half.

"*Tay* . . . Ter . . . *Tay* . . . Ter . . ."

On the bus ride home I was once again seated next to him. Somewhere on the interstate south of Grand Coteau, a car passed in the lane on the side of the bus with a young woman breast-feeding her child in the passenger seat. The car's interior light was on, making her hard to miss.

"Hey look!" Marco Miller shouted, "That lady's got her boob out."

In an instant we all moved to the left side, upsetting the balance and making it feel as if we were going to tip over. The baby must've been around six months old, and the woman had her breast poking through a flap in her bra. It was the first time I'd ever seen a mother and child this way, and I found it exciting and repulsive both at once. This seemed an act for animals, not people. True, people were animals, or so Dead Eye Dud had taught us. But I couldn't believe we were *that* kind of animal. I had to fight off a gag impulse, even as I was awed by the heavy engorged breast and the nipple the color of an Allegheny plum.

The coaches hollered for us to get back to our seats, and when I returned to mine I realized that Tater was the only player on our side who hadn't rushed over for a look. He was sitting forward with his head on his arms, and he was sobbing into his pads.

I understood who the woman in the wheelchair was.

I never took him for a liar, but he really did have a talent for keeping secrets. How else could he have gone so long without telling me his mother was alive? Angie and I discussed the subject that night when we got home. She'd worked out all the answers in her head, and she presented one in the form of a question: "If Pops tried to kill Mama and then killed himself, would you want to talk about it?"

"That wouldn't happen."

"But just saying it did."

"Then I would talk to you about it."

"Anybody else?"

She had me. "No."

I was as frustrated as I'd ever been. I knew I couldn't approach Tater for a thorough personal accounting without expecting to be laughed at or challenged to a fight. I supposed I could've asked Angie to get the story out of him, but it would've been underhanded, and I didn't do things that way. Having no other option, I decided to talk to Coach Cadet. I needed to clean out my locker the next morning, anyway.

I put my personal effects in paper shopping bags, then walked to his office. He was watching film; I could hear the projector through the door. I knocked, and he hollered for me to come in.

When he saw who it was, he put down his clicker and had me turn on the ceiling light.

"That lady in the wheelchair when we played Lafayette High?" I said. "That was Tater Henry's mother, Coach."

The coils in his chair squeaked as he leaned back and brought his arms over his head. "Sit down," he said.

"All the time I've known him I believed she was dead."

He was quiet as he sat appraising me. I could tell he was trying to figure out what I was after.

"Her name is Alma Henry," he said. "She is indeed his mother. She lives in a government-run facility over on the north end."

"She lives in town?"

"It's a place for poor people who can't afford the medical attention they need. Chateau Something. The lady Tater lives with . . . his aunt? The two of them go and see her every Sunday after church for lunch. Alma has only partial eyesight. Tater told me the aunt made the arrangements to have her travel in a van to see him play against Lafayette. It was Tater's first start and he wanted his mom to be there. You can appreciate that, can't you, Rodney?"

"Yes, sir. But I thought his father killed her. That's what I always believed."

"Do you have private things you don't like to talk about?"

"I'm sure I do, but she's his mother, Coach."

He picked a rubber band off the desk and began to roll it around with his index fingers. "He came to me a few days before the game and asked if I would mind if she was there. It's hard to read Tater sometimes, but I think he was worried his teammates would fix on her and make a big deal of it. 'Your daddy tried to murder your mama?' 'He blew the side of her face off with a shotgun?' Things like that. Definitely not the kind of distraction anybody would want before a game with the best football team in the state." He kept rolling the band. "Anyway, I'm glad she could make it. He was a warrior that night, and I'm sure it did a world of good for them both."

"He had a twin, he told me."

"I don't know anything about that. I thought it was just him."

"She died when they were born."

He shook his head. "News to me."

I got up to leave. I went to flip off the light, and I heard the coils in his chair squeak again. "You said it was a girl?"

"Yes, sir. He told me her name was Rosalie."

A metal filing cabinet stood against the wall. He opened a drawer and pulled out a manila folder. TATUM HENRY was written across the tab in orange ink. Coach Cadet kept one of these files for every player on the team. I saw familiar papers inside, mostly questionnaires and consent and medical forms our parents had been required to fill out before we could go out for the team.

Coach leaned back in the chair. "She died, you say? Rosalie?"

"Yes, sir. And he lived, and I guess . . . Well, I wondered if it had something to do with why Tater seemed so secretive sometimes. Like there was a connection between what he lost and who he was, if that makes sense."

Coach glanced up from the papers. "R-o-s-a-l-i-e?" He wrote the name on the side of the form.

"I don't know how to spell it."

"There well could've been a twin. I don't have any reason to believe that story isn't true. But this questionnaire was filled out and signed by the aunt. And it says right here there's a brother." He pointed to the place on the page, and now he began to mumble to himself. "Robert Battier. Are you kidding me?" He said it this way: *Batch-yay.* "Could've been a half brother, I suppose, which would explain the different last names."

"You've lost me, Coach."

"Robert Battier," he said, louder this time. "Tater's brother."

"Don't know him."

"Robert Battier might've been the best football player J. S. Clark ever produced. He was several years ahead of you boys, would've long since been gone by the time of integration. He carried them to the semifinals for the black schools, then got busted for drugs and kicked off the team." He waved the paper between us. "I don't read these things, and I definitely never knew he and Tater were related. This is a shock. An absolute, unmitigated shock. Of course without him, Clark went on to lose the championship. And Robert sat in the parish prison for a good, long while before they let him out."

"Why haven't I ever heard of him?"

"Because he went to Clark, son, and nobody who's white cared what went on over there. The newspaper didn't even cover them."

He returned the document to the file and started playing with the rubber band again. "Crazy turd. It's coming back to me now. Robert goes missing the week before the biggest game in the school's history, and the principal finally calls the cops to help find him. They find him, all right. He's holed up in a vacant house, and so high on marijuana he can't even tell them his name." *Merry-ja-wanna*, Coach said it. "What a waste of a human life. They say he was smooth."

"Smooth, Coach?"

He seemed to be trying to remember something else. "That's right," he said. "And everybody called him that."

The next weekend Angie got word that she'd won a blue ribbon for an oil painting she'd entered in the Yambilee's arts-and-crafts competition. It was a large canvas done in oils showing Mama's dresses thrown on top of a chair. Up close it looked like a jumbled abstract, but as you stepped back you could make out the colors, patterns, and textures of the outfits, and a picture revealed itself. Angie called it *All Kinds* and Pops made a frame for it out of scrap boards he kept under the house. The prize was for her age group, but she'd also been named first runner-up for Best in Show.

Angie had been reluctant to enter the competition. "It's incendiary," she'd said of her painting. "I hope people don't think I'm a communist."

I thought I understood what she was trying to say in the picture, but Mama and Pops didn't seem to. *All Kinds* to them simply meant all kinds of dresses.

"I wish I had the energy to pick up more," Mama said.

"Me? I wish we could afford help," Pops said. He winked at Angie. "See there, baby? You really got us thinking. That's what art can do."

The weekend turned out to be a time of recognition and honor for me as well. My first year as a starter on the football team had begun with a long string of defeats but ended on a positive note when the league's coaches named me first-team all-district in a unanimous vote. I received the news in a phone call from Coach Cadet.

"You keep working hard and putting the time in, and you'll be one of the all-time greats before it's over," he said.

Tater had played in only two games, but they were enough to earn him a spot among the league's honorable mentions. The quarterbacks who were named to the first and second teams had both received scholarships to play major-college ball. While it was true that their passing and rushing totals for the season were twice as high as Tater's, it was also true that they'd played in eight more games.

On Saturday, Pops let Angie and me borrow the Cameo, and we drove straight to the Yambilee grounds for a look at her painting. It was on display in the Yamatorium, a cavernous World War II–era Quonset hut with a metal bas-relief over the front door showing a sweet potato with a happy face. The festival featured various competitions along with the art show, including the Yambilee Queen beauty pageant and contests for the best-looking yams. There was also a category for most unique yam, which honored the potato that best resembled an animal or human being. One recent winner bore an uncanny likeness to Richard Nixon, and a picture of it ran in the local paper alongside a photo of the president.

We found *All Kinds* hanging from a Peg-Board right as you entered the building. Two ribbons hung from its weathered cypress frame, a blue one and a red one. Next to it was the painting that had won Best in Show—a brightly colored acrylic depicting sweet potatoes spilling from a crate.

Angie posed with *All Kinds*, and I snapped some pictures with the family Instamatic. Then I stood in front, and she aimed the camera at me, chest blown up big in a demonstration of pride.

Next we gave the camera to a man we knew from church, and he photographed us standing on either side of the picture.

"You should've won two blues," I said. "Yours is way better than the one with the potatoes."

"Art is so subjective," she said.

"But it's clear to me, Ang. Clear as day. The one of the potatoes is propaganda. Yours is profound and challenging. It's unfair you didn't win, and anybody with a pair of eyes can see it."

"The most beautiful thing in the world to one person is sometimes the least appealing to another," she declared. Then she glanced at me and shrugged. "To be honest, I don't like finishing second to those potatoes either. But I didn't paint *All Kinds* for everybody else. I painted it for me."

The Yambilee also had a fair with amusement rides like bumper cars and a Ferris wheel and carnival games where you basically depleted your life savings trying to win a stuffed animal. I played a lot of Skee-Ball after Angie and I first left the Yamatorium, but it was the ring toss that obsessed me. This was the game where for a dollar you threw three small rings at sticks standing up on a platform. The goal was to get the rings to fall over the top of the sticks and to slide down to the bottom, making you a winner. But all of my rings, which really were plastic napkin holders, bounced off the finials decorating the canes and clattered to the ground. I'd already gone through twelve bucks when Angie pulled me away, and as we spun into the midway I nearly bumped into Tater.

"Your brother's a bigger fool than I thought," he said to Angie.

I was surprised to see him. Blacks usually waited until Sunday to go to the fair. Whites pretty much had it to themselves on Friday and Saturday.

"I really wanted a cane," I told him.

"Then go to Low's and buy one. They can't cost more than a quarter."

"But I wanted to *win* one," I said. "Anybody can buy one."

He was wearing a strange mix of clothes—equal parts cowboy and soul brother. His shirt was a silk number printed with a Day-Glo tropical pattern, but his pants were old straight-leg Levi's bleached almost white. He had on his TATER HENRY belt and his feed-store cap, and his shoes were black patent-leather platforms polished to a mirror finish. It was a fashion statement that revealed what an idiot he was about fashion.

"I went and saw your painting a minute ago," he said to Angie. "I bet it feels good, winning those ribbons. I'm proud of you, Angie."

"Thank you, Tater. You're sweet to say so."

He seemed to be trying to remember the rest of what he'd planned to tell her. "I like the palette. And you built up the paint surface real good. I bet you got three whole tubes of paint squeezed out on that surface. You know what they call that in Italy, don't you?"

"Impasto?" she asked, pretending not to be sure.

He smiled. "Sounds like that other name for noodles, doesn't it?"

They wouldn't let me try again for a cane, so we cruised the length of the midway to where a dilapidated mobile home stood back a ways in the weeds with a sign on a door that said HAUNTED HOUSE. We walked through it in our usual formation, that being an "ass-backward Oreo cookie," and screamed bloody murder at the petrified cat and glow-in-the-dark skulls and skeletons. Then we groused about how unscary it was when we realized we'd reached the end.

Angie wanted to ride the Ferris wheel, so we joined the line and waited until it was our turn to be seated. Because of the ride's popularity, the woman taking tickets made sure every passenger car was filled. She sat two people in each one. "You three together?" the woman asked.

Tater nodded.

"Then you two boys take that car there"—she pointed to the one—"and I'll put you next to this little lady here." She pulled Angie toward a car already holding a passenger.

The woman had mixed up the order to make sure Angie and Tater weren't seated together. I might've complained had I been able to put into words what bothered me. Until Tater came along, I would've thought she was doing the right thing.

I watched the operator hit the switch, and we jerked upward, a gray burn cloud rising up from the motor and with it the smell of oil. "Something's been bugging me all week," I said as we climbed. "I need to talk to you about it."

"Just so long as it's not about my mother," he said.

"You should've told me she was still alive, Tater."

"I never told you she wasn't."

"You gave me that impression."

"I didn't give you that at all. You went and got it yourself somehow. I never told you anything about her."

"Same goes for Robert Battier, too, huh?"

He had no defense. He shook his head but didn't say anything.

It was dark now and from the top of the turn I could see the Eunice Highway and the headlights of cars backed up and waiting to enter the Yamatorium parking lot. I could see the fields bordered by man-made canals dredged for irrigation and overgrown now with blackberry brambles. Off in the distance, a movie was playing on the outdoor screen at the Yam Drive-In. Up in the sky, lights beat on the wings of a plane, and I wondered what passengers inside saw when they looked down at us. I had never flown in a plane before, had never left the state, had never traveled beyond the places I was instructed to go. Did they see only a scattering of color on the prairie? Or could they see enough to make out individual people, like Tater and Angie and me floating in circles?

"We must look like little baby ants to them," I said, "our lives no more important."

But Tater didn't seem interested. Something else had occupied his mind. He barely smiled.

"Where'd you learn so much about painting, anyway?" I asked. "Palette and paint surface and pasta primavera and all that?"

"Book at the house."

"You actually read an art book? Who does that?"

"I wanted to be able to talk to Angie about her pictures. I know how much they mean to her."

We had a crossbar keeping us pinned in our seats, but he was able to slip out of it and stand up. The wheel climbed to the top of its second rotation, and he put a hand on either side of his mouth and yelled as loudly as he could. It wasn't a yell that said anything, and it probably got lost on the ground to the roar of the wheel's motor, but Angie heard it, and she stood up and started yelling along with him.

I'd have joined them had I been small enough to squeeze from under the crossbar.

Mama had put our curfew at eight o'clock, but by seven we'd hit all the rides, tried all the games, eaten everything that looked good, and spent all our money. We returned to the Yamatorium for one last look at *All Kinds*, and this time I had Tater stand with Angie in front of the painting. She and I had posed on either side, but they stood next to each other in front of it. Their eyes weren't on the camera, and they weren't on the painting behind them. Instead they looked at each other.

He accepted our offer of a lift home but insisted on riding in back. He pulled his cap down even lower on his head, then he sat leaning against the bulkhead, legs extended, ankles crossed. I steered the Cameo toward the highway, and Angie reached over and touched me on the arm.

"Stop, Rodney. I want to get out."

"Why?

"I want to sit in back with Tater."

I hit the brakes harder than I needed to and pulled over on the shoulder. She got out and climbed up over the tailgate, and she settled in next to him. In the rearview mirror I could see them sitting there without so much as their shoulders touching, but I saw more than that. A couple of feet separated them, just like when they'd posed for the photo. And yet blood was burning hot in my face, and I felt like stepping outside and asking them what the hell they thought they were doing.

I rolled down my window and let the air in. I gulped at it like it was water to drink. I didn't want to believe the view in the rearview any longer, so I turned in my seat and got the one through the glass.

Light from the highway spread out over them. The breeze was blowing Angie's hair in her face, a few long strands of it stuck to her lips. Out past her in the distance the carnival twinkled like a cloud of fireflies, and the Ferris wheel had just started up again. Tater tilted his head back and met my eyes with his.

"That's my sister," I said, pointing.

He didn't seem to understand.

"That's Angie," I said.

She looked up at me too. They were both smiling—at least for a moment.

That was the winter we went to see *Romeo and Juliet*.

The movie was two years old by now, but it was finally playing at the Delta, and no girl I knew was more excited about seeing Leonard Whiting on the screen than Angie. Whiting was the English actor who starred as Romeo, and she adored every small, pretty piece of him.

We always got movies months or years after their release, but this hadn't diminished the intensity of Angie's admiration for Whiting. The walls of her bedroom were still covered with photos of him torn from teen magazines. She still sketched his portrait when she found time to doodle. And on the hi-fi in the living room she still played the film's soundtrack over and over. The music was so depressing it made her stand at the window, looking out at the rain falling on the ligustrums. When the album played a part where Whiting said his lines, tears rolled down her cheeks.

"Isn't he gorgeous?" she asked me about an hour before we left for the show. She was holding up the album cover. It showed Whiting with Olivia Hussey, the girl who played Juliet.

"What kind of name is Hussy?" I asked her.

"It's not Hussy, you bozo. It's Hussey." But both pronunciations sounded the same to me, even when she used an English accent.

Angie's friend Julie had come down sick this morning, and Angie had recruited me to go in her place. It was the first Friday of the Christmas holidays, and we were off from school until after New Year's. I probably would've declined the invitation if not for that moment with Angie and Tater at the Yambilee. It was all I thought about anymore, even though I'd decided that I'd overreacted. What they had was innocent. It was impossible that Angie would want to be with Tater. She liked guys like Leonard Whiting, and she never would've done that to Mama and Pops and me. Even forgetting that she was family, Angie was the prettiest girl in town. What would she want with a black dude whose father had shot his mother, then himself, and who could have a girl from his own race like Patrice Jolivette as a girlfriend?

Nope, it didn't add up.

Thank God it didn't add up.

The picture show had a huge marquee in front that said DELTA in blinking lights. Expecting a sellout, we arrived more than an hour early and bought tickets, and already moviegoers were waiting out front in two lines. The larger line counted about thirty people, only a few of them black. They were waiting for the main doors to open on the gilded lobby dressed with scarlet carpeting and deco-era furnishings. I counted six people in the second line. Every one of them was black and standing by a door with a sign over it that said BALCONY SEATING. Until a year or two ago the sign had said COLORED ENTRANCE, and you could still make out the shadow of the old words under the new paint.

The Delta had integrated along with the other businesses in town, but whenever I went there I still noticed few black patrons watching movies on the main floor. Miss Nettie was among those waiting today for balcony seating. A moment passed before I recognized her under the floppy black hat that sat on her head like a crow, and in heavy winter clothes that made her look bigger than I remembered. She'd spotted me, though.

"Romeo, oh, Romeo," she said in her best Olivia Hussey imitation, and I laughed because she got it just right—better than Angie, anyway.

Not waiting for me to introduce them, Angie stepped over and offered Miss Nettie her hand.

"I'm Angie, Tater's friend," she said, drawing the attention of the moviegoers in the larger line.

"So you're Rodney's twin," Miss Nettie said, identifying Angie as I would have.

Angie nodded. "Isn't Leonard Whiting the most beautiful thing you ever saw?" she asked.

"You should write him a letter. Stick your picture in with it."

I wanted to disappear, but suddenly the doors opened and the line lurched forward. "Showtime," I said to Angie.

She gave no indication of having heard me. Despite my gesturing for her to come back and reclaim her place, she stayed where she was.

I finally surrendered and joined them when only three people stood between me and the man in the velvet tuxedo taking tickets.

"And what about you, Rodney?" Miss Nettie said. "You going to write a letter to Olivia Hussey? I got a stamp if you need one."

The balcony entrance opened only after the other line had moved inside. We climbed a flight of hollow stairs to seats in poor condition, their red covers threadbare, stuffing spilling from tears, so fat, rusty coils poked your backside.

Miss Nettie sat between Angie and me. Because of my size, they let me take the aisle seat, and I stretched my legs out and relaxed as well as I could in the lumpy chair.

"Why don't you just sit downstairs?" I asked Miss Nettie.

"They didn't want me before, they're not about to get me now. To heck with that. Uh-uh. I won't give them the satisfaction."

I slept through most of the movie, which was even harder to watch than I'd expected. The actors spoke in English, but I understood little of what they said, and what I did understand didn't make sense.

When the end came and the two young lovers die, Angie and Miss Nettie were holding hands and sobbing. Unable to bear it, I got up and went downstairs and waited under the marquee where it was warm. Angie and Miss Nettie eventually emerged with bloodshot eyes, whimpering, their fingers still entwined.

It was Angie's bright idea to go swimming again.

School was still out, and one afternoon the two of us joined Tater for lunch on the patio at the Little Chef. We were eating pizzaburgers and drinking malts, and the jukebox was playing Dusty Springfield, and as usual Angie, who wore heavy eyeliner and a leather headband that pushed her bangs down to the upper rims of her eyeballs, was holding court. It was true that she'd consumed a lot of sugar this afternoon, but the two large strawberry malts weren't solely responsible for her excitement. New Year's Eve was two days away, and she'd cooked up a plan for the night.

"We're in the pool floating on our backs in deep water and watching the stars in the sky," she said in her Olivia Hussey voice. "We lose track of time until fireworks begin to explode. Ah, the happy moment has found us at last. It's no longer nineteen seventy, pilgrims—thank God! It's nineteen seventy-one. We've straddled the years while suspended between earth and sky. Thus from my lips to thine, we'll never forget it, I can assure thee."

"We'll forget it, milady, if we drown," Tater said.

They'd been plugging old English words and phrases into the conversation, with no care to whether they made sense. "Thy yonder bayou reeks," Tater had said earlier. "Yes, but mine pizzaburger is such glad tiding."

Angie sucked the last of her malt. Then she removed the key for the pool yard from under her blouse—proof that she'd been plotting the swim since at least before lunch.

"Oh, God," I groaned. "You're serious, aren't you? Why can't we just be like everybody else and steal some cooking sherry from the kitchen cabinet? And won't it be cold out? Is the pool even heated? I don't remember it being heated."

"Rodney, you might look like a full-grown man three times the size of most full-grown men, but you're still such a child. Isn't he a child, Tater?"

When it came to getting her way, Angie didn't have to work very hard. Sometimes all she had to do was smile and bat her eyelids, as she was doing now.

"Right," Tater said. "Rodney is still a child. But he sure is good at opening up holes for me to run through."

"Still thanking your offensive line, are you?" Angie said.

"Got to, milady."

It often happened that winter felt like summer in our part of the state, and such was the case when the big day arrived. Pops, off from work, offered to let us take the Cameo, but Angie's vision had us traveling to the park on bikes—"In keeping with tradition," as she described it.

We left at 11:00 p.m. and saw neither the paperman on his route, nor bugs swarming under the streetlights. Large populations of kids, up past their bedtime, shot rockets from glass Coke bottles, and the air smelled of cooked sulfur. The temperature was in the middle sixties. We wore swimsuits under jeans and long-sleeve shirts. Beach towels hung from our necks.

Tater was waiting at the fence when we rode up and stashed our bikes under the bleachers. I sensed resignation in his posture, in how he held the links and stared straight ahead. Angie and I scrambled up a grassy incline to meet him, and now I understood why. There was no water in the pool; black leaves lay in drifts and clumps on the bottom. "Maybe we can stand in the deep end," I said, "look up when the fireworks start, and pretend that we're—how did you put it, Angie . . . ?"

"Suspended between earth and sky," Tater said.

Angie glanced at her watch. "Tater, take my bike. Rodney, you big galoot, do you think your tires can support us both?"

We took a moment to inspect them. The bike was a Schwinn Continental ten-speed with reinforced rims on the tires. "I guess it depends on where we're going, Angie," I said. "Where are we going?" But somehow I already knew.

There was a private swim and tennis club in our neighborhood, built only recently in response to integration and the specter of blacks sharing the water with whites at South City Park.

Members used the pool year-round. One of our neighbors went there each morning to exercise, including those days when there was frost on the ground. It had to be heated.

Angie and I knew the place well enough to avoid the main entrance gate, which stood at the end of a residential street and was bedecked with wooden plaques welcoming members only and threatening police against those who entered without permission.

With Tater fast on my tail, I rode with Angie indelicately perched on my bike's crossbar. We pedaled up to Helen Street and past our house where lights were burning in every window to a dirt lane that led to the rear of the club. We rode past kids who gawked at us, and one aimed a penny rocket in Tater's direction but sailed it high.

"Go home, you!" I heard a boy shout in a rough Cajun accent. But these kids didn't worry me much. What worried me was what their parents would do.

As I pumped the pedals I leaned forward with Angie pressed

against my chest, and caught a hint of baby shampoo and Crepe de Chine.

"I keep having this vision," I said. "A man strides out in the street, raises a rifle to his shoulder, and picks us off one after the other."

"You mean like skeet?" Tater asked.

"Yeah, like skeet."

His laughter told me what he thought about my vision.

From the path we walked our bikes to the hurricane fence surrounding the pool. Like the one in the park, the fence had strands of barbed wire on top. We threw our towels over the barbs and scaled it with ease. There now were only minutes to go before midnight. We stripped down to our suits and entered the water.

The pool was larger than the public one. It broke into an L where competitive diving boards stood on the edge of a deep bay, and in the darkness you could see black lines for race lanes painted on the bottom. Angie swam a couple of laps and made as much noise with her strokes and kicks as she had at the other pool. Tater and I were more reticent and chose to stay in the shallow end with our heads barely above water, looking for trouble in the night. When we dared to speak it was in a whisper.

"Have you considered an escape route?" I asked.

"Jump the fence and run like hell," Tater said. "Pretend we're playing Lafayette again, and Abe Lincoln is the end zone."

We couldn't see the moon or stars for the cloud cover, and when midnight struck and the fireworks started, we couldn't see them either. We weren't floating on our backs as Angie had planned.

Instead the three of us were leaning back against the pool's apron with our arms stretched out and our heads up, eyes on a black sky. There were no exploding blossoms of light. There were no streaks of color to convince us that our reward was worth the risk we'd taken.

"Here's to the best year of our lives," Angie said, lifting an imaginary toast.

Thirty minutes later, I was first out of the water. Our clothes were on the other side of the pool. When I glanced back at Angie and Tater, I saw them move closer together. More accurately, I saw Angie move closer to Tater and position herself in front of him. The sky was still banging with so much noise that I couldn't hear what they were saying. They were two shadowy forms that coalesced and became one, and from my vantage point clear across the pool, she appeared to kiss him or maybe to whisper in his ear. Now the neighborhood fireworks seemed to intensify, as if the volume had been turned up, and the sky must've been clearing because a bolt of color suddenly found them.

I almost felt like puking. I wanted to tell them to stop, but no words would come out. At this very moment, I knew, my parents were home celebrating at the kitchen table with glasses of wine from the A&P.

Yes, it was a new year and the world was changing. I knew that. But I also knew that I wasn't ready to see my sister with a black guy, even if he was my best friend.

I'd heard the explosions, but not the car at the club's entrance or the metal gate scraping the blacktop or the cop's feet on the walkway as he climbed a small hill to the pool. The beam of his flashlight went to me first, then to Tater and Angie. The man didn't speak for a minute. Then the light went out. Had he seen what I saw?

"Get out the water," he said. "Both of you. Rodney, come stand over here by the fence. Angela Boulet, what the hell are you doing, girl?" He waited, but there was no answer. When he spoke again his voice was louder and higher pitched. "Get out, I said."

By now I knew who he was. Charlie LeBlanc was a cop in town. He and Pops had grown up together and remained friends. They fished together in the summer. They passed the collection baskets at Queen of Angels on Sunday and served the community as members of the Knights of Columbus. Only two months before, I'd spotted him in the stadium at the New Iberia game.

He was still watching Angie. The two-piece she had on didn't hide much, and the effort of climbing out of the pool revealed even more.

"Hello, Mr. Charlie," she said as she moved past him. She picked her clothes off the ground and started to get dressed. "Are you taking us to jail, Mr. Charlie? Please don't take us to jail."

"Tater Henry," Charlie LeBlanc said now, as if just recognizing him.

"Please, Mr. Charlie."

He brought the light up to her face. "Angie, be quiet."

The three of us stood along the fence, once again in our familiar configuration with Tater in the middle, and faced out like criminals in a lineup.

"Did we break the law, Mr. Charlie?"

"Yes, you broke the law."

"We're trespassing?"

"That and other things—more serious things." Charlie LeBlanc brought the light up to Tater's face and held it there until Tater closed his eyes. "Good as your parents are," Charlie LeBlanc said. He was still looking at Tater, even though he seemed to be talking to Angie. "Hard as they try, much as they've sacrificed. People said it would happen. I didn't believe it. But look at you."

"What would happen, Mr. Charlie?" It was weird, but she didn't sound scared. She didn't look it either.

He moved the light away from Tater. "Are those yours?" he asked. His light was shining on the bikes on the other side of the fence.

"Angie's and mine," I answered.

"What about you?" he asked Tater. "Did you ride a bike here?"

"I borrowed Angie's."

"I rode with Rodney," Angie explained. Then she said, "It was all my idea, Mr. Charlie. I need to be clear about that."

"Angie, if you know what's good for you, girl, you won't say another word."

"Tell me what would happen, Mr. Charlie," she said, sounding downright defiant now.

"Shut up!" he yelled.

Tater went to sit in the front seat, but Charlie LeBlanc made him get in the back. Angie and I started on our bikes for Helen Street, and the cop car followed us. We didn't pedal fast; neither of us was in a hurry to get home. The neighborhood kids had gone inside, and the night was cooler now and you could see more than just clouds in the sky. At the house, the carport light was on and inside a light shone over the kitchen sink. You could see it through the lace in the window. There was no one looking out.

We lay the bikes down in front of the Cameo and walked back to the street and the car idling by the curb. Charlie LeBlanc's window was rolled down, and I could smell cigarette smoke.

"Are you taking him home or to the jail?" Angie said.

"I never thought I'd see the day," Charlie LeBlanc said. "I mean, I thought I might, but I never thought it would be you, Angie."

"You're confusing me again, Mr. Charlie."

"No, I'm not," he said. He was still looking at Angie when he said, "There aren't any colored girls good enough for you, Tater Henry?"

"We were just in the water talking," he answered.

"Up North in the big cities they tell me you see the black buck with the white lady like that and nobody pays it any old mind. But we don't live there, do we?"

They'd camped a lot, Pops and Charlie LeBlanc, back when they were boys. I remembered the pictures. Mr. Charlie standing in front of a tent, Pops next to him, holding a string of fish, a fire going with a pan on top. They'd both run off and joined the army after high school. And they'd gone to Korea together, returned home at the same time, and married local girls. Like brothers, they were.

"What's this all about, Angie?" Mr. Charlie asked.

"I don't know what you mean," she said.

"What is it you see in them? I guess that's the mystery here."

"The mystery?" she asked.

"I always heard that if a white girl went with a black, it's over for her, and no white will ever touch her again as long as she lives. You ever heard that, Rodney?"

"No, sir."

"You believe it, though, don't you?"

I didn't say anything.

"But you believe it, don't you, Rodney?"

I still kept quiet. I kept quiet, and Angie wouldn't stop staring at me.

They drove off, and we stood in the yard and watched them all the way up to Dunbar Street. Light from the streetlamps shone through the windshield, and I caught a glimpse of Tater as the car turned left, its headlights sweeping over the houses.

"You're a coward, Rodney," Angie said in a plain voice, as if it were a fact that finally needed stating.

I followed her inside, and she made enough noise to make certain Mama and Pops knew we were there. They came down the hall in their nightclothes and stood in the middle of the kitchen. Angie was crying, but it wasn't because she was afraid of Pops. She was afraid for Tater, and she kept pleading with Pops to get dressed and drive us downtown to the police station. Instead Pops went to the sink and drank a glass of tap water, then rinsed out the glass and set it upside down on the drain pan to dry. He was in no hurry to do anything, and

I could tell now that neither he nor Mama had been sleeping. Next he opened a cabinet door and removed a tin of coffee. He filled the electric pot with water and spooned some grounds into the basket on top.

Mama, meanwhile, had started pulling bacon and eggs out of the refrigerator. Her skillet was already on the stove. She turned a knob and used a match to light one of the burners, then she warmed the skillet over the flame and lay lengths of the bacon across the surface in neat rows.

And the whole time Angie stood there crying and pleading with Pops to do something. Mama slid a chair out from the table and helped her to sit.

By now I understood who had called Charlie LeBlanc. And Angie must've realized it, too. She stopped crying and sat up taller. I offered her some paper napkins to wipe her face, but she pushed it away.

"You called him," she said to Pops.

He had poured himself some coffee. There was a smile on his face as he brought the cup to his lips.

"You called him!" Angie screamed. "How could you? How could you—"

But Pops threw his cup crashing to the floor and was on top of her before she could say more. Hands on his knees, he brought his face right up to hers and seemed to pin her down in her seat with it. "I will put you out on the street before I let you get away with this, little sister."

"Get away from me. Rodney . . . *Rodney*, get him away. . . ."

He stood up and waited to see if I had it in me. I couldn't look at either of them.

"I didn't think so," he said.

The cup lay in pieces on the floor, and coffee was dripping from the bottom cabinets. I thought it was over. But she said quietly, "Rodney," and started crying again.

Mama came over and positioned herself between them. "Go to the room," she said. She was talking to Pops. "Go," she said, trying to keep calm. "Right now. Go to the bedroom."

I cleaned the floor after he left. I put the pieces from the broken cup in a brown paper bag, and I sopped up the coffee with a sponge. Then I wiped everything with a damp towel.

The house had gone quiet, and Mama started cooking again. She scrambled the eggs in the bacon grease and reheated some leftover biscuits on the stovetop and served them dripping with oleo and cane syrup. It was almost 3:00 a.m. We usually said grace before meals, but we didn't now.

Angie sat without eating. Her shoulders were shaking although her sobs were silent. "Mr. Charlie wouldn't hurt him, would he, Mama?" she said.

"No."

"He wouldn't, would he?"

And Mama shook her head.

★

CHAPTER THREE

★

He left the house about two hours after we went to bed. My door was open, and I could hear him tell Mama he was going to the lease to hunt rabbits. The lease was some acreage in Acadia Parish where he and a couple of men from the plant had hunting rights. I heard him remove his shotgun and a box of shells from the rack in the living room. I heard him ask Mama if he should wake up Angie and try to talk sense to her. I heard Mama tell him no.

He let the Cameo warm up a long time in the carport, and as soon as he was gone Angie came to my room. "Get up," she said. "You're coming with me." She stood over my bed and nudged my shoulder with her knee. "Let's go, Rodney. Rodney, let's go. Don't you need to see for yourself that Tater's okay?"

It was wrong how Pops had treated her, but I could still think of about a hundred guys that I'd have preferred for her to be in love with, every one of them white. I got up and dressed, and minutes later I found myself riding after her down the street.

"Can I start over with you?" she said as we headed down Dunbar toward the bayou.

"You don't have to start over with me, Angie."

"No, Rodney. That's what you should be asking me—can I forgive you and let you start over? Don't you want to redeem yourself for last night?"

I was never one for public spectacles, so I wasn't pleased when she threw her bike down, ran up on Tater's porch, and started pounding on the door and calling his name. Her voice was desperate again. And I knew she was imagining the worst—Tater hanging by a rope from a tree in the Thistlethwaite Reserve, or Tater bound and thrown from a bridge for animals to dispose of his body.

I kept revisiting the look in Charlie LeBlanc's eyes when he held the light on them in the pool. I wanted to see through to his brain and find what was there, but the exercise didn't get me any closer to the truth. His eyes had probably revealed little more than my own, and I didn't care to consider what that meant.

Angie and I sat on the porch with our legs hanging over the side. She was operating on less sleep than I was, and I had never been so tired.

"Tater," she called again, throwing her head back to get more volume. "Please, Tater, open the door. Open the door, Tater. Open the door."

A man stepped out from the house across the street. He was holding a kitten, mewling for food.

"He's in there," he said, and pointed with the hand holding the cat. "Try the back."

And now we could feel vibrations in the floorboards, and in that moment we knew he was home and the fear washed away.

"Just let us know you're all right," Angie said again.

"I'm all right," he said, answering from the middle part of the house. He was in the bedroom, judging from the distance.

"Did he do anything to you, Tater?"

"No."

"Are you sure?"

He didn't answer for a minute, then the door creaked open. "Yeah, I'm sure," he said. He was wearing orange gym shorts from school with a tiger emblem on one leg and the Bigfoot T-shirt I'd given him.

"I'm so sorry," Angie said. "What did I do? Just tell me you forgive me."

"Nothing to forgive," he said. He stepped out onto the porch, and I looked him over for evidence of a beating, but there was none. He waved at the old man across the street, and the man went back inside.

"Y'all really know that guy?" Tater asked. And we knew he was talking about Charlie LeBlanc. "He starts on me again. Then a call comes on his radio—trailer house on the Lewisburg Road is burning. So he stops on Parkview Drive and tells me to get out. He goes, 'Next time find yourself a nice colored girl to go skinny-dipping with,' and takes off. I walked the rest of the way home." He looked back through the open door. "Y'all want some cornflakes?"

"I want a hug," Angie said, and moved closer to him.

He seemed uncertain but still opened his arms, and she started crying again the way she had at home. Holding her in a loose embrace, not sure how to console her, he glanced at me from over her shoulder, and I shook my head.

When you stood next to him and allowed for familiarity again—when you came back around to the understanding that, yes, here was a friend—all the emotion that had led to wild screaming and a cup crashing on the floor began to register as a waste. And as I looked at them standing together in each other's arms, I realized that by trying to stop them, we really had only encouraged them. It was them against us now, and they would win that one every time.

I got on my bike and started pedaling, taking the usual route and taking it slow in case Angie wanted to catch up. It wasn't long before I heard the clattering of her bike as she closed in on me. I went to say something, and she shot right past me, going twice my speed. I stood on the pedals and started pumping harder. I tried to close the gap. She could've slowed down had she wanted to. After a while I let her go and stopped trying.

The school had an awards ceremony in the gymnasium at the end of the year, and seniors were called up to a portable stage and given trophies and certificates for their various accomplishments, if you could call categories such as Best Dressed and Prettiest Eyes accomplishments.

The keynote speaker was a dentist in town who'd recently been crowned champion of a statewide Toastmasters speech competition. Known by his patients as a timid man, the dentist was loud and fearless with a podium in front of him, and kids in the audience who went to him for regular care expressed shock at the intensity of his delivery. The theme of his talk was the importance of pursuing your dreams. He wanted us to dream big. If you dreamed big, he said, there was no telling what you might achieve. You might even surprise yourself and become president of the United States. You might become an astronaut and walk on the moon.

The whole student body was there—seniors in metal folding chairs on the floor and underclassmen in the bleachers. The black kids sitting around me seemed less impressed with the dentist than the white kids did. Some of them were pretending to be asleep. It bothered me that he could look out and see students making an obvious effort to ridicule him. Our school was better than that, and he had a positive message, besides, even if it did assume that the world was a fair place that dealt with everyone equally and really did reward merit no matter who you were.

Tater was sitting next to me in the bleachers. I glanced over at him, and he brought his mouth up to my ear. "First thing I plan to do when I'm president . . . ?" he whispered.

I waited for what promised to be a line loaded with racial content, such as "Free the slaves" or "Call everybody in from the cotton fields."

Instead he said, "Find out about aliens and UFOs. I always wondered."

"Then what?"

"Find out if James Earl Ray acted alone. That never seemed right. Same for Lee Harvey Oswald. I'd need to see the secret files on those two. And next I'd want to know the truth about Bigfoot. They have that film of him walking in the woods. Was that real or fake? I'd have the CIA work on it and give me a report."

At the end of his speech, the dentist locked eyes with somebody in the audience. "Do you want to produce a rock album that lands on top of the charts?" he asked. Now he pointed to another kid. "Do you want to climb Mount Everest, world's tallest peak?" He must've hit twenty others with similar questions. "Do you want to win an Olympic gold medal? Do you want to swim from the tip of Florida to Cuba in shark-infested waters and gain your country's respect and admiration?"

I thought of Coach Cadet, pointing at us the same way and asking if we were turds. Most of the students the dentist was singling out would've been happy to get into trade school or the army. But now he had Cedric Joubert discovering a cure for cancer, when everybody knew that Cedric, who had his challenges, had no future but to pump gas at his dad's Esso station.

The white kids gave the dentist a standing ovation, and I saw Robbie Brown, the white basketball coach who was being sued by his black assistant, rubbing his arms, as if to get rid of gooseflesh. A portion of the black kids—a very small portion, I should say—displayed their approval with tepid applause, but most of them just seemed glad it was over.

"What do you really want to do?" I said to Tater as the dentist was stepping down from the stage.

"When I'm president?"

"No, man. With your life."

"I want to win state in football," he said.

"That's it? Win state, and you can die?"

"No. Winning state is first. Winning the national championship in college is second. And winning the Super Bowl as a pro is third."

"It's good that your ambitions are modest."

"I don't see why I can't do it. I mean, you take out the end zones, and a football field is but a hundred yards long, right? It's a hundred yards in California and New York, and it's a hundred yards in Louisiana and Alabama and Mississippi. They don't shorten it if you're white, and they don't make it longer if you're black. It's the same for a banker's son like Marco and for a kid like me who never knew his dad. Everybody says change has arrived, and I'm hoping that's true, but right now when I'm out there playing, it's the only time I feel like things are fair."

What do you say to something like that? If you're me, you say nothing. Or you wait a while and try to come up with a clever reply to make you stop from thinking so much. I waited. "Maybe when football's over you can become a dentist," I said.

But Tater didn't laugh. He was somewhere else, and I was pretty sure I'd never been there before.

Like everything else at the school, race played a role in who got what at the awards ceremony. The year before, black parents had complained that the school gave almost all the awards to white students. So this year the principal and his staff, aiming to be more racially sensitive, had decided to celebrate a white and a black in each category, and in doing so segregated the student body even more.

There was a Most Likely to Succeed (White) and a Most Likely to Succeed (Black). There also were double winners for Most Beautiful and Most Handsome, but other categories, such as Best

Personality and Best Dressed, counted four winners for each because awards went to Black Male, Black Female, White Male, and White Female. The day reached a high point in absurdity when Best Smile was announced. There was a three-way tie among White Females and a two-way tie among Black Males, so the school honored seven people, none of whom seemed very happy to share the award. None of the Best Smile recipients were smiling, in any case, when they were called up to the stage.

Orville Jagneaux claimed the trophy for Most Athletic (White Male). And Most Athletic (Black Male) went to Albert Johnston, a senior long-distance runner who'd been the only athlete in school to win a state title. While Albert had been outstanding, Tater easily was the school's best black athlete. As a starting point guard on the basketball team, he'd averaged eighteen points a game; he was our top sprinter and long jumper in track; and he'd been a major contributor in baseball, hitting a team-high .513 and stealing a school-record twenty-two bases. Students booed when Albert's name was called. Then our side of the gym—the side where the junior class was sitting—struck up a familiar chant.

"*Tay!*" kids shouted.

"Ter," answered others.

Poor Albert took it hard. Shoulders slumped, head hanging so low his chin touched his chest, he looked defeated as he walked up to the podium to receive his award. I wondered how to get the student body to cut him a break, but then Tater rose to his feet, stepped up on the bench where we were sitting, and started applauding. Positioned in the middle of his classmates at center court, he put some fingers in his mouth and wolf-whistled. Everybody stopped and looked at him, and in that moment he pointed to Albert who was up on the stage. "Al . . . *Bert*!" he shouted. "Al . . . *Bert* . . . Al . . . *Bert* . . ."

The calls for Tater ended, and I shot to my feet next to him and yelled *"Bert"* after each time he yelled "Al."

In no time the whole gym was chanting Albert's name.

The school didn't even attempt to have a prom. Instead the front office gave permission to the students to stage their own, as long as they were held at venues that weren't school property. White leaders rented out the VFW Hall. Black leaders booked a church community center on the north end.

Both proms were open to juniors and seniors, and no less than three people invited Angie to go with them to the white prom. One after another she turned them down, explaining that she had other plans. This wasn't true, but she said it with such sincerity that none of her suitors questioned her.

I'd invited Regina Perrault, but she'd politely declined and used the same excuse as Angie—she had other plans. Regina sounded genuinely aggrieved, which helped with my disappointment, but I later learned that she, in fact, was going with a former boyfriend, Shane Gautreaux. Shane had graduated the year before and now was a Marine Corps private waiting for deployment to Vietnam. Angie encouraged me to invite someone else and rattled off a list of candidates, but for me it was Regina or no one. I decided to stay home and lick my wounds instead.

It was the actual day of the prom before I realized that Angie wasn't going because she didn't want me to be at home alone when she was out having a good time.

"They're just friends," she said.

"Who are?"

"Regina and Shane. She asked him because he's shipping out soon."

I didn't want to talk about it. "What are our plans?"

"I was going to ask you." Before I could make a suggestion she said, "What if we crashed the parties?"

"Don't you mean party?"

She didn't answer. More than four months had passed since our encounter with Charlie LeBlanc, and she'd successfully recovered from the experience by focusing on her studies and after-school activities, often chocking her days so full that Johnny Carson was deep into his monologue before she surrendered and went to bed. We still had classes with Tater, and still sat next to him, but I didn't notice any tension of the romantic sort between them. For all I knew it had been repressed into oblivion, and I found myself hoping for that.

One day after track practice, Tater and I were walking to the locker room when he told me he was exhausted because he'd stayed up late the night before talking to Patrice Jolivette on the phone. Thrilled to hear it, I shared the news with Mama, knowing that she'd pass it on to Pops. I just wanted things to be normal at home—normal, as we knew it.

"Is it true he's with somebody else?" Pops asked me.

I knew he meant Tater. "I believe he is."

"Thank God in heaven," Pops said. "Remind me to light a candle next time we're at church."

I'm not sure why, but I didn't tell Angie about Tater and Patrice. She'd been getting a lot of attention from guys at schools, and I suppose I thought none of us would benefit from a discussion about Tater's current status. I didn't want to distract her, I guess it was, and I hoped she would explore the possibility of another relationship. One of her admirers was Donnie Landry, a senior who'd taken her to see *Gone with the Wind* when it returned for its annual showing at the Delta. Donnie owned his own car, and on weekend nights he and Angie often went for drives around town, returning to Helen Street with just enough time to make curfew.

I asked her once if they ever went parking out on Nap's Lane, and the only answer she gave me was a giggle. I'd thought Donnie might be gay, but her reaction told me I was wrong.

"What do y'all do out there?"

"What does anybody do?" she replied.

"Do y'all make out or something?"

"I'm suddenly very uncomfortable with this conversation," she said. But it was an answer, the one I'd hoped for.

Mama said she wanted us home by midnight, which seemed generous considering our usual 10:30 p.m. Saturday curfew. We began the evening at the Little Chef, then headed out to the VFW Hall on North Liberty Street. I was driving, which prevented me from seeing much, but the prom was exactly what you'd expect from a large social given by a school like ours. Girls wore homemade formals with corsages either pinned to their gowns or held to their wrists with elastic bands, and the boys wore mostly pastel-colored suits with shirts open at the neck or finished with narrow sock ties. There seemed to be as many people outside drinking and smoking under the trees as there were inside. Through the open front door I glimpsed a rock band in matching red outfits playing on stage, and out in the night I heard the thumping of a bass guitar and caught occasional phrases from a singer struggling with "Like to Get to Know You" by Spanky and Our Gang.

On our third pass in front of the building, I spotted Regina through the door. I'd heard people say she looked like the model Jean Shrimpton but with a more voluptuous figure. Now I felt blood vessels clamp shut in my neck at the sight of her slow-dancing with the smartly uniformed Shane Gautreaux, and then a dizzy spell came on. Part of me wanted to rush the place and hit Shane the way I hit the blocking sled. But another part—the one where my sanity resided—wanted to leave the prom as fast as possible. That was the part that prevailed.

Next we drove across town to the church center where the black prom was being held. I made a couple of laps around the building and then found a place to park. The building's walls were mostly windows, and there were no curtains to keep us from seeing inside. Mood lights were strategically placed in the corners of the room; it was just dark enough to make out figures moving around. Most everyone was dancing, while a few drank punch and ate finger sandwiches at tables arranged along the back wall. The scene was nearly identical to the one we'd found at the VFW Hall, except here instead of a band there was a deejay spinning records. And everyone was black.

We listened to songs by the Delfonics and Freda Payne, and then one from the Jackson 5. It was "I'll Be There," which inspired shouts and squeals as everybody stormed the dance floor. Even Angie and I found ourselves brandishing invisible microphones and exaggerating the effort it took to get the words out: *"I'll be there, I'll be there, just call my name, I'll be there."*

"How are we any different than they are?" she said when the song ended. "I mean, how are we, really? Remember what Dead Eye Dud said in biology class about skin color? He said it was decoration, nothing more, nothing less."

Something in the building had caught her attention, and I turned away from her now to see it. In the back of the room, positioned above one of the mood lights, I could make out the familiar, well-formed figure of Tater Henry dancing with the equally impressive Patrice Jolivette. Tater hadn't told me about his plans to attend the prom, but there he was in a suit, the front of his shirt open halfway down to his navel. I hesitated to look at Angie for fear of her reaction.

"He needs to stick to playing ball," she said.

"It's true. The dude can't dance a lick."

Certain it was time to leave, I started the engine and engaged the clutch, but she reached over and killed the motor. Then she removed the key from the ignition.

"Let's watch a while longer," she said. "Please. It's kind of cute."

Not that I hadn't had plenty of opportunities before, but this was the perfect time to ask her how she felt about him, even though if I were honest, it was a question I didn't want answered. As long as I didn't know with certainty, the possibility existed that her feelings for him were no different than my own.

"It looks like he's stomping roaches," I said to her instead. "Stomping and missing. God, he's almost as bad as me."

She'd only started to reply when a figure broke from the dance floor and went straight at Tater, knocking him to the ground and upsetting the lamp, which thrust that part of the room in darkness. The music stopped. Cries rang out. I saw a table with food tip over. Then Tater appeared again—or rather a shadow of Tater—and he was pummeling the guy who'd attacked him. He had the upper hand now. The guy curled up with his arms covering his head, and Tater kept striking him, driving punches wherever he could fit them. I felt the old impulse to help him out, but it was obvious he didn't need me. He might've been a boxer hitting a speed bag, his fists moved so fast. Then several figures converged on Tater and pulled him away, and my brain processed the hulking silhouettes and gave me names—Randall Wallace and Stanley Redd, football teammates. A moment later Tater came crashing through the center's doors with Randall and Stanley attending to him. Patrice appeared next, and finally a crowd of excited kids tumbled out.

Angie pushed her door open, but I reached over and grabbed the handle and pulled it closed again.

"It's not our place," I said.

"What does that mean, Rodney?"

"You're not going out there."

"Who would do that to him? Who would just run up and knock him to the ground like that? Did you see? He wasn't doing anything."

"Give me the key, Angie."

She was still watching the building as she held it out to me. I started the engine and shifted to first.

"Who does it, Rodney? Why?"

In the building now the overhead lights came on, even as the music started playing and dancers returned to the floor. I could see a couple of people I recognized from school helping up the person who'd struck Tater.

His hair was teased out to a size twice as large as everybody else's, and he wore chains around his neck. The family resemblance was uncanny.

"It's always something," Pops said the next day at the kitchen table.

He'd heard about the fight, and now he was weighing in.

"If it's not this," he said, "then it's that. Why does so much happen to that boy? He shows up and there's automatically a score to settle."

That seemed to do it for Angie. She got up and left.

Mama had cooked a pot roast and mashed potatoes, and we'd returned from mass only an hour before. I'd hoped for a quiet meal without the subject of race dominating yet another conservation. Still, I couldn't help but consider Pops's words, especially since he kept repeating them in an effort to bait me: "Always something, huh, Rodney? Is it *in* them? I wish somebody would tell me."

I considered the litany of things Tater had been through since we'd known him. And I understood what Pops was getting at, even though I would've put it differently. Tater's guilt or innocence didn't matter; they weren't even the issue. What mattered in most instances was his skin color. And what mattered every other time had even less to do with who he was.

"Angie, come back to this table right now, young lady," Pops called out.

Her response was no response. We could hear it from the kitchen.

Tater called later that afternoon as Angie and I were doing homework. Not wishing to rile Pops any more, Mama came to my room and whispered that it was for me. I went to the kitchen phone.

"I saw this truck last night heading south with two white people in it," Tater said. "The driver looked like Bigfoot. He also looked like he was in a hurry. I'm sorry if the passenger saw what I think she saw."

"Why'd he do it?" I asked.

"You'd have to ask him, Rodney. And while you're at it, find out why he busted your leg open that day with his car door. The dude's crazy."

"I know he's crazy, Tater. But what is it between the two of you? What happened that he's still coming after you?"

"Nothing happened," he said, "except that my mother took his father away from his mom and him, and then disappeared for good once he shot her and turned the gun on himself. Robert blames me. He's always blamed me."

"But you were a baby."

"That's right, I was."

"And in his mind you were the cause of it?"

"Yeah. Me. Tater Henry. I did it."

Perhaps because we'd been to church that morning, I tried to remember the story in the Bible about brothers who compete for their father's love. I hadn't been much of a catechism student, and now I couldn't remember if it was Cain and Abel or the prodigal son. In any case, it was the one where only confusion and heartache came to the good son in the end.

Angie appeared in the kitchen and held her hand out for the receiver. I gave it to her.

"You need dance lessons," she said.

I heard laughter and a muffled reply.

Then she said, "Of course I will. But I think Patrice might object. Clear it with her first, will you? I don't want her to come after me the way your brother did last night."

Another inaudible answer.

"Okay, *half* brother. I stand corrected."

It was hours later, long after I'd gone to bed, when she came into my room and stood next to me in the dark. I'd been sleeping off the chaos of the night before, and it took a while for me to understand that I wasn't alone. She must've just had a bath and washed and blow-dried her hair. She was combing it out, giving it the required strokes.

"Rodney," she said, "I want you to know that I've had it with your contradictions. You have to do better."

"My who?" I said into my pillow.

"Your contradictions. How do you live with them, Rodney? How do you live with yourself for that matter?"

"I just do, Angie. Will you let me sleep now?"

It wasn't the answer she wanted. "You can love him, but I can't? You can want to protect him, but I can't get close? Why is that? We're twins."

"Yes, but I'm the boy twin. And you're the girl twin."

"You're the boy twin? You're also the worst kind of hypocrite. I would also say you're something else, but I'm not here to call you names."

She had me now. I sat up and turned on the lamp. "I wish you'd stop thinking about only yourself, Angie. Think about Mama and Pops for a minute. They have to live in this town. Pops could have problems at the plant. Mama could lose work. People will shun them. And what about me? I won't be able to walk the halls at school without people saying things. And you know what things. It's not cool, Angie. Do you know one white person at school—no, make that in town, the whole, entire town . . . Do you know one white person who's with a black?"

"Yes."

"And who is that?"

"Jules Taylor Rich," she said, naming a local attorney.

"Yeah, but Jules Taylor Rich had to go all the way to Wisconsin to find her. That's where they met—in Madison, Wisconsin, at the college there. Ask Mama if you don't believe me. That woman doesn't have a friend in town, Angie. The blacks have nothing to do with her and the whites don't either. And people look at their children . . . well, like they're Martians." I was awake now. I was good and awake. "You've taken it far enough."

"But I've taken it nowhere."

"In this case nowhere is farther along than you need to be. Aren't there any other boys for you to fall in love with? What about Donnie?"

"Why Donnie? Because he's white?"

"Yes, because he's white."

She started combing her hair again. I could hear numbers as she ticked them off under her breath: "Fifty-three . . . fifty-four . . . fifty-five . . . fifty-six . . ."

She counted all the way to a hundred before letting herself out of the room, but I couldn't get back to sleep. I lay awake thinking about what a hypocrite I was. She'd said I was something else, too, without naming it, and I knew what it was and knew she was right.

I was a racist.

Yeah. That was the word.

I needed a summer job, so Pops helped me get a part-time gig at the plant, loading tractor-trailer rigs. After a week the manager asked me if I knew any other high school boys looking for work, and I recruited Tater.

It was weird how I felt about him. One moment I burned with resentment for the troubles he'd brought to my life, and the next he was the guy I liked hanging around with better than anybody else.

We usually started the day at around 5:30 a.m. to avoid the heat.

Pops was still on the job when we punched in, which meant that for the first few weeks, with the Cameo tied up, Tater and I had to get to work on bikes. I rode mine, and he rode Angie's. She'd let him borrow it until we could figure out a solution to our transportation problem.

It was Pops who came to the rescue. One day, when he should've been sleeping, he hopped a ride with a neighbor to a used-car dealership out on the Ville Platte Road and returned home with a four-door Mercury Comet. It had a hundred and sixty thousand miles on the odometer, but the engine had been rebuilt, and the body and tires were good. And it was the family car we'd needed for years. Pops wanted to help me out, but he was also tired of Mama's complaints about the four of us having to go to church crammed on a bench seat made for three.

"I'm not giving her to you," he said of the Cameo, "but she's yours to use for now. Share her with your sister, and take your mother wherever she needs to go. You'll have to pay for gas and help with the insurance."

So Tater returned the bike to Angie, and I picked him up each morning and drove him to the job. We rarely worked past 10:00 a.m., then we had doughnuts and chocolate milk at a bakery in town, and reported to the weight room at school. Done with lifting by noon, I dropped him off at home and returned to Helen Street for lunch and a two-hour nap. Then I went back to his house at around three o'clock and retrieved him a second time, now for baseball practice.

We'd graduated from the Babe Ruth League to American Legion, which meant we were playing teams from other towns. Pops let me drive the Cameo to away games, and I loaded two teammates in the cab and fit more in back, along with the team's equipment. There usually were three or four cars in our away-game caravans, each of them packed with teenage boys in pinstriped baseball uniforms, but one time I was the only player who could get a vehicle and I had to drive the entire team, fourteen guys total. We had five up front and the rest in back. Good thing the game was just twenty minutes down the road in Rayne. Avoiding the interstate, where I was sure a state trooper would pull us over, I drove the truck down less-traveled roads to Shuteston and Church Point, then shot southward through rice fields until we arrived at the ballpark.

We were the Warriors, and our coach, Danny Arnaud, told me I was the largest player in team history, which dated back nearly forty years. Coach Arnaud took more pride in this than I did. The local paper ran a story about how he had to special-order my uniform (XXXL), spikes (size 18), and batting helmet (8 ½). They were so expensive that most of the money I made at the plant that summer went to paying for them. As I read the story, I kept seeing a made-up picture of Regina Perrault shaking her head in disgust as she sat with the paper and calculated my measurements. If she was reading right (now I was imagining her thoughts), my head was almost as big around as her waist. Like a fairy in a children's book, she could take a bubble bath in my shoe.

Time in tractor-trailer rigs and the weight room had reduced my bulk and made me leaner and more muscular, but I was still a behemoth and, to some, a freak. During batting practice before games, I put on shows, hitting balls over the fences and deep into the cane and bean fields where the parks had been carved. Most of the balls were lost until harvest time, when the combines came through and kicked them up. Even players for the other teams paused to watch me take batting practice. I led the Warriors that summer with twenty-nine home runs, a fairly sizable number if you considered we played a thirty-five-game schedule. As the season went on, fan attendance grew to where it was standing room only. They came and stood along the fence and took pictures with their pocket cameras, the flashes going off when I came up to bat.

While many, I'm sure, came to see "the Boog Powell of Cajun Country," as one newspaper columnist called me, even more came to see Tater, who the same columnist had labeled "the Roberto Clemente of Acadiana." Tater's batting average was .547, the best in our region, and he was so adept at stealing bases that most catchers let him advance without bothering to challenge him.

Deep into the season I noticed that it wasn't only regular folks who were coming to see us play. College recruiters also started turning out, the identity of the schools they represented stitched in bold lettering over the pockets of their polo shirts and on the crowns of their caps. They wanted us for baseball, but then a football coach, LSU's Beauregard Jeune, attended one of our home games.

Coach Jeune paid at the gate. Then he walked through a mob of fans and took a seat at the top of the bleachers. People kept approaching him for autographs, and the game announcer welcomed him in the voice that he usually reserved for home runs. Some of the locals started chanting, "*El Less Hugh . . . El Less Hugh . . . El Less Hugh . . .*" And Coach Jeune stood and waved to them like a politician on the stump.

The NCAA had a rule prohibiting football coaches from speaking to high school talent in the summer, but Coach Jeune didn't need to visit with Tater and me. That he showed up told us all we needed to know.

My mother's parents had a small cattle ranch outside of town on the Sunset Road, and every Saturday that summer, Tater and I camped in an old army tent under the pecan trees that stood along a bayou at the back of the property. We made sure to pack well for these adventures and brought along a Coleman lantern, a gas cookstove, and an ice chest filled with boudin, frozen fish, and candy bars. The heavy canvas tent trapped suffocating levels of heat and moisture, and some nights never did cool down below eighty degrees, but we managed the conditions without any difficulty because we'd become inured to it after our mornings at the plant and afternoons playing ball in the sun.

My grandparents' house stood at the front of the ranch, and you reached the bayou on a rutted dirt lane that ran a mile back between a wire fence and the grassy fields where the cows grazed. We lay on quilts under the stars and listened to Zydeco and Cajun music on Miss Nettie's transistor radio, and a few nights after it got dark we had visits from Angie and Mama, who arrived in the Comet, trailing clouds of dust. The car's headlights grew larger and brighter the closer they got. A cottonmouth infestation made the bayou too dangerous to swim, and I knew that the real reason they came out was to allay any fears that wild animals had made a meal of us in the night. They brought leftovers from supper and an occasional dessert, such as fudge bars, melting in a minnow bucket filled with ice.

"What are y'all doing?" Angie asked this one night when she stepped from the car.

"We're camping," I said. "What does it look like?"

"But what are you *doing*?"

Only now did I understand that she'd intended the question for Tater.

"Camping," he said. "Doing what you do when you camp."

She wouldn't stop. "Such as *what*?" He started to answer, but she cut him off. "Where do you use the bathroom, for instance?"

"Wherever they like," Mama answered. "Let's move on, baby."

But Angie was still waiting for Tater's reply.

"Behind trees," he said at last. He looked off at an old oak thirty yards away. A roll of toilet paper sat on the tree's roots.

"We usually designate one for that purpose," I explained.

"Can you imagine what life must be like for your bathroom tree?" she said. "You're standing along the bayou, minding your own business and making the world a pretty place and processing loads of carbon dioxide and putting oxygen in the air, when all of a sudden you two show up. It must be traumatizing."

I supposed she was hoping for laughs. She got none.

"Where's Pops?" I asked.

Neither of them answered, which told me he'd decided to stay home. It was his way of protesting, I knew. He didn't want his daughter involved with Tater, and he wasn't happy about his son's involvement with him either. "Why can't you go camping with T-Boy or one of those?" he'd asked me, producing the same silence that lately I answered most of his questions with.

Angie hopped to her feet and brushed off the seat of her pants. "I'm ready when you are," she said to Mama. Then she ran ahead to the Comet.

"I'm so sorry," Mama said to Tater.

It was hard to tell whether she meant for just now or for other things. Tater put his arm around her shoulders and led her to the car. "Don't worry about it, Mrs. Boulet," he said. "I sure don't worry about it."

I didn't know what to make of Angie. She might've been a cheerleader at school, but she usually was a modest, private, serious-minded girl, and the type who made every effort to distract attention from the fact that she even used the bathroom. When we shopped with Mama at the A&P, Angie hid the toilet paper under other items in the buggy. The bathroom at home was always spick-and-span because she kept it that way, and I never once heard her pass gas let alone belch.

I wondered if she was trying to be one of the guys, talking the way she thought we did when members of polite society weren't around. It didn't register that she might've been calculating whether she would be comfortable on a campout until the next Saturday when she showed up at our campsite alone. She arrived in the Comet, and rather than leftover supper and frozen dairy bars, she brought two six packs of beer. The cans were warm, and I figured she'd raided the stash Pops kept stored in the shed. By now Tater and I had already drunk the pint of tequila that Tater had pilfered from Miss Nettie, so the beer was much appreciated. Angie made room for the cans in the ice chest, then she removed a grocery bag from the car, holding a change of clothes, toiletries, and a family-size bottle of mosquito repellant.

"Which tree is it tonight?" she asked, getting right to the point.

Tater pointed to a towering pecan with a large trunk, excellent for privacy. "If you want to spare the tree's feelings," he said, "there's an abandoned outhouse in that overgrown stand of chicken trees on the edge of the pasture. Only problem, last time I stopped by, there was a moccasin coiled up on the seat."

Had I wanted Angie to camp with us, I'd have invited her. I didn't feel like arguing in front of Tater, but she needed to let us know her plans for the night.

"I told them I was going to a slumber party at Julie's house," she said. "There really is one, and I really did go. But I left after an hour and came here."

"So you didn't lie. That's what you're saying."

"I didn't lie. No. In the morning, if Mama asks how it went, I'll tell her—truthfully again—how boring it was and that will be that."

"And what about Pops? What will you tell him?"

"He won't ask," she said. "But if he does, I'll tell him it's none of his business."

She sprayed repellant all over her body, then gave me the bottle to cover her backside. I'd never seen her drink before, and I struggled now with the sight of her holding a Schlitz Tall Boy. Something about her manner smacked of the provocateur, the young rebel wanting to upset the status quo.

"Pops would blow his top if you talked to him like that," I said.

She laughed and slurped her beer. "Then I should make sure to do it."

We arranged the quilts around the fire and lay on them with our hands folded behind our heads and stared off at so many stars clotting the sky, it seemed they were one star. We really got after the beer, and we listened to the radio until midnight when KSLO went off the air. It was the only station in town, and we were so far out in the sticks that finding a replacement with good reception wasn't easy. Tater worked the dial until he found a channel out of Lafayette playing "Layla" by Derek and the Dominos, and he jumped to his feet and reached for Angie's hand, which she surrendered without hesitation.

They danced around the fire like a pair of drunk, hungry cannibals gearing up for a late-night repast—yeah, one that basically amounted to each other. In the hot firelight you could see how beautiful they both were. Tater wore hiking boots, jean cutoffs, and a light T-shirt adorned with an Indian warbonnet and the word WARRIORS across the chest. Angie had rolled her white shorts up to the points of her hips, and her halter top, as I'd warned her in a whisper earlier, "just isn't working hard enough to keep you from spilling out." Bare feet stamping the grass, she moved without her usual grace, and instead demonstrated that at the core of every smart, pretty girl was a hellion needing only beer and a campfire to set her free.

"Don't you wish I'd brought Regina with me?" Angie asked me when the song ended. She fell to the ground in a swoon and lay panting against me. "My brother is in love with Regina Perrault," she said.

Her eyes were closed, and I wasn't sure if she was making a general statement of fact or edifying Tater on the subject.

"This explains why the more he drinks, the more he mumbles her name," he said.

"I don't understand genetics," Angie said. "Whenever I see an attractive girl—Regina is definitely that—I check out her brothers to see what they're like. I do this because I have such a handsome, desirable twin, and I have this fantasy about the two of us double-dating. Anyway, Regina's brother, Carl, is a year ahead of us, and he's just not in her league in the cute department."

"I like Carl," I said. "Good dude."

She wasn't listening. "Because if Rodney ever does pursue Regina, I thought it might be interesting if there was a male equivalent in the Perrault family *pour moi.* We could keep the twin thing going in perpetuity and have a large wedding ceremony—you know, a two-for-the-price-of-one kind of deal, and save Pops some money. Then Rodney and I could have dinner together every Sunday and stuff like that."

"And wear the same clothes," Tater said. "All four of you."

"No more beer for me," I announced. "No more for you either," I said to Angie.

"I don't think I could hold Carl's hand, let alone kiss him," she replied, then threw an arm across my chest and fell asleep.

I slept too. And when I awoke, hours later, she and Tater were sitting on a quilt a few feet away from me, closer to the fire. Head wildly tumbling from the beer and tequila, I had a hard time comprehending what they were doing, which was so extraordinary I wondered if I was dreaming.

Tater's legs were crossed under him, and Angie, positioned behind him, was removing leeches from his body. Fat, black, and glistening, the leeches counted in the dozens, and blood smudged Tater's skin where they had latched on. As she picked each one off, she flicked it in the fire, making sparks shoot up. The leeches had anchored to the exposed areas of his body, and suddenly it occurred to me that if he had them, I likely had them too. I stood and frantically started brushing my arms and face with my hands. I ran in place, the way we did at football practice, knees pumping high, feet light on the turf. Angie and Tater let me continue for a while before stopping me with laughs. This was the same moment I saw the sun topping the trees and coloring the dirt road that ran on the side of the fields.

"How long did I sleep?" I asked.

Angie was working on his upper torso now, her face screwed up in disgust. "Four hours maybe. Five at most."

I saw fresh wood on the fire, the blaze stronger than when I fell off.

I felt poisoned, like I'd substituted the Schlitz with rat killer. "Where'd your little friends come from?" I asked, then lay back and covered my face with my hands.

"We went swimming in the pond," Angie said.

She meant the watering hole where the cows went to drink. Now it was my turn to laugh, despite the load of pain it dropped on my cranium. "The cows do more than just drink in there. At least we have trees to hide behind when we need to do those things."

"Oh, God," she said. "We walked right in it, spent a long time in it."

"That explains why the bottom was so soft," Tater said.

"Where are your leeches?" I said to her, asking a question that I immediately knew I'd never pose to another human being for as long as I lived.

"Tater was a gentleman," she answered. "He insisted on taking mine off first, then I went to work on his."

She finished and stood up, and I noticed that she'd wrapped a towel around her middle and knotted it at her waist. Still, a thin trickle of blood ran from her inner thigh past her knee. I wondered if it was the result of a leech's damage or the beginning of her menstrual cycle. I glanced at Tater. He was checking his legs for more leeches. Hoping to avoid his attention, I held my gaze on the blood on Angie's leg. She looked down, quickly toweled it off, then fled for the bathroom tree.

I checked her toiletries to see if she'd come prepared, but there was only facial tissue. I knew her well enough to know that she was as "regular as clockwork," as I'd heard her say to Mama. It seemed unlikely that she didn't know her period was coming.

When she returned to the fire, she was holding the towel in a bundle in her arms. "I'd better go," she said. "Pops will want the car. And I need a bath in the worst way."

"You'll miss breakfast," Tater said. "We always scramble eggs."

"I don't want to get in trouble."

I stayed on the quilt. Tater gave her a hug good-bye.

She left with a maelstrom of dust in her wake.

★★★

The baseball season ended in Baker on August 7, when we lost in a regional tournament to the hardest-throwing pitcher in the state. Only Tater, with a pair of singles, was able to hit him. It was my worst day all summer. I grounded out twice and struck out my next time up. After the strikeout, I threw my helmet from the batter's box to the dugout in a fit of frustration, and Coach Arnaud pulled me from the game.

"What is wrong with you?" he asked in front of my teammates. "You're the last person I'd expect that from."

I considered running down the list of things that were wrong with me, beginning with the fact that I couldn't sleep at night for fear of dreaming about leeches and my sister's blood, but I preferred to have him think of me as a hothead than a psycho so I apologized and dropped it.

Angie and I celebrated our seventeenth birthday five days later. It was the same day that two-a-day practices for football began, and Mama and Pops waited to throw us a party until after the afternoon workout was done. A dozen or so classmates showed up, as many of them black as white. Pops never explained why, but he stayed outside the entire time, turning links of pork sausage on the barbecue and sucking on his lumpy cigarettes. Tater and Rubin and the other guys hung out with me in the living room, and the girls helped Mama with the potato salad in the kitchen. Minutes before we sat down to eat, Patrice Jolivette showed up at the front door. She'd driven all the way from Baton Rouge, where she was undergoing freshman orientation at Southern University. Angie was so happy to see her that she broke into tears.

Angie had told everyone not to bring gifts, but Tater defied her order. He presented us with custom-made T-shirts with a big Oreo cookie on the front of each one. Angie's shirt was number one and mine was number three. They were both black. "Long live the Oreos!" somebody shouted as we were holding up the shirts. Then Tater made a big production of revealing that he'd come to the party wearing his own Oreo shirt under his dress shirt. It was number two, wouldn't you know, and it was the same white as the cookie's cream filling.

We made po'boys with the barbecued sausage on foot-long tubes of crusty French bread, and each serving of potato salad came with an artful sprinkling of warm, crushed bacon on top. Ever since we were babies Mama had insisted on doubling the candles on the cake, to give each of us a chance to blow out our own, and today's total came to thirty-four. Angie's were the pink ones on the right side; mine were the blue on the left. We counted to three and blew in unison and got the job done, and then we annihilated the lemon *doberge* cake that Mama had baked that morning. Rubin and I ate most of the cake by ourselves. I answered every piece he ate with one of my own.

"Just another excuse to compete," I explained to the others.

"Don't eat the candles," Angie said. "They're made of wax."

"Did somebody say candles?" asked Rubin. And this, of course, prompted the two of us to pretend to make a meal of them.

Pops never did come inside. After he finished cooking he moved his lawn chair away from the hot pit and placed it in front of his garden.

Surrounded by tomato plants, a bottle of mosquito repellant at his feet, he was content to stay outside until the guests left. It was almost 10:00 p.m. when I went out and told him we were taking Tater home.

"He can't walk?" he said.

"It's too far. And we had practice today."

"Then don't be long, Rodney," he said. He'd stood in barbecue smoke for hours, and he could barely keep his eyes open. "Don't let your sister—"

"I won't, Pops."

He was squinting. "Thank you, son." And he patted me on the shoulder.

In the truck, Tater sat between Angie and me. We had our first workout tomorrow at 8:00 a.m., and I was already dreading it. The muscles in my legs were sore, and a cramp stabbed my calf every time I lifted my foot to work the clutch. Even worse was how my head felt. It would take a while to get used to wearing a helmet again. We'd just turned left on Dunbar Street, heading toward Parkview Drive, when I heard music approaching from behind us. As always with Smooth, I heard the car before I saw it, and by the time I saw it he was already sitting on my back bumper.

We crossed the bridge and came to a stop. Smooth revved his engine and pulled up beside us in the next lane. In the night, his car looked sinister, with its white stripes floating against a field of gleaming black, and the darkened windshield reflecting a silvery sky.

"This ends now," Tater said. "Let me out."

"No!" Angie screamed.

I turned right onto Parkview, and Smooth turned with us, staying even with the Cameo in the next lane as I worked through the gears and began to pick up speed. The street was quiet tonight and there was no oncoming traffic. He followed us going the speed limit for about a quarter of a mile. Hoping to shake him, I stupidly decided to punch the accelerator and hold it against the floorboard. But the Cameo was no dragster. Smooth stayed with me all the way down the street until he suddenly braked, cut his wheel hard to the right, and pulled up on my tail.

We now were at the intersection of Bertheaud and Parkview—the corner, it occurred to me, where affluent, white Parkview transitioned to mostly black Railroad Avenue. Smooth couldn't have been more than a few inches off the back bumper.

"I'll teach him," Tater said. "Come on, Angie. Let me out."

Tater made a move to get past her. She blocked him. "No," she said.

"Rodney?"

"No way, brother." I leaned forward and hugged the wheel. I turned left and crossed the tracks, Smooth still hanging close. I stopped in front of Tater's house and cracked my door, and the gleaming black car shot past us, its stereo blasting "Patches" by Clarence Carter, a song I'd halfway liked until now.

He parked in the middle of the street, about sixty yards away, his foot on the brake pedal, lighting the fronts of the little houses, and seemed to be contemplating his next move. We stood huddled outside and waited, as Clarence Carter wailed on:

"He said Patches
I'm dependin' on you, son
To pull the family through
My son, it's all left up to you"

Then without a word Tater broke from Angie and me and went running toward him. He showed classic form as his knees came up high and his arms pumped close against his ribcage to help him accelerate.

"No, Tater," Angie called out. And in that instant Smooth dropped to a shooter's stance, held a handgun out in front of him, and opened fire. The *pop pop pop* of the pistol sent me diving against Angie, and I could see Tater fall to the street as I tumbled with her into the weeds. Smooth squeezed off a few more rounds and then was gone, rounding the corner with a squeal of tires, music receding in the night.

Tater was sitting on the blacktop and feeling his body to make sure he hadn't been hit. "I'm fine," he said before we even reached him.

"Tater . . . *Tater* . . ."

"He missed on purpose. They all went over my head."

He and Angie held each other. Whimpering and shaking with fear, she ran her hands over his face, and he did the same to hers.

Along the length of the street, porch lights came on, but nobody stepped outside. The man across from Tater's house watched us from his front window. I thought how odd we must've looked in our Oreo

T-shirts, moments after being shot at. I leaned back against the hood and listened for Smooth's return, but there was nothing: no music and no sounds of a car speeding. "We need to call the police," I said.

Tater was standing by the side of the road now, Angie leaning against him. He had his arms around her.

They're still together, I thought. *They've always been together.*

"Can I use the phone in your house?" I said. "Let's call them."

"No,"Tater said. He turned back to me. "It wouldn't do any good."

"The guy just shot at you, and you won't call the police?"

"He shot over me, and it wouldn't help. I can't count the number of times me and my auntie called them before. Most times we're lucky if they even show up. No, man, there are other ways to handle it."

"Like at the prom? Like how you did it then?"

Tater patted his chest. "He's two up on me. It's my turn next."

"I'm with Tater," Angie said.

"Yeah, Ang," I said. "You are, aren't you?"

"I mean I agree with him. I don't see the point in calling the police either. Suppose they send Mr. Charlie again. Is that what you want?"

They must've been pretending all these months. The real reason she hadn't gone to the prom wasn't because she hadn't wanted me to spend the night alone. It was because of Tater. If she couldn't go with him, she wasn't going to go with anyone. And Tater's thing with Patrice? That was all a show too. He'd used her the same way Angie had used Donnie Landry—to give the appearance that it was over between them and they'd moved on, to mollify Pops, and maybe even to get me off their backs.

I was too tired to argue with them, and besides, Tater was probably right—if the rest of them were anything like Charlie LeBlanc, the cops wouldn't do.

My hamstring was starting to tighten up, and I knew I had to get off my feet. "Let's go home, Angie," I said.

"Not yet. Just a little more time, please."

"But Pops is waiting."

That was all it took.

On the drive back to Helen Street, I kept checking for Smooth in the rearview mirror, and I saw his ghost car pulling up behind me, even though it wasn't really there. Still crazier was how I couldn't get the song "Patches" out of my head.

"I know you wouldn't tell Pops," she said, "but please don't tell Mama, either. Will you promise me, Rodney?"

In the light from the dash she looked years younger, like a little kid.

"They don't need to worry, do they?" she said. "I've already made them worry enough."

We were back on Dunbar Street now, crossing the bridge over the bayou. "You're right they'd worry," I said. "And who knows, Angie? This time Pops might really stop you from ever seeing Tater again."

She let out a sob from deep inside. I thought I knew everything about her, but this was a sound I'd never heard before. "That too," she whispered.

Nothing else passed between us, but I stopped talking to her, and she stopped talking to me.

We couldn't very well avoid each other at home, and yet we did somehow. When I had an errand to run in town, I no longer invited her to join me. We didn't visit the Little Chef or go to mass together, and she stopped coming to me with her drawings and paintings for approval. Our Oreo shirts, still new, went unworn. I drove her to school in the morning, but the only voice in the cab came from the deejay on the radio. Our seating order in class changed. I let the two of them sit together, while I found a desk on the other side of the room.

There was turmoil in my head like I'd never known. Even with football to keep me occupied, I thought I was losing it.

I decided he didn't love her the way she loved him. Yes, he loved her, but it was another kind. I did believe she was in love with him, and desirous of him, desperately so. I believed she wanted to be his girlfriend. Because she could be so serious and single-minded, she probably also dreamed about a future with him after they graduated and left town. But I never got the same from him. Angie offered something else—the family he never had, maybe the sister he'd lost. If he was in love with her, why didn't he look at her the way other guys looked at the girls they wanted?

He had a phone at home, but he rarely called. Was he afraid Pops would answer? I supposed it could've been Pops, but I'd always had the impression that Tater wasn't afraid of anyone.

I didn't want to believe she'd given her virginity to him that night by the bayou, but in my weak moments, despite piles of evidence to the contrary, I couldn't help myself. I revisited their words and actions and became convinced that they'd made love on a quilt only a few feet away from me while I was sleeping off a drunk. "I don't want to get in trouble," she'd said shortly before leaving. Had she been talking about Pops and the Comet or about getting pregnant?

It was also possible that they'd had their moment earlier, with leeches devouring them, in that vat of cow waste. If this was true, they deserved the leeches. She had always promised to wait until she got married, as I had promised. Mama instilled this in both of us, indoctrinated us with its importance and sold us on its virtue.

And he was black. More than everything else, Tater Henry was black.

These thoughts banged around my head at practice when I should've been focused on becoming a better football player.

We were in team drills going against the number one defense. I was faced off against Rubin Lazarus, a man who had the power to hurt me, and I kept obsessing about my sister. I saw her dancing with Tater to "Layla." I watched her pick leeches off his chest. The play was a dropback pass, and Rubin came at me hard, and I slammed my headgear into the breastplate of his shoulder pads and knocked him back a step. He staggered, then charged again. I hit him a second time.

Why didn't she talk to me anymore? Did she really think I was a racist? What made me a racist? I had black friends, didn't I? What about Rubin here? And would Tater be such a great player without me blocking for him, protecting him from harm when he set up to pass, clearing the way when he ran with the ball?

If I was such a racist, why did I get along so well with black people? And why did I like so many of the ones I knew?

Everybody loved him because he was gifted. They loved her because she was beautiful. The two of them understood each other better than I understood either of them, and I'd by lying if I said that didn't bother me. She'd always said we were "one and the same and nobody without each other." Now we didn't even talk.

Another pass play began. Rubin charged, and this time I caught him under his birdcage and popped his chinstrap off. His head jerked back; his helmet tumbled away. It looked like a head ripped from its body, rolling until it finally stopped at Coach Valentine's feet.

Would I be decapitating people if I were such a lousy human being?

In the locker room after practice a kid laughed at me. "What's funny?" I asked.

I knew it was because of Angie. Word had gotten around: She'd made it with a brother. The prettiest girl in the school—Rodney Boulet's twin sister—and she had gone with the opposite race.

That's right. The opposite race.

I got out of my pads. I stripped off my hip girdle and jock strap and sweat-wet socks. Then I showered and returned to my locker, a towel around my waist. The kid started up again. Now he was pointing at me, and I pointed back before uncorking a roar and running to the other side of the room. I should've grabbed him by the neck the way that unhappy dad had grabbed Tater at the swim meet. But instead I bumped him with my chest and drove him back into the wall, pinning him there. "Not another word about it," I said. "Not another, you hear?"

I might've crushed him had Jasper Bacquet and some others not pulled me away. The kid fell to the ground, gasping for air. "The way you gave Big Rube jelly legs, man," he said, struggling to breathe. "You blew him up, Rodney. On account of that, my brother. Jesus. What is wrong with you, Rodney? You made that dude look weak."

And then he reached out and put his hand on the top of my foot. He started to pet me the way you'd pet a dog or a cat, his hand massaging me from my ankle down to my toes. It was such a weird thing to do, and so pathetic that I suddenly felt sorry for him.

I mean, who pets your foot?

We opened our senior season with the Jamboree. The three teams on the round-robin schedule took turns playing one another over six fifteen-minute periods, so we actually had to face two opponents—Port Barre to start and then Ville Platte to end the evening. Even though the Jamboree was really just a scrimmage, it held great importance to my teammates and me because we were beginning a new year filled with the usual dream of winning every game and claiming the state title. Other schools had come from nowhere to do it. Why couldn't we?

For Tater and Rubin and me, the Jamboree also was the beginning of recruiting. College coaches would be on hand to evaluate our every move, and we needed to impress them.

"This one sets the tone for all the rest to come," Coach Cadet told us on the bus ride from school to the stadium. "You can't win them all without winning the first one, and that's our mandate tonight. It starts here and it starts now."

Coach had been using the word "mandate" since two-a-days, dropping it in pep talks, writing it on the grease board followed by exclamation points. I'd asked Pops what it meant, and he'd shrugged his shoulders and said, "Isn't that a tropical fruit with a big nut in the middle?" Things had been stressful at home, but he still was good for an occasional laugh. I checked the dictionary. "All right, then," Pops said after I read him the definition. "I'll have to remember that."

As Tater and I were leading the team in stretches beforehand, I noticed him looking off in the direction of the cheerleaders. Angie's hair was pulled back and held in a ponytail, and she wore a garter on her right thigh. Because she was my sister I didn't always see her the way others did. But to them Angie was the type who made the world speed up while she moved through it in slow motion. Tater could make all the long runs and throws he wanted tonight. And I could pile-drive any number of defensive linemen into the dirt. For most people in the stadium nothing we did would be halfway as exciting as the sight of her standing on the sideline with pom-poms at her hips.

We finished loosening up and started for the sideline, and Coach Valentine came up behind me and tapped the back of my shoulder pads. "Must be hard, huh, Rodney?"

"What's that, Coach?"

"Having a sister look like Angie. I wouldn't want her out of my sight either."

Until this moment I hadn't realized I was staring.

"She still dating Tater?" he asked.

"She never dated him."

"Really?" His face flashed surprise, and I knew he wasn't kidding.

"No, Coach."

He extended a hand for me to shake. "I'm counting on big things from you tonight."

He meant to be nice, but the conversation set off a burn in my gut. Angie dating Tater? Where on earth had he heard that? Was that what people were saying?

Before kickoff there was a ceremony on the field, recognizing Marco Miller's father, the banker who'd donated money to help stage the event. As Mr. and Mrs. Miller were walking out to midfield to receive a plaque, I broke with team protocol and left the end zone and ran over to where Angie was standing. "Coach Valentine just told me he heard you were dating Tater. Crazy, huh?"

"Coach Valentine said what, Rodney?"

"That the two of you were dating?"

I knew her face. I knew its expressions. The one she was wearing now said: "Get away from me, you moron."

I ran back to my teammates. "Coach Valentine thinks Angie's exclusive with Tater," I said to T-Boy Bertrand, who, like everybody else, was waiting for Marco Miller's parents to get off the field.

"I heard that too," he said.

"You heard that?"

He had taken a knee with his helmet on the ground by his side, and he was propping himself up by the helmet's face mask.

"You really heard that?" I asked. "Who told you that?"

"I don't know, Rodney. I just heard it around."

"They might be very good friends, but I'm not sure it's anything more than that."

"Well . . . sure, man. Yeah. They're friends."

Moments before kickoff, the players for Port Barre jumped around and slapped helmets and gave an appearance of wanting to give us a contest, but it was clear from our first offensive play that they were outmatched. I barely bumped their defensive tackle, and he fell over on his back, eyes clamped shut to the horror of it all.

Tater, meanwhile, faked a sweep to the weak side, then ran around end for sixty-three yards and a touchdown. He jogged past the cheerleaders on his way to the bench, and Angie jumped and fell against him, forcing him to take her in his arms. It was a clumsy gesture that was repeated by yet more girls. We kicked the PAT, and I approached Tater on the sideline.

"Listen," I said, "I have to know. What happened the night we went camping?"

"The night we went camping? Which night?"

"The night Angie stayed with us. When you got the leeches."

He removed his helmet and stepped up to within inches of my face. He seemed to be trying to find words to respond. But after a while he shook his head and walked away.

"Did something happen while I was sleeping?" I yelled after him.

The crowd went up suddenly; our defense had intercepted the ball. Coach Valentine was calling for the offense to get back out on the field.

It had been drilled into me since junior high that the huddle was the quarterback's domain and only he had the authority to speak in it. Linemen kept their mouths shut until the play was called and the count given. Only then, as you were approaching the line, did you have permission to say anything. Now, instead of making calls based on my reading of the defensive front, I addressed my quarterback again.

"What happened, Tater? Tell me, man. Get it off your chest."

He stood behind center as his linemen calculated their splits and formed the no man's land between the offense and defense. He'd called a pass play, a quick slant over the middle to T-Boy, and I set up now with my left hand planted on the ground. On this play you wanted to sell the defense on the run, then surprise them with the pass, and I leaned forward to give the impression that I was ready to sprint out of my stance. Tater started calling signals.

"What happened?" I shouted, waiting until the moment before the ball was snapped.

To my immediate left I felt T-Boy come out fast and chip the man in front of me with a forearm shiver. He cut across the middle just behind the linebackers who'd charged the line hard in response to Tater's belly fake to Jasper, and now T-Boy was wide open with only the safety to beat. Tater usually jumped off his feet to make this pass and threw it over the center, but tonight he pivoted a notch to his left and aimed the ball at me, firing it as hard as he could into the back of my helmet. The ball hit right on target and careened to the ground, prompting whistles from the officials who signaled the play dead.

"You think that lets you off the hook?" I said on my way back to the huddle.

"Get your head in the game, Rodney."

"What happened with Angie?"

"Will you let it go?"

"Let it go?" I shouted. "Let it go? What happened with Angie, Tater?"

We huddled and he called the same play, and once again he threw the ball at my helmet. Except for the impact, which whipped my head forward a bit, shooting a small, dull charge into my neck, I really didn't feel much of anything. But now I could hear the coaches shouting and the fans hurling insults.

Louie Boudreaux ran in from the sideline with the next play, and we gathered for Tater's third-down call. It was the same pass to T-Boy. I glanced at the sideline and spotted Coach Cadet standing among my teammates with his arms crossed, earphones pulled off his head and wrapped around his neck. Under the stadium lights his pink face had the polished texture of marble. His teeth gnashed what everybody assumed was gum; I knew it was Rolaids. Curly Trussell stood next to him, as if waiting to be put in. Coach had also pulled Rubin Lazarus by his side. Rubin was our best defensive player, but he also was my backup on offense.

"Let's try it one more time," Tater said in the huddle. He usually made eye contact with each of us, but he was looking at only me now. "T-Boy, break off my pump fake and take it straight up the field, will you?"

One of the disadvantages of playing my position was being unable to see the action develop behind me. But when I glimpsed the ball sail over center, I knew Tater was finally running the play according to design. He would've pretended to take aim at my helmet again, and that would explain why Port Barre's linebackers and strong safety crashed the line of scrimmage and left T-Boy alone to run his route. T-Boy was wide open in space now, and Tater timed the pass perfectly, laying the ball a step in front of him. T-Boy pulled it in without breaking stride and ran untouched for a touchdown.

After the PAT, Coach Cadet grabbed my jersey as I was moving past him toward the bench. "What was that about?"

"Ask Tater, Coach."

"What happened out there?" Coach said when Tater reached the sideline.

"Ball slipped out of my hand. Sorry, Coach."

"You run the play as I call it, you hear me, son?"

"Yes, sir," Tater said.

"No more, you understand?"

"Yes, sir."

I grabbed a cup of water and plopped down on the bench. Tater sat next to me.

"I might not be good enough for your sister," he said, "but it's not because I'm black. I'm not good enough because she's Angie, do you hear me?"

I dropped the empty cup between my feet and put my helmet back on. I should've apologized. I should've told him I didn't want to be the way I was. But Port Barre had turned the ball over again, and the coaches were calling us back onto the field.

★★★

I could never sleep after games, and tonight was no different. In the locker room earlier I'd swallowed a handful of salt tablets to fight cramps, but they weren't working. My hamstrings kept seizing up on me, and the muscles in my neck bunched up in knots and pulled against my skull. As I lay in bed trying to get my body to relax, I could hear Angie through the wall behind my head. She was playing records in the living room—not loud, but loud enough to let me know she was there.

I finally got up. Still wearing her cheerleader uniform, garter hanging loose at her ankle, she was sitting on the sofa in the dark. Mama had been working on a collection of bridesmaid dresses, and the cranberry-red outfits covering the furniture made the room look like Christmas had come early.

"I don't know how to do that with a boy," Angie said. She'd obviously been waiting for me. "How am I supposed to know how to do that, Rodney?"

"You're asking me?"

"I've never even had a date—not a real one. But I have notions about how things should be when I do give myself to someone. And these notions, you should know, don't have me covered with mosquito repellant on a hot night next to a bayou crawling with water moccasins and my dumb, drunk brother snoring on a blanket a few feet away. They don't have me giving away something so precious in a cow pond, either, with leeches sucking on me."

"He shouldn't have said anything," I said.

"I'm *good*."

"I know that."

"I'll always be good. This doesn't mean I don't have carnal thoughts. But I haven't acted on them. Still, though—and this is important, Rodney: Wouldn't I still be me? Wouldn't I still be good?"

"Angie?" I walked over and stood in front of her. "Forgive me, Angie. I don't know what's wrong with me lately."

"I never touched him that way. And he never touched me. But what if I had? And what if he had?"

"I don't know."

"Do we know a better person than Tater Henry? Do we have a better friend? And who is more handsome and down-to-earth? Who's more popular?"

I shook my head.

"Who works harder, Rodney? Who *tries* harder?"

"Nobody."

She got up and put on *Romeo and Juliet*. I wished she'd chosen something else; I was beginning to hate that album. But now wasn't the time for me to question her choices.

"I'm embarrassed, Angie," I said. "Why am I this way? Where did it come from?"

She cleared some room for me on the couch, and we sat next to each other. "Do you really want an answer?" she asked.

I shook my head, and she wrapped her arms around my head and pulled me against her chest, then she started rocking in a gentle motion, like a mother would do, and after a while I could hear her reciting lines from the soundtrack.

In the morning I wouldn't remember falling asleep, but we woke up together on the floor, with the stereo needle, having run out of grooves, bouncing against the paper label at the middle of the record. I had my left arm around Angie's waist, and a couple of Mama's bridesmaid dresses covered our legs.

"I'll change," I told her. "I'll do better."

But she didn't hear me, she was still asleep.

I kissed her face, then went down the hall to soak in the tub.

In the team meeting that afternoon Coach Cadet reviewed the game film from the Jamboree with little commentary. But when he reached the plays where Tater threw the ball against my helmet, he used the clicker to repeat the action over and over. A low rumble of laughter accompanied each screening. Coach Cadet also seemed amused. He touched the back of his head every time the ball spanked my helmet.

"Either one of you want to explain what's happening here?" he asked.

Tater and I were sitting on different sides of the room. When neither of us spoke up, Coach rewound the tape for another look.

"What am I seeing?" he asked. "Are the throws misfires, or is Rodney out of position?" We watched it again. "It's one or the other," he said.

Neither of us answered, and we had the pleasure of yet another review.

"Tater? Rodney? Somebody needs to own it or we spend the rest of our lives here trying to figure it out."

Tater was taking aim at my head a fifteenth time when I heard the projector malfunction and a block of white light filled the screen. The film had torn in half, a common occurrence when Coach got too familiar with it.

Somebody turned on the overhead light and for a moment I kept my head down, not wanting my teammates to see my face burning red. But then as Coach Cadet patched the tape, I felt myself rising to my feet, and I heard myself calling the room to attention. "I need to say something," I announced.

The locker room went silent. I looked around from man to man before finally coming to Tater.

"What happened last night was my fault, and I got what I deserved. Tater, you should've thrown a brick at me instead of a football." I waited until the laughter stopped. "I'm sorry, Tater. I hope you'll forgive me"—he was already nodding—"and I hope the rest of you will forgive me too."

Coach had fixed the tape. He started playing it again, and I was glad to see that he had moved past the passes hitting my head.

"So in other words you were out of position," he said.

"Yes, Coach. I was out of position."

On Sunday after mass we picked up Tater and Miss Nettie in the Comet and drove with them to Soileau's Dinner Club. Angie had talked Tater into letting us join them on their weekly visit with his mother, and now we were retrieving the lunches Miss Nettie had ordered to bring with us—fried shrimp salads, pecan pie, and sweet tea.

Despite our insistence on paying, Miss Nettie said she would walk home if we didn't let her treat. While she and Tater were inside, Angie bought a copy of the local paper from a newsstand by the front door. The paper wasn't published on Saturdays so the story about the Jamboree had not appeared until this morning, two days after the fact. I'd seen it earlier at home, but apparently Angie hadn't.

There was a photo of Tater and me on the front page, with a caption that read: *Henry, Boulet lead Tigers in Jamboree blowout; LSU's Beau Jeune says they're going places.* Tater and I were shown sitting next to each other on the bench. I recognized the moment—it had come after the series when he'd thrown the ball at me. The photo gave the impression that Tater was lecturing me about the game, when in fact he had been lecturing me about my attitude. The actual subject of his remarks, who looked especially fetching today in a simple white dress that Mama had made, held my face in her hands and kissed the corner of my mouth.

"I'm proud of you," she said. "My word, you're going places. Wherever might that be?"

Tater and Miss Nettie returned to the car, carrying a stack of white cardboard boxes. Miss Nettie sat in front with me, Tater in back with Angie. Angie leaned over the seat, holding the paper for Miss Nettie to read.

"Boy, you need a haircut," Miss Nettie said to Tater as she studied the photo. "I knew Rodney was special, but what's this Beau Jeune saying about you?" She mumbled the words "going places" under her breath, then turned to Tater with a smile. "Don't let it go to your head."

Chateau De Chene must've been built about six or seven years before, at the same time the government was constructing housing projects around town. It was a long, low-slung building of red brick and white-board trim, with a jumble of television antennae on the roof. It stood at the end of an alley of ancient oak trees with massive limbs hanging low to the ground.

"Whenever you see trees like this," Miss Nettie said as we drove down the alley now covered with a cement drive, "you know the place was a plantation once, where there was a big house for the white people and little cabins for the slaves."

Race again. It didn't matter that shrimp salad and pecan pie were on the menu, there was no escaping the subject. I parked and walked around the car and opened Miss Nettie's door.

"Maybe I shouldn't have mentioned that," she said, offering her hand. "But we're all family here, aren't we, Rodney?"

"Yes, ma'am. That we are."

She led us into the building and down a hall to a room with a label that said ALMA HENRY on the door.

"Hey, Mama," Tater said. His mother was sitting in a wheelchair; he stooped down to kiss her. "You look pretty today, Mama."

"You lie," she said.

"No, I swear, Mama. You do."

I wished I'd prepared myself for the reality of her condition. She had only half a face, with one small hole and a mound of tortured flesh where her nose should've been. Even though she was wearing sunglasses, the light was bright enough in the room to let you see past one lens to the sewn-shut socket that once held her right eye. I wondered if the bumps on her skin were birdshot. Her left ear had not been damaged, but what remained of the right one was a mass of red, fleshy tissue.

Miss Nettie leaned over and hugged her now, then she came up tall. "Angie, Rodney, this is Alma, Tater's mom."

"So nice to meet you, Mrs. Henry," Angie said.

"I was never married," she said. She waited a moment. "Why don't you just call me Alma?"

I stepped up and offered my hand. "Pleasure to meet you, Alma."

"Pleasure's all mine, Big Rod."

She wasn't as old as our mother. She might've been thirty-three or thirty-four, but it wouldn't have surprised me to learn that she was actually years younger.

"It's a nice day," Tater said. "Why don't we go outside and eat at one of the picnic tables under the trees. Sound good?"

She nodded. "I don't mind the bugs if you don't mind the bugs."

Miss Nettie helped her put on the same hat that she'd worn to the game last year, its lace veil covering her head and puddling on her shoulders. Pushing her chair at a slow pace, Tater led us down a corridor and out of the building to a metal table that was bolted to a concrete slab in the ground. I was carrying the food, and the smell of fried shrimp was so good I thought I might have to stop and sample it. We'd forgotten the tea in the car. Angie went now to get it.

"Such a pretty girl," Alma said.

She was looking at me, but Tater said, "Thank you," before I could reply.

We talked about the Jamboree and the recruiters who'd come to see us play. We talked about our classes at school and our teachers and friends. Alma knew we called ourselves the Oreos, and she seemed familiar with the name of every friend we mentioned. In order to eat she had to pull up her veil, and it didn't take long to get used to looking at her, to take her as she was. From the undamaged part of her face you could see that she'd probably once been a beauty herself. A breeze came up and helped with the heat. I ate and let them talk, and even though the salad had its merits I wished I'd ordered something more substantial, like a T-bone steak and a stuffed baked potato.

"I had an interesting thing happen this morning," Alma said. "There was a phone call for me at the nurses' station. They come in and say it's important, so they roll me down the hall to get it. Anyway, it's a sportswriter at the paper, and he tells me Coach Jeune has a message for me. I said, 'He can't call me his own self?'"

"What did he say, Mama?"

"Just that he liked what he saw. And that he would come out and visit me as soon as he could, when he can get away from Baton Rouge and his own boys." She laughed now. "I told that man to tell Beau Jeune he was welcome anytime."

"I'm going to be the first black quarterback to ever play for LSU," Tater said.

"I know you will, baby."

"And when I'm in the pros and making some serious money, I'm going to buy you your own house, and we'll have our own nurses and wheelchair ramps and a cook who comes in the evening to make us supper."

"Oh, yes."

"It'll have two stories," he said.

"Two? How do you expect me to get up them stairs, boy?"

"The elevator."

"That's right. All right."

"And in the kitchen we'll have counters low enough so you can get your own water at the sink."

"Oh, yes."

"And a white picket fence, and what else?" he said.

"A flower garden."

He sipped his tea. It was clear they'd indulged this fantasy many times before, and even though they seemed to be enjoying themselves, the exchange made me sad. There was no way any of it was going to happen unless a pill came out that let him change the color of his skin.

"Don't forget my cat," Alma said.

"What kind you want, Mama? A Siamese?"

"An apple-headed Siamese."

"I'll buy you two. How's that sound?"

"I like that."

"You want a dog?"

"I'm not a dog person. Don't ask me why."

"Not even a golden retriever?"

"Well, all right, then."

I noticed as we ate that Alma had difficulty handling her fork and bringing it up to her mouth, and it occurred to me that she likely also suffered from nerve and muscle damage. But she worked through it and used the arm, anyway, sometimes employing her left hand to support it. I also noticed that neither Tater nor Miss Nettie helped her. They seemed to know better than to try.

"Tater came first, his sister, Rosalie, second," Alma announced suddenly as she was working on her pie. "I looked up and could see in the nurse's eyes that something wasn't right. She probably would've grown up to be like you, Angie—a cheerleader at the high school, rooting for her brother and Big Rod here."

"She would be my friend," Angie said.

"I know she would, baby," Alma Henry said. She sat looking at Angie. "Do you know I don't own—and have never owned—a picture of their daddy?"

"He was no good," Miss Nettie said.

"That's true," Alma said, although something about her expression told me she didn't believe it.

"When he was little," Miss Nettie said, "Tater would cry and ask me what his daddy looked like, and I'd tell him to go look in the mirror, to get right up to the glass and look close, to *stare*, he would see him there."

"Was his dad an athlete?" I asked.

"Not that I know of," Alma said. "To be honest with you, he was more a tomcat than anything." She lowered her plastic fork and laughed with her good hand covering her mouth. "Rodney, would you like the rest of my pie?"

"No, ma'am."

"Are you sure?"

"Yes, ma'am."

But she slid it over, and I looked to see how much was left. You hated to waste anything as good as that.

"I met him walking home from school," she said. "I was fifteen—that's all, just a baby. He pulls up in his car and asks if I need a ride. How many times have I interrogated myself why I didn't tell him no? But that would mean there would be no you, wouldn't it, Tater?"

He didn't answer.

"Robert Battier was his name, same as the name he gave that first boy. He was ten years older than me. He worked as a deliveryman. I didn't even know he had a wife and child until I was ninth months pregnant. Not eight months, mind you. *Nine* months. And big out to here." She showed us with her hands. "It was one of them things where if he couldn't have me, nobody else could. He came to my mama's house—she was still alive then—and he had all these grocery bags lined up on the backseat, waiting to be delivered. He had some ground meat in there for Lois Duplechain. I can still see her name written out on a slip on a bag—*Lois Duplechain*. He had other perishable items. Your milk, ice cream, oleo. You think I'm crazy for remembering that, don't you?"

"No, ma'am," Angie said.

"Sounds so stupid now. Me worrying about the cold things in his car, when I had a baby in the house. I screamed at him to leave. I told him I was going to call the police. He opened the back door and threw the bags out in the yard. I think he knew he would be losing more than just me, when he did that. He would also lose his job. I have a lot to be mad about, but I'm just glad he didn't go after my baby. Some men do that, you know?"

"Yes, they do," Miss Nettie said. "It's on the news every day of the week."

"You get the newspaper, Angie?" Alma asked.

"My father does."

"You like it when Tater's in there?"

Angie nodded. She looked down at her plate. "It's wonderful."

When we returned to the building, a crowd was waiting for us in the hallway. Most were elderly, but there were some young people too. Like Alma, the young ones had injuries that required medical attention and kept them institutionalized. I couldn't figure out why they'd gathered in the hall, staring and smiling at us, but then I noticed the newspapers. They were also holding ink pens.

"Could you sign this for me?" an old man said, holding out the section of the paper with the picture of Tater and me.

I was a Bigfoot. I'd never signed an autograph before. But I enjoyed these first ones. Tater and I must've signed fifty that morning, and all the while Angie stood behind Alma Henry, holding the handles of her wheelchair.

We went on a run like the school had never seen before. To start the regular season, we beat Crowley in the rain at home. Then came easy road wins over Franklin and Morgan City. Next up was Lafayette Northside, where it was 57–0 at half, and 71–12 at the end. Tater ran three quarterback sneaks for touchdowns the next week against A team from Baton Rouge. Before the last of them, Coach Cadet called time-out and had me join him and Tater on the sideline.

"See their miserable excuse for a coach over there?" he said. "He's the biggest turd that ever walked a sideline, maybe even the planet. And I would like nothing more than to drop a load of shame on him tonight. Rodney, I want you to hold your man and draw the flag."

"You want me to hold him, Coach?"

"Yes, Rodney, *hold* him. Hold him like this." And he grabbed my jersey and yanked me toward him. "We're on our own 26. We get a penalty and that puts the ball on the 1. Tater, after the ref steps it off I want you to run the quarterback sneak. And make it pretty, will you?"

Tater made it pretty, all right. It was so pretty the coach for the other team threw his cap at the ground even before Tater crossed the goal line. Next he shot the bird at Coach Cadet from across the field and drew a flag for unsportsmanlike conduct. Then in arguing with the officials he was ejected from the game. All this made it perhaps the prettiest play Coach Cadet had ever seen.

Tater's run was also the longest for a quarterback in school history, and because a run from scrimmage can't be longer than ninety-nine yards, it tied state and national marks and put him in the record books for all time. It also put him back in the news—"from Haynesville up high to Boothville-Venice down low," as Coach Valentine put it, naming places at different ends of the state. When local TV stations showed highlights and scoreboards that Friday night, Tater's run was the top story on every program.

We had an open date the next weekend, and over the days leading up to it, he and I welcomed recruiters into our homes. Most of the big schools that wanted him, like Michigan, Illinois, and Rutgers, were from up North, while the major colleges that were pursuing me hardest were in the South and Southwest—Oklahoma, Texas A&M, Ole Miss, and Alabama. Our phones at home rang day and night. Sometimes when we left the locker room after practice, the recruiters were lined up outside, waiting for a minute of our time. That was what they all asked for—just a minute. But when we gave it to them, they tried to convince us to give them the next four years of our lives. Not that Tater and I ever complained. There was no way Miss Nettie could pay for his college education, and Mama and Pops had both Angie and me to worry about. Coach Cadet stored our mail from recruiters in matching metal washtubs in his office, one with Tater's name marked on the side, the other with mine. The letters counted in the hundreds, and they all seemed to say the same thing: We can't win without you.

He and I both wanted to stay in the state and play for LSU, but we knew it was best to keep our options open. While we didn't have a pact to sign with the same program, I couldn't imagine the two of us splitting up and going to different places. He made me better, and I liked to think I did the same for him. "Where would I be without my offensive line?" might've been his favorite line. But everybody knew he was really saying, "Where would I be without Rodney Boulet?"

One night that week, Beau Jeune came back to town, stopping first at Tater's for a meeting with him and Miss Nettie, then driving over to Helen Street for a fried catfish dinner with my family and me. Coach Jeune had left practice early to make the hour-long drive, and he arrived wearing a baby-blue sport coat thrown over a mesh shirt trimmed in LSU's purple and gold, and you could see the indentation around the top of his head left by a baseball cap. He seemed to understand how important it was to win over Mama, and he honed in on her as soon as he walked in the house, complimenting her on things I'd never noticed before, such as the handmade doilies on the arms of the sofa and the color of our telephone, which was avocado. We ate at the kitchen table, then moved over to the living room, which Mama and Angie had cleaned up and organized earlier that afternoon. Mama served chicory coffee from a silver tray, then she and Angie retired to their rooms and left the coach alone with Pops and me.

It was quite a thing to hear someone I respected so much tell me that I ranked as the top prospect on his list, a pitch I was sure he'd tried out on other blue-chip talent, but one I still very much appreciated.

"What about Tater?" I asked, interrupting Coach Jeune's spiel about my golden future as a Tiger. "Where does he rank?"

"That one's special, ain't he?" Coach Jeune said. "That kind of raw talent you don't see every day. The sky's the limit for that young man."

Pops sank deeper in his seat. "You don't really see a boy like him playing quarterback in Baton Rouge, do you?" he asked.

"You mean a black?"

"Right."

"I don't completely rule it out, Mr. Boulet. Not yet I don't."

"Sign him and see what happens," Pops said.

All of a sudden Coach Jeune seemed to remember that he'd really come to see me. He turned in his chair. "Can this stay in the room with us, Rodney?"

"Yes, sir."

"I like Tater, I like him a lot. But I keep asking myself if he might not be out of position. He has the arm strength and the intelligence and all the other intangibles to play quarterback, but he's absolutely at his best when he's carrying the ball." He put his cup on the coffee table and leaned forward in his chair. "Can't you just see him taking the pitch out of the I-formation and turning the corner, Rodney?"

"I'm just a night watchman at a plant," Pops interrupted, "but I can tell you the world ain't ready for one at LSU."

"The world," Coach Jeune said, as if he'd just now heard of the place. "Isn't that where if you don't win ten games a year, the Board of Supervisors convenes an emergency session and hires somebody else?"

Mama wrapped some catfish in aluminum foil for him to take in case he got hungry on the road. He left a media guide for the 1971 season on the coffee table and gave Mama and Angie hugs on his way outside. Pops only had about ten minutes to get ready for work, so that finally gave Coach Jeune and me some time alone.

We walked to his Cadillac parked along the curb and stood in the lamplight. "We'd love an early commitment from you, Rodney," he said. "I know it would influence a lot of quality young men who haven't made their minds up yet, and my recruiting coordinator tells me it would be a knockout punch to Alabama. Every year they sneak in this state and steal some of our best boys, and your commitment would go a long way to putting an end to that."

"I'd commit to you tonight, Coach, if you gave me your commitment to play Tater at quarterback."

I was looking right at him when I spoke, and even in the strange light I could see how surprised he was by the offer. I could also see how tempted he was to accept it. But in the end he only gave me the same uneasy smile he'd given Pops earlier.

"I'll take that under consideration," he said, "but I suppose I should first tell you straight up about my reservations. Your dad's position is shared by a lot of people, Rodney—I'd even say by most of them. The proposition of a black boy quarterbacking my football team stops being about the game and becomes about something else."

"I don't know why race has to matter, Coach. Isn't the field the same one hundred yards for the black players as well as the white ones?" I should've given Tater credit for the line. But instead I said, "Have you told him you weren't sure where to play him?"

"No, I have not."

"The northern schools all say he's a quarterback. Most of the ones down here avoid answering the question when he brings it up. Ole Miss told him he projected as a cornerback, and he asked them not to come around anymore."

The Sedan de Ville, white with purple and gold trim, was as long as our house. He got in and pulled the door closed. The electric window came down.

He'd set Mama's catfish on the seat next to him, with the foil peeled open. "Let me talk to some people, Rodney. Everybody might not want it. But everybody's not Beau Jeune, now, are they?"

On Thursday Tater and I kept with tradition and met again to watch film in my bedroom. Mama made redfish sauce piquant, and we ate in the room with the reel rolling for the second half. When we were finished, Angie came in to take our trays away, and as she was leaving, Tater said, "My auntie knows Clifton Chenier. You heard of Clifton Chenier before, huh, Angie?"

She nodded.

"He's playing at Richard's in Lawtell this Saturday. He told her we should come." A second or two passed and he said, "You and Rodney and me."

"We can't go to bars," I said.

"It's a dance club more than a bar. They'll also be serving barbecue, my auntie says. We can eat and hang out and listen to the music. They won't bother with us as long as we don't order a real drink—you know, a beer or whatnot."

Angie never could hide much. "We'll have to get permission," she said, then let out a squeal as she pulled the door closed behind her.

Richard's, pronounced *Ree-shard's*, wasn't a place I'd ever thought about visiting. You saw it on trips to Eunice, standing back past a ditch in the shade of some loblolly pines, its tin roof covered with rust, aluminum windows facing out. Some of the faster kids at school went to the all-white Southern Club, also on that road, but Richard's attracted mostly black people from nearby towns like Frilot Cove, Swords, and Mallett. Many of these people had French ancestry and French surnames, and the musicians among them had taken Cajun music, jazzed it up with a saxophone and a rub board, and turned it into Zydeco, a French word that meant "snap bean." Chenier's admirers called him the "King of Zydeco," although that wasn't saying much. Zydeco was just being discovered outside the region, and locally its popularity had made little headway into the white community. No one I knew listened to it.

We knew better than to ask Pops for the green light, so we waited until he'd left for work that night and ambushed Mama as she was getting ready for bed. Seated at her vanity, rubbing cream on her face, she looked at us in the mirror as we entered the room and stood next to each other in a show of solidarity. I let Angie do the talking.

"I'll need to discuss this with your father," Mama said in a harder tone than usual.

"He'll just say no," Angie said.

"And in this case he'd probably be right to." She turned in her chair and faced Angie, her mask of cream shining against the frosty white bulbs. "Is this a good idea?"

"I swear nothing will happen," Angie said. "We'll come home early. Rodney will protect me, won't you, Rodney?"

"Anybody gets too close," I said, "and I'll give them one of these." And now I punched the air with a forearm.

In the morning Mama waited until Pops had gone to the bathroom for his shower before giving us an answer. We were in the

Cameo, letting the engine warm. She came outside still dressed in her robe and tapped on my window. I lowered it.

"Don't make me regret this, but I'm giving you permission to go. You can't drink, and you have to be home by midnight. And you must never tell your father. *Comprends?*"

"*Comprends,*" Angie and I said in unison.

"One more thing," Mama said. She held up a finger. "Don't forget who you are. Will you promise me?"

"Promise," Angie and I answered at once.

But on the drive to school that morning, as Angie rattled on about how much fun we were going to have, Mama's warning messed with my head a little. Over the years coaches had told me to remember who I was when they wanted to stress the importance of staying humble and showing class after big wins, but her command sounded different and had an undertone that left me confused.

Don't forget who you are. . . .

Did she mean we shouldn't forget that we were white? It didn't sound like her. Besides, I'd already decided that the one thing we weren't likely to forget in a roadhouse filled with black people was the color of our skin.

It was too cold for Tater to ride in back, so he and Miss Nettie squeezed in the cab with us. As we drove out west of town, we listened to Cajun music on the radio, the songs punctuated by wails and moans that had the four of us wailing and moaning along with them. We arrived at the club at around seven thirty, early enough to beat the crowd and to claim a table by the stage. On the side of the red-painted building, a couple of men were standing by a huge barbecue pit with no less than three smokestacks on the lid. They were drinking bottled beer and listening to LSU–Kentucky on the radio. We followed Miss Nettie to the door, where admission was three dollars a head. Just inside, Patrice Jolivette stood waiting, and she and Angie fell into each other's arms.

"You're home," Angie said. "Oh, I've missed you so much. How did you know we would be here tonight?"

Tater held up his right hand, as if taking an oath. "Guilty as charged," he said. "I thought I should invite another girl. Ain't no way you can keep up with me by yourself, Angie Boulet." Then he did a little dance that spun him around in a circle.

"Somebody's been practicing," Angie told him.

Miss Nettie ordered a whiskey sour for herself and Cokes for the rest of us. We also had pulled pork sandwiches still hot from the pit and dripping barbecue sauce. People kept filing in, some of them familiar faces from town. One lady was a server in the lunchroom at school. It was the first time I'd ever seen her without a hairnet, and Angie had to tell me who she was. I also spotted the man who made deliveries in our neighborhood for Clover Farm Dairy. During the day he was dressed all in white, carrying milk bottles in wire crates, but tonight his black suit, black western boots, and turquoise rings gave a different image.

"He looks like the dude from *Shaft* gone country," Tater said, and that about covered it.

I suppose the thing that surprised me most about the place was the diversity of the crowd. You had old men in cowboy outfits and young ones in nylon shirts and bell-bottom pants. Some of the women looked like they'd just put their hoes down and left the farm, while others had fancy ways about them and fancy hairdos and clothes. At around nine o'clock, Clifton Chenier and his band came through a back door and mounted the stage. Chenier played blues accordion, and the one he harnessed to his shoulders looked like a fireplace bellows grafted onto a piano keyboard. He wore a white dress shirt with a bolo tie, white pants, and black church shoes, and his hair, which glistened with oil in the hot lights, was swept back in a Little Richard pompadour. Several men walked up to the stage to greet him. "What's happenin', soul," Chenier said to each of them.

I've pretty well established here that I'm a large person, a Sasquatch, a tractor-trailer rig, a monster, and a load. I've been called all these names. But no one ever accused me of being a dancer. Chenier had barely hit the first note of "Bon Ton Roulet" when I lured Miss Nettie out on the floor and got things started. She might've put me to shame had shame been a possibility for me. Tater, Angie, and Patrice soon joined us, and for the next half hour we swapped partners from one song to the next as both couples and trios, allowing for any number of combinations except the one that had me dancing with Tater.

When Chenier arrived at "Louisiana Blues," it was my turn with Patrice, and what luck I had that it was a slow one. I held her close because that was my job, and Tater held Angie close because that was his. Even Miss Nettie was feeling it, tied up with the milkman who went ahead and nibbled on her ear while he was at it.

"Come hug me, Nettie," Chenier called out between songs. She ran up to the stage and did as she was told, and then he broke into "*Zydeco Sont Pas Salles*", which if my eighth-grade French was correct, translated to "Snap beans aren't salty."

"Cut a rug with me, Rodney," Miss Nettie said, then she and I were going at it again, dominating the floor and pulverizing anybody who got in the way.

I never had a better workout. When Angie and Patrice finally conked out, and Miss Nettie's sore feet put her in a chair, Tater and I recruited other women in the club and gave them spins on the dance floor. Sweat poured down our faces and soaked our shirts, and all the while Chenier's accordion kept driving us.

A clock over the bar said eleven thirty, and that meant it was time to go. Angie and Patrice returned for one last dance, dragging an exhausted Miss Nettie by the hand. The song, "Jolie Blonde", was about a pretty blonde, and suddenly all eyes were on Angie.

"Where would I be without my offensive line?" Tater yelled as we stumbled out the door when it was over.

He jumped on my back and wrapped his arms around my neck, and I took off running with him under the pines.

★

CHAPTER FOUR

★

Against Eunice the next week, he got sick.

We were playing on the road, and although it now was October, we still had to deal with more heat and humidity than seemed fair, even for people accustomed to suffering because of the weather. I struggled to catch my breath between plays, and I saw misery on the faces of my teammates and the guys across the line.

Tater was the best-conditioned athlete on our team, but he was seriously winded in the first half, and in the huddle his voice was so thin it was hard to make him out. It sounded like he'd had the wind knocked out of him and couldn't get it back, and when he made calls at the line he had to drop his voice to a lower register to project the words and numbers. I saw him grimacing in pain, and on the sideline he adjusted the straps on his shoulder pads to give them a looser fit. As usual he outperformed everybody else on the field and seemed able to score at will, but his obvious discomfort had me worried.

"You coming down with the flu?" I asked.

He didn't answer.

"You have us twenty-one points ahead. It wouldn't be the end of the world if you sat out the rest of the game."

"I can't do that."

"Why not?"

He sat, thinking about it. "People paid good money to see me play. Wouldn't want to disappoint them."

Late in the third quarter, he broke free on a quarterback draw and was racing down the sideline when he suddenly collapsed. He landed on his back and fumbled the ball, and Eunice recovered. I thought he'd slipped. But he tried to stand and quickly went down again, staggering, then falling sideways like a boxer who'd taken one on the side of the head. By the time I got to him he was vomiting. His helmet was still on, and the stuff was shooting out through the bars of his face mask.

"Stomach virus," Coach Cadet said.

Rubin ran out from the sideline to help, and he and I threw Tater's arms over our shoulders and carried him to the bench. Two other players on the team had come down with the same thing, and we brought Tater to where they were pulling guard duty by the water buckets.

"I ain't staying here," he said.

"Yes, you are," I told him. I carried his helmet to a faucet on the side of the bleachers and washed it off. When I looked up I could see faces in the crowd, looking down at me as if for an explanation. Pops got up from his seat and took two steps at a time coming down.

"That didn't look right," he said.

"There's a virus going around."

"It looked like he passed out cold on his feet."

"He probably did. Alfred and Timmy are sick with it too."

"Yeah, but still—"

"It's always something, huh, Pops?"

It was a cheap shot, and I wished I could take it back as soon as I said it, but he was already climbing back up to his seat.

Our team doctor hadn't made the trip, but the one for Eunice came over to look at Tater. I saw him shine a penlight in his eyes. He did a few other things and asked some questions: "Did you take a shot to the head?"

"No, sir."

"Are you woozy?"

"I was earlier, but I'm not now."

"Are you cramping?"

"I had me some, nothing too bad. They went away. I promise I feel good, Doc. Can I go back in the game?"

The ice in our coolers had already melted, so the doctor dipped a towel in our drinking water, wrung it out, and draped it over Tater's head. "You're done for the night, son. Not another play, you understand?"

Tater gave no indication that he'd heard him, much less understood.

"I'm going to the concession stand on the other side of the field to get you some ice to suck on," the doctor said. "You stay here and keep still. You want to be well enough to play next week, don't you?"

The doctor walked over and said something to Coach Cadet. They both turned and looked at Tater. Curly Trussell, expelled from school the week before when he was caught with pot in his locker, was no longer available as a replacement, so Coach called over sophomore Jay

Meche and told him Tater was done and the offense was now his to run.

"I ain't done, Coach!" Tater yelled from the bench. "Coach, I ain't done."

But he was done.

The doctor returned and wrapped Tater's head with another cold towel and gave him a cup of ice. And for the rest of the game Tater sucked on the ice and sat staring at the ground. He looked up only when the offense came off the field and he had words of encouragement for Jay or when he wanted to slap our hands after a score.

"Do you remember what Huey Long said before he died?" Tater asked me on the bus ride home.

The late Louisiana governor and US senator, assassinated in 1935, was the last person you'd expect anybody to bring up during a long drive across the prairie after a football game. But Tater seemed to want an answer, and I couldn't provide one.

"Come on, Rodney. You should've learned this in Louisiana history class. That man had shot him in a hallway at the State Capitol, and Huey Long was in the hospital. He opened his eyes and said, 'I can't die yet. I got too much left to do.' And then not long after, he was gone."

"But all you've got is a bug, Tater. Nobody shot you."

He laughed, the first time tonight. "But I understand where he was coming from. I can't be getting sick now, Rodney. I got too much left to do."

By Monday he felt better and was able to practice. On Thursday I had him over for film, and he was in such good spirits, and seemed so much like the old Tater again, that none of us thought to ask how he was feeling. I usually drove him home afterward, but as we were getting ready to leave, a charley horse gripped my right calf and dropped me to the floor.

"I'll take him," Angie said.

"No," Pops said. He walked ahead of her into the kitchen and removed the truck keys from the table. "Let me."

"I'll be right back. I promise."

"No, Angie."

"It'll take fifteen minutes, twenty tops."

"Not tonight."

Yelping for the pain, I staggered to the living room and fell on the couch. I glimpsed Tater's face as he was going through the door to the carport. It twitched as if against tears, and he gave his head a shake. I considered running out after him, but I worried that it would only lead to the admission that went: "Pops won't let Angie drive you by herself because as her father it is his duty to protect her virtue and her future." Instead I shouted, "Remember to always carry out your fakes. Their Sam linebacker gets fooled easily." But he was already outside.

Angie started kneading the spasm with her knuckles. "I could've taken him," she said. "Nothing would've happened."

"It's late. They'd worry."

"Late isn't why and you know it."

I stopped myself from mentioning Smooth. It would've been like calling her a liar.

I thought of a story Mama liked to tell about when we were little. Our baby cribs had stood next to each other, with the head of mine touching the foot of Angie's. Mama had walked in one day and found Angie sticking her foot through the slats of her crib into mine. Upset at the sound of my crying, she had offered me her toes to suck. "And you were going to town," Mama always said. "I worried that you would never let her have her foot back."

Until now I never doubted that Angie would do practically anything for me, and that she'd put me above anyone else. But tonight I wasn't so sure that still held true. Tonight I was just in her way.

She worked on my lower leg until Pops came back. He walked into the kitchen and dropped the keys on the table. At the sound of them hitting the boards, she whipped her head to the side, as if she'd been slapped. "I won't always be seventeen," she said. "Do you think he realizes that?"

"I think he would trade you for Angie at seven or Angie at twenty-seven, but Angie at seventeen makes him nervous."

She went to the kitchen sink and washed her hands. Pops had to report to work in the next hour; he was drinking coffee at the table.

"What did you and Tater talk about?" she asked.

"He told me that was the best gumbo he ever ate in his life."

"That's it? He liked the gumbo?"

Pops brought his cup to his lips but stopped before taking a sip. "Oh." And now he smiled at Angie. "He said he liked your peach pie, too."

★★★

The Acadiana Wreckin' Rams fought hard to keep it close. They ran a Veer offense that gave our defense fits, but they weren't as strong on the other side of the ball, where they had a healthy Tater to deal with.

He threw two touchdown passes and ran for slightly more than a hundred yards—a great night for most quarterbacks but just an ordinary one for him. People were so spoiled by his performances that they thought he was slacking when he didn't have five touchdown passes and two hundred rushing yards. The polls for Class AAAA had us ranked second behind Shreveport's Byrd High, which had been treating schools in the state's northern redneck parishes in the same fashion that we'd been treating the Cajun ones in the south.

After the game we took the bus back to school. I left the showers and found Coach Jeune waiting at my locker; his recruiting coordinator, Nolan Moore, was talking to Tater in a far corner of the room. As a rule Coach Cadet didn't allow recruiters into our private area, but by now I knew what he wanted for Tater and me. The recruiting blitz had been as exhausting for him as it had been for us, and he'd been encouraging us to end it. More to the point, he wanted us to verbally commit to LSU and "put all the other schools out of their misery," as he'd told us just a couple of days before.

"I'm ready for that commitment, Rodney," Coach Jeune began. He shuffled up close to me, until he was inches from my face. "You have mine if I have yours."

"You would do that, Coach?"

"I would and I will. How long did you say the field was?"

"A hundred yards, Coach."

"Tater's a quarterback and a great one. If people don't like it . . . well, tough." I could tell he wasn't joking, even though he laughed and said, "They always say the most popular person in the state of Louisiana is the head football coach at LSU the week after he wins a big game. Well, we won big last week and that means I can do whatever the heck I want. I want Tater Henry to be my quarterback, and I want you blocking for him."

I had a home visit scheduled with Alabama the next week, but who did I know in Tuscaloosa? Would Angie and the folks get to see me play if I went there? Where was Tuscaloosa, anyway?

"Okay, Coach. It's a deal."

"You're committing?"

"I give you my word. Now comes the hard part—telling all those recruiters to stop coming around. I hate to let them down."

He looked over at Tater, who was still hearing it from Nolan Moore. "Tell him you've committed, Rodney. Go on, son. Do it now."

Still wearing only a bath towel, I walked over and waited until Nolan Moore understood that it was my turn. He walked outside with Coach Jeune.

"Who do we know in Michigan and Ohio and all those other places?" I asked Tater.

Tater shook his head. "Not a soul."

"Where is Eugene, Oregon?"

"I have no idea."

"Coach Jeune says you're a quarterback and he wants me protecting you, Tater."

He seemed to have a hard time believing it, and for a moment I thought he was going to cry. "I should call my auntie," he said.

"It's history," I said. "If a black man were elected governor and moved into the mansion, it's as big as that. Maybe bigger." I put my hands on his shoulders and gave him a shake. "LSU will have a black quarterback next year."

"And his name is Tater Henry," said Tater.

To celebrate we went to the Little Chef and hung out until closing time. Tater spent most of the night at a patio table, eating free food with Rubin, whose presence there made him the second black player to be invited to the postgame party. "Hallelujah," I heard Rubin tell one of the guys. "The floodgates have opened now."

The week before, Rubin had committed to the University of Southwestern Louisiana, and he already had a homemade Ragin' Cajuns tattoo on his arm, the words still red and puffy where he'd carved himself with the needle. When it was time to leave, Tater came over to where I'd parked and asked if he could go home with Angie and me. I looked at my watch, even though I knew the time.

"We'll need permission," I said. "And shouldn't you talk to Miss Nettie first?"

"I already did. Mr. and Mrs. Miller are out of town for the weekend, so she's staying at their place."

Angie opened her door and turned sideways in the seat to let him squeeze past her. "Get in," she said. "If you're good enough for Tigertown, I guess you're good enough for Helen Street."

Pops was at the plant, and Mama was already in bed. I didn't see the point in waking her to tell her we had company. If I drove him home in an hour or two, they wouldn't even have to know he'd been there. And if they did find out, I could tell them we'd invited him to the house for leftovers.

It was true that we were hungry, but it was also true that we were always hungry, even after we'd just eaten. Mama had prepared a crawfish casserole and left it in the refrigerator, and Angie warmed it in the oven and toasted some Evangeline Maid bread topped with tabs of butter. We ate in the living room with the stereo turned down low. For dessert Tater and I had ice cream—two bowls each—then we helped Angie with the dishes. Next we put on more records and wasted an hour discussing the merits of various album covers. Angie's favorite was the one for *Romeo and Juliet*. "Do you mind if I put it on?" she said to Tater.

"Me?" He pointed to his chest. "It's your house, Angie."

The part of the album she chose to play meant nothing to me, but it was one from late in the story, with Juliet doing most of the talking.

Angie walked to the middle of the room and waited a moment before she started reciting lines. She'd performed for Tater and me nearly a year before at the Little Chef, but tonight she seemed to feel the words more deeply than she had then, and she delivered them as if they were her own. Shakespeare hadn't scripted them centuries ago; she was making them up on the fly now. Even her accent was more believable, and she spoke less like an actress with a role to interpret than a teenage girl in love.

To his credit, Tater was able to keep it together. He didn't laugh once, although every now and then he said, "Wow," to compliment her.

The words just kept coming.

Something something.

Something else.

I gave up and moved from a chair to the couch. I'd played a football game tonight, and played hard, and I could feel my body telling me it had had enough.

"Here it comes," I said to myself. And then she started to cry, as she always did when listening to the soundtrack. It was more a purge than a few tears, and frankly I was shocked to see it. She'd told me before that she cried because the language was so beautiful and full of meaning, but it seemed she was crying now for all the wrongs of the world, none less than the ones in her own life that were depriving her of happiness. Her vulnerability seemed authentic, and it had me wondering if I should get up and hug her.

But it was Tater who took her in his arms. He whispered to calm her down, but by now she was hysterical. He had one hand on the middle of her back, the other on her head, holding her against his chest.

"Are you ready to go home?" she asked.

"If you tell me you're going to be all right."

"I'm just emotional. It's hormones, I'm sure."

She walked to the kitchen for the keys. I started for the door, but she stopped me. "Can't I take him home by myself for once?"

It was an impossible spot to be in. If I told her no, it would be like making a confession about how I felt about black people. And I didn't want to make Tater doubt me again. But if I said yes, I was inviting other problems. Pops, to start.

"Angie, don't forget who you are," I said.

"I won't, Mama."

Any other time and I wouldn't have let her get away with it.

"Tater, don't forget she's my sister."

"Right," he said. "And you don't forget it either. See you later, Rodney."

There was no sleeping now. I went to the kitchen and ate more of the casserole. As a matter of fact, I finished it off.

She was gone for nearly three hours. She made sure to come home before Mama got up and Pops returned from the plant. Hearing the Cameo in the carport, I turned off the lamp in the living room and slipped into my room. I didn't want her to think I'd been waiting up, and I didn't want to talk.

I expected her to put the record back on. I lay in bed waiting for the actors' voices to reach me through the wall behind my head. And then Angie's voice to join them, the way it always did. But instead I felt the floor vibrate as she walked down the hall to her bedroom.

I heard her door close. And finally I heard her lock it.

Next up were Comeaux, New Iberia, and Lafayette, then the playoffs—Terrebonne, Sulphur, and Brother Martin. The hometown crowds grew more animated with each win, the headlines in the local paper bolder. Workers at the stadium added portable bleachers along the sidelines and end zones, but even those filled up well before kick-off, and spectators had to stand wherever there was room.

Fourteen school buses followed us to Houma for the game with Terrebonne. They were loaded with the band, the Tigerettes baton-twirling troupe, and the pep squad, which counted about a hundred girls. Cars packed with fans trailed the buses in a long procession that choked the bayou roads to the south and east.

Tater turned seventeen that day, and the windows of more than a few cars were decorated with birthday wishes and pictures of orange-and-black cakes burning candles. All through the game Angie led our fans in the singing of "Happy Birthday to You." Tater waited until late in the fourth quarter to stand on the bench and acknowledge them with a bow. Had the game been closer, Coach Cadet would've squawked, but by then Tater had put us ahead by thirty-seven points. Rather than upbraid him for showboating, Coach stood on the bench next to him and joined in the singing, his voice loudest of all.

The next week at school Tater and Angie tirelessly exchanged notes with each other during classes, passing them back and forth while our teachers stuck to their lectures and pretended not to notice. On a whim I passed a note of my own to Regina Perrault, and she promptly answered with a smiley face. That was the day I collected my books and moved again. I gave a death stare to the kid who occupied the desk behind her, and he promptly found a new place in the back row. Angie and Tater could have each other. I didn't need anyone as long as Regina was within reach or at least within view.

Before the pep rally for the Sulphur game, I sat cross-legged on the gym floor and offered a shoulder to a tearful Patrice Jolivette, who'd skipped classes at Southern and returned home for the day. She'd hoped to surprise Tater and Angie, but instead it was they who surprised her. After her wails died down, I had a hard time finding the right words to console her.

"I can't believe she would do me like that," she said.

"You're not the only one in shock."

"What happened?" she blurted out, as if she'd just witnessed an accident. Then she wept with her face pressed against my arm.

It was winter now, and they met in the park after practice, some days when it was already dark outside. Angie rode her bike; Tater walked.

They wore matching purple pullovers and sweatpants stamped with LSU logos that showed animated tigers wearing crowns. Few people used the picnic grounds because of the weather, so they usually had that section of the park to themselves. They sat in the open pavilion down by the bayou and pressed their bodies against each other to keep warm. On especially cold days they gathered kindling and made fires in the big brick pit. You could smell smoke on Angie's clothes when she came home later and gave me all the details about their meetings. If there was enough light, she brought a sketchbook and her paint box and made pictures. I went into her room once when she wasn't home and sneaked a look at her finished books, thinking they would be filled with portraits of Tater, but they mostly showed trees and birds and the bayou. She did draw his hands, though, and included the tape on his fingers, the nails torn up from where he'd banged them against helmets. She used a lot of different colors to get his skin right. I saw browns and yellows and the rich undertone she'd once talked about that went into getting the color right.

"You never asked me where I plan to go to college," she told me one night.

"I didn't think I needed to."

"It's LSU."

"I'm glad, Angie. I'm sure Tater is too."

"Yeah," she said, stretching out the word. I thought that was the end of it, but then she said, "I wonder if LSU is ready for us."

I looked at her. "For you and me? Or for you and Tater?"

When she didn't answer, I knew the answer.

"I don't know, Angie," I said. "Baton Rouge is a city, but it's not the most sophisticated place in the world. It's still the South. It's also the Deep South. You won't be able to go out together without people gawking. Some will make comments."

"Let them," she said quietly.

"Let them? You want that?"

"Yeah," she said, and faced me now. "Let them."

The next day Pops said he wanted to see what they were up to at the park. I got in the truck and went with him.

He parked on Market Street in front of the pool house, and we walked past it and the pool and entered the woods that ran down to the bayou. At the bayou we left our trail and started for the barbecue pits. We moved from tree to tree, using the trunks for cover. I experienced a bump of déjà vu and recalled tracking prey with Pops on hunts in the Atchafalaya Basin. We didn't get close enough for them to see us, and what we saw were two silent figures sitting across from each other at a picnic table with schoolbooks open between them. A Coleman lantern—ours probably—stood at the middle of the table and burned a bright white light.

"They're studying," I whispered.

He didn't answer.

"Innocent enough," I said.

Even in the darkness I could see the color come up in his face. I followed him back to the Cameo along the same route, and once we got inside the cab he said, "That's your sister down there, Rodney," as if to challenge me to do something about it.

On the drive home I thought about those words—"*That's your sister down there, Rodney.*" And I understood that while I had seen Angie and Tater studying for an exam, Pops had seen his daughter out in public with a black guy.

She always returned home before supper, her lipstick fresh and her hair in place, her clothes in perfect order. She and Tater talked again later before it was time for bed. She called him from the kitchen phone. I once heard her whisper "I do too" into the receiver. But I never heard her tell him she loved him.

He still came by on Thursdays, and now he added Sunday to the schedule. He was mine the first day and Angie's the second. Mama had a rule against letting boys in Angie's room or girls in mine, so they sat in the living room and played records. He never held her hand, never kissed her, never so much as brushed against her. He never stayed late. "Thank you, Mrs. Boulet," he always said before leaving.

The more we saw of Tater, the less we saw of Pops. He put in longer hours at the plant, and on his days off he made more hunts and fishing trips. The freezer in the carport couldn't hold more fish and game, so he went from house to house in the neighborhood, giving it away. "No tomatoes till summer," he'd say, "but how about some rabbit meat for the winter stew?"

He found chores to tend to when he was home, most of them unnecessary. One day I returned from practice and found him on the roof brushing silver radiator paint on the vent stacks. "I don't know how to make him stop," Mama said.

But she, too, was allowing work to consume her. Debutante season was only a few months away and she accepted more bal masque commissions than she was capable of finishing. Bolts of fabric stood in the corners of the living room; lace and taffeta covered every surface. If you wanted to watch TV, you had to move the pile of dresses from the top of the Zenith.

I never heard Mama or Pops say a word to Angie about Tater. And only once did I hear them speak to each other about him. They were talking in their bedroom, and I was listening out in the hall, my ear close to the door. "When will it run its course?" Pops said. "When will it end? I swear I can't take it anymore." Sometimes I could see the pain in his eyes when we sat down to supper in the evening. And I saw it when we filed into Queen of Angels on Sunday and claimed our usual seats three rows from the altar. Once at mass Pops wasn't able to stand with the rest of the congregation and join the line to receive Communion. I would later tell Regina he seemed paralyzed.

"Are you okay?" Mama asked him on the drive home.

"No. No, I'm not. Are you okay?"

And all the while Angie was sitting there in back, her face turned to the window, even though her eyes were closed.

One evening when she wasn't home, Pops asked me to help him carry the hi-fi to her room. "I'm sick of hearing it," he said. In the weeks leading up to this day, Angie had removed the magazine clippings showing Leonard Whiting and replaced them with a large collection of newspaper stories that chronicled the football season, and many included photos of Tater in action. I found only a few that showed me, captured, as usual, in the inglorious throes of blocking for my quarterback. One headline, tacked to the gypsum board over Angie's headboard, had appeared in the paper earlier this week. TATER ON THE PROWL, it said.

"Makes him sound like an escaped convict terrorizing the community," Pops told me. "Gentlemen, lock your doors and load your weapons. And hide your little girls," he added, with what sounded like a laugh.

He led me out into the hall and pulled the door closed, then he returned to the living room and got on his knees and started cleaning the floor where the hi-fi had stood. We never talked about much outside of sports in their seasons. He could tell you the Astros' lineup and batting averages, he knew the team rosters for LSU and the Saints, he could ramble on about sacalait and bull bream. But ask him anything personal and he either became evasive or disarmed your questions with long silences that had you wishing you'd kept your mouth shut.

"I once knew this colored guy named Carnel Williams," he said.

"Who?"

"Carnel Williams. He worked at the ice plant. One night Carnel—" He stopped and waited until I was looking at him. "Do you want to hear my story, Rodney?"

"Sure, Pops."

"Well, Carnel goes out one night to the honky-tonk. He's got three other colored boys with him, and they get in a head-on crash on the way home. Carnel's trapped behind the wheel, and they pronounce him dead at the scene. The next day in the paper there's a headline on the front page: 'Local Man Killed in Automobile Accident'. It's a long story describing what happened, and you read all the way down to the end and find out that four Negroes also died. And you understand that, in fact, five people were killed in this wreck—the white man in one car, and in the other Carnel and his friends." He paused. "My point being, whenever you get to thinking that your old man is prejudiced, and whenever you wonder why I am the way I am, I want you to remember that story. It will give you some perspective."

"Why do we not like them, Pops?" I asked.

"You're not speaking for me when you make a statement like that."

"It wasn't a statement, it was a question."

"Who are we talking about, Rodney? Are we on Carnel and his friends or is it blacks in general now?"

"Blacks in general. Why don't we like them? Could you tell me?"

He gave no answer, as I knew he would. "I've stopped always looking for the differences, Pops."

"The blacks never did anything to me."

"Then why do you leave the house when Tater comes over? He walks over a mile to get here. He's always polite and respectful. He leaves early."

"What was the question again?"

"You've been leaving the house when he comes over."

"Have I?"

He also left our games before they were finished, disappearing into dark parking lots where he rolled cigarettes and smoked them, staring off at the sky. He wasn't there when we left the locker room at game's end, either. A victory gauntlet stretched from the stadium to the bus, but Pops never joined it.

I didn't mention these absences now. I felt almost privileged that he'd gone this far with me. He pulled a handkerchief from his back pocket and used it to pick up the husk of a dead cockroach.

"It's either an inherited thing or a behavior we learn when we're kids," I said. "It's one or the other. Which one would you say it is?"

"You've lost me, Rodney."

"No, I haven't. The way we automatically feel about them, without giving them a chance first."

"You'll need to go get the dictionary. What were my choices again?"

We moved a chair to the place where the hi-fi had been. I could see his biceps bunch up, then stretch out in bands. He suddenly seemed very old, like a person from another time. He could've been a character in a black-and-white movie that played on TV late at night when no one was watching.

Something in his face changed. His lips bunched up; a twitch came to his chin. He looked down at the handkerchief and seemed to be trying to decide what to do with it. "Everything is moving so fast," he said. "I try to keep up, I really do. But I feel like it's run me by. I stand there saying, 'Wait, wait, wait for me,' but nobody does."

"What kind of people are we, Pops?"

"I don't want your sister to throw her life away, Rodney."

"But it's Tater, Pops."

He'd fought with the 23rd Infantry Regiment at Heartbreak Ridge. On the top shelf of the closet he shared with Mama there was a wooden box filled with medals. But here he was now with tears running down his face and his son watching.

The cheerleaders continued to decorate the gym anew each week, and on Thursday they left messages in our lockers, wishing us well in the upcoming game. The messages were written out in crayon on slips of colored construction paper, rolled up tight and tied off with ribbons and stuffed into the ventilation holes in the cubbies at the top of our lockers. After Terrebone, Regina broke from the group's tradition of anonymity and signed her notes to me with a monogram.

After Sulphur, she drew hearts instead of stars and glued sprinkles on the hearts and shot arrows through them. She also added perfume. As a matter of fact, she added so much that my teammates ribbed me mercilessly about it, no one more than Rubin, who held Regina's scented note to his face, inhaled deeply, then staggered backward across the locker room, as if drunk and angling for a place to fall.

"I'll get you for that," I said to him.

Still stumbling, he came over and kissed the top of my head.

Not counting the games, the Friday pep rallies were my favorite part of the week. When we walked out on the gym floor as a team, the crowd hopped to its feet and greeted us with so much noise you thought the Plexiglas basketball goals were going to shatter. All the guys combed their hair, wore cologne, and kept their jerseys tucked into their jeans. Everybody was loose and goofing off the way it should be the day before the biggest game of your life. The principal and Coach Cadet gave speeches, then the senior team leaders got up and said a few words. Or most of them did. Driven to panic by the prospect of having to speak to a large group, I'd succeeded in avoiding that chore until our semifinal game with Brother Martin. Even though I'd told Coach Cadet I wouldn't do it, he introduced me, anyway, after announcing that Tater and I had been named consensus all-Americans.

The crowd was making such a racket that Coach couldn't hear me wailing in protest. Then Angie and another girl ran out and pulled me from my seat, and next thing you know I was standing on the little stage, looking out at bedlam. A bit of sickness seized my stomach, but I contained it somehow. And I managed to open my mouth and force words out, my impromptu remarks astonishing no one more than myself.

"We have God on our side," I announced like a preacher before his flock. But even as the spectators responded with a roar, I stood there wondering: Why would God choose us? Why would He favor a public school team over one from a Catholic school? Would He really prefer a crummy town like ours to a big, beautiful city like New Orleans?

"And with God on our side," I went on, "we can't lose. Remember I told you that." I pointed a finger at the ceiling as I walked back to my seat.

Dumbass.

Tater came next. He stepped up to the mike and had to wait for the cheering to subside and the crowd to sit down. His jersey was baggy on him, the number 11 cut short by the fat black belt at his waistline. He looked out not only at an audience of his schoolmates but of their parents and siblings, as well as supporters from the town and alumni swept up by our success. He cleared his throat.

"First, I'd like to recognize my offensive line," he said. "I can assure you I'd be nothing without the Bigfeet—Rodney and the rest of them guys. Second, I'd like to make a promise. This school has never won state as far as I know, but I promise you today that my teammates and I are going to change that. Nothing can stop us—nothing, you hear me? Come see us if you're not doing anything Friday night."

I'd heard more impassioned speeches from Tater before but none as effective. He hadn't guaranteed the title but promised it, and that was more like him, and exactly what they wanted—unfailing confidence with a touch of humility. A wild eruption followed, and up came the band with "Hold That Tiger." The rest of the team had been sitting in folding chairs on the gym floor, but now everybody rushed to their feet and charged him. And so did the crowd, spilling out to where he stood under hanging lamps decorated with orange-and-black streamers. Some of the guys hoisted Tater onto their shoulders and paraded him around, as if we'd already won. This didn't go over well with Coach Cadet, who commandeered the mike and announced that the pep rally was over and for everybody to report back to class.

"Don't hurt him, for God's sake," he said. "We need him. Please. *Please*. We need him."

We won by ten points, which put us in the championship game the next week. Afterward, Regina and I danced a slow one on the patio at the Little Chef. The metal overhang was strung with multicolored Christmas lights, and they warmed the top of my head as we moved across the floor. The weather had turned cold, and I removed my letterman jacket and draped it over her shoulders. The coat swallowed her up and reached down past her knees. And when the party ended, she left with it. In our world a girl wore your letterman jacket only when the two of you were a couple.

"Does that make it official?" Tater asked as we stood next to each other in the lot and watched Regina drive away.

I was too overcome to reply.

The next night I drove her to my grandparents' place and parked under the trees by the bayou in back. Regina was the first girl I ever kissed, and I understood at last what the fuss was all about. When we weren't making out, I told her stories about No Face, Bonepicker, and the Loup Garou, all local legends whose terrifying mythologies succeeded in driving Regina closer to me. The night was alive with ghosts, but we'd arrived at a place where neither of us was scared.

We kissed each other with such fierce and hungry abandon that the flesh around my mouth became desensitized. I was so happy that I wished the same happiness for my sister, and I was ashamed for standing in her way.

"When you're young," Regina told me, pushing my hand away, "there should always be something left to look forward to."

"When you're young," I repeated, certain that we would be so forever.

Two days before our game with Byrd, they met for the last time in the park. It was cold and the wind blew from the north, trapping leaves against the fences of the tennis courts and baseball fields and chasing off the bayou's usual odor of sludge and waste. They rummaged for kindling and downed branches and carried them to the open pavilion and made a fire in the massive pit. They dragged a picnic table close to the blaze and sat next to each other on top with their feet resting on the bench seat. Neither was wearing gloves. Tater opened his jacket and she put her arms inside and warmed her hands.

They were sitting together this way when an old car pulled up. Four young men stepped out, and then a fifth emerged from behind the wheel. It was Curly Trussell, who'd enrolled at one of the new all-white academies in town after his expulsion from our school. The blowing wind and crackling fire kept Angie from hearing Curly and his friends until they were "right on top of us," she told me later.

Dressed alike in school uniforms, they looked more like a debate team than a pack of hoodlums. Curly was holding a wooden club about eighteen inches long with rings carved on the handle. He walked up to within a few feet of where Angie and Tater were sitting and slammed the club against one of the wooden columns holding up the pavilion. The sound was like a shotgun blast, and it so frightened Tater and Angie that they jumped from their table and stumbled out into the grass. The boys followed them, and Curly slapped the column a second time.

"Who told you you could burn a fire in our pit?" the smallest of them said. "That's my pit." He pointed.

Angie reached for Tater's hand, and this brought Curly closer. He was standing in front of them now, and the four others formed a circle around them. Curly kept tapping the club against the palm of his hand.

"My pit, my park," the boy said. "What makes you think you're good enough? Because you play football? Oh, wow. He plays football."

Tater didn't respond, and Curly pointed the club at him. "How about it, my brother? Are you good enough?"

"Good enough for what?"

"For me to beat your brains in," Curly said. "Let's start there." He jabbed the air between them. "Good enough for Angie Boulet, then?" he said. "You good enough for some of that, my brother?"

"Yeah," Tater answered. "I think I am. But I'm prejudiced."

"He's prejudiced," Curly said to his friends. "Y'all hear that? The brother's prejudiced. How does that work?" He laughed even as his expression turned cold.

He seemed to be trying to decide which one of them to strike first, Angie or Tater.

It was at this moment that Angie cocked her head back and spat at Curly, catching him in the right eye. He lunged at her with the club raised, and she went at him, leading with her head and butting him in the middle of his face. Blood shot from his nose and mouth as he dropped to the ground and lay screaming at the feet of his friends. Angie picked up the club and offered it to the other ones—"Take it, come on"—but they backed away. She took a step toward the smallest kid, pretending to want him next, and he took off running for the car. The others carried Curly away.

After they were gone Angie sat with Tater in front of the dying fire. She cried and he did too, reminded once again what they were up against. There was a red mark turning into a bruise on her upper forehead near the hairline. Tater brought his face close to hers and inspected it.

"Does it hurt?" he asked.

"Yes, it hurts."

The skin hadn't broken and there wasn't blood. And I would barely notice it later at home when she covered it with makeup and combed over it with her bangs. Tater blew against the injury, then kissed it, his mouth barely touching. "Does it still hurt?"

"A little," she said.

He kissed her there again. "What about now?"

"No," she said. "Not now."

They waited for the cops to come with lights flashing and sirens wailing, but none did. They waited for Curly and his friends to return, but they didn't show either.

They stayed until the fire died down to embers and it was too dark to look for more wood.

We traveled to Shreveport in a pair of Greyhound Scenicruisers chartered by the booster club. Upperclassmen occupied the lead bus; sophomores and freshmen filled the rear one. Everybody wore navy sport coats with gray or khaki slacks and white shirts; neckties also were mandatory. The drive took nearly five hours, and Tater slept most of the way, his head tipped sideways on my shoulder. When he was awake, we played a Cajun card game called bourré.

We both used the toilet in the rear of the cabin, but we did so less out of necessity than curiosity. Neither of us had ever seen a bathroom in a bus before. We stopped in Alexandria for lunch at the Piccadilly Cafeteria, our only break and chance to inhale fresh air. There was a large parking lot in front of the restaurant, and after heavy meals of hamburger steak and seafood gumbo, we threw passes with a football while waiting for the driver to finish up inside. I got in line behind several other players and waited my turn, then with my tie flapping over my shoulder I jogged between queues of parked cars and caught Tater's pass, though not without bobbling it. To make sure everybody remembered, I slammed the ball against the asphalt and celebrated my pretend touchdown with a dance. I seemed to rate laughs and applause from everybody but Coach Cadet, who unceremoniously led me back to the bus by an earlobe.

In Shreveport the buses took us first to the stadium for a walk-through, then to the hotel where we would be staying the night. It was the Shreveporter on Greenwood Road, and Coach Cadet, who'd assigned two players to each room, had made Tater and me the only racially mixed pair. He handed out the room keys while we were still on the bus. "Either of you have a problem with this arrangement?" he asked. He was standing in the aisle, hand held out in front of him, keys lying side by side in his open palm.

"I don't, as long as Rodney agrees not to hog the bed," Tater said.

"It's not just one bed, Tater. It's two beds. They're doubles." Coach Cadet looked at me. "Can you handle a whole night with this knucklehead, Rodney?"

"I'm a team player. If it helps us win state, then I'll do it, Coach."

That evening we had a spaghetti supper on the hotel's dining terrace, and afterward Tater and I watched game film in our room, setting up the projector on a pile of phone books on one of the beds and throwing the light against a bare wall. Byrd's best player was defensive lineman Truman Millicent, the man I would be assigned to block. He was primarily used as a tackle in their base fifty defense, but he also lined up as an end in passing situations when his explosive speed off the snap made him a threat to sack the quarterback. Byrd's last opponent had tried to slow him down with double teams and help from the fullback, but Truman still recorded four sacks in the game. One sequence in particular would play over and over in my head tonight: Truman shucking a block, making quick work of the quarterback, then leaping to his feet and pumping his fists in the air.

"Dude's scary," I said.

"I bet he's saying the same thing about you."

"He's No Face and the Bonepicker rolled into one."

"Look at me, Rodney." I did as instructed. "You can handle him."

We cut off the lights at ten o'clock. But about two hours later, he and I were still awake. Visions of Truman had kept me up, but Tater had someone else on his mind. He rolled over on his side and faced me in the dark.

"I'm in love with her, you know?" he said.

I let a minute go by. "Yeah," I said, "I know."

Some guys for the other side liked to acknowledge you at the start of a game. You broke the huddle and stepped up to the line of scrimmage, and they greeted you like an old friend. Others glared and muttered and tried to intimidate. If they spoke coherently, it was almost always to reveal some recent moral failure on the part of your mother. Fewer still gave up nothing. Truman Millicent was one of these. He stood only a few feet away from me, but he didn't allow for eye contact. I wondered if he was shy. His hands rested on his hips, his heavily muscled biceps twitching like animals trapped under the skin of his arms.

"Good luck," I said, hoping to engage him. He didn't respond.

The whole time I stood there sizing him up, he was watching Tater.

It was freezing that night in Independence Stadium—the ground was frozen and so was the rain that swept across the field and sat in brown puddles on the crest. Coach Cadet had decided to defy the weather conditions and open the game with a pass, a call I believed would work until I dropped back in pass protection and felt Truman blow by me like so much wind. Swim moves to the outside had always been easy for me to handle, but the same move to the inside gave me fits. Truman would've picked this up on film. I thought I heard him laugh as he shucked me and dropped Tater for a nine-yard loss.

I'd gone the whole year without giving up a sack, and I'd forgotten how awful it made you feel. I was cursing so much I was lucky the refs didn't flag me for unsportsmanlike conduct. Refs can forgive some words, but they don't like it when you take the Lord's name in vain, even when you're shouting the insult at yourself.

Still straddling Tater, Truman swatted celebratory fists at the air. Lemuel Weeks, the guard who played next to me, ran over and pushed him out of the way, and then I helped Tater to his feet and pulled the grass and mud from his face mask. If you're playing hard, the words "I'm sorry" should never leave your mouth. But I did tell Tater that I wouldn't let it happen again. And by the look in my eyes he had to know I meant it.

We approached the line for the second play. "I hope you enjoyed your moment in the sunshine, Truman," I said and glanced up at the black sky dumping rain, "because it'll be the last time you touch him tonight."

Truman still didn't look at me, but he did speak. "Just shut up and play, Boulet," he said, pronouncing it "Bullet," which set off a whistle screaming in my head.

In his pregame speech in a cold stadium locker room, Coach Cadet had said the game tonight would be the one we remembered when we were old men looking back on our lives. But we'd run only one offensive play and already I had lost all awareness of a future or a past, and instead I was living the moment with such clarity and purpose that I felt like a wild beast without a mind to anything but its next meal.

Tater had called for a "strong left 71 option," which meant the play would develop right behind Lemuel and me on the left side of the line. Byrd was showing a five-man front, with a nose guard, two tackles, and two ends. T-Boy's assignment was to brush past the end and try to tie up the strong safety. Tater would then determine what to do with the ball by how the unblocked end played him. If the end went after the pitchman, who in this case was Jasper, then Tater would tuck the ball and run. But if the end's responsibility was the quarterback, then Tater would pitch the ball to Jasper. In either case, my burden was to make sure Truman didn't disrupt the play by penetrating the line. It had looked easy enough when Coach Valentine drew it up on the grease board in position meetings. But Truman was just a letter *T* in those diagrams, and in the flesh he was way more ball player than I cared to contemplate.

As Tater was calling out signals, I heard one of the linebackers calling out his own for the defense, and Truman shifted from directly in front of me to my right shoulder, shading the gap. Eugene snapped the ball, and I crashed down hard on Truman as he plowed into the space between Lemuel and me. Truman staggered back a step absorbing my helmet, my face mask striking between the seven and the nine on his jersey, then I steered him farther inside until he collapsed against the pile. Tater, meanwhile, had pitched the ball to Jasper for a seventeen-yard gain. As Truman lay under me, eating chunks of sod, I thought I'd educate him on the proper way to say my name. I removed my mouthpiece and smiled at him.

"It's Boulet," I said, emphasizing the French accent. "My ancestors came to this country from France in the seventeen hundreds."

He was silent except for a strange wheezing that might've meant he was having trouble breathing.

By the start of the second quarter, Truman's legs were spent and so was his will, and by the fourth, crusts of black blood rimmed his nostrils and his lips were dry and swollen.

"Boo-lay," I said every time I knocked him down.

"Bullet," he said whenever he got the better of me.

The weather and the field made it a sloppy game, and so did nerves. Most of the guys couldn't loosen up because they couldn't forget how much was at stake. Tater, usually so composed with everything on the line, kept putting too much on his passes and sailing them high. His runs had a schizophrenic quality in how he stacked moves on top of one another and made unnecessary cuts when taking an opponent head-on or blowing past him would've served him better. Going for broke when safe-and-steady was more in order, he threw an interception that Byrd returned for a touchdown. Trying to force other big plays, he fumbled twice. "Settle down, son," Coach Cadet must've yelled a hundred times from the sideline.

The score was 13–8, Byrd, with less than two minutes left to play when Rubin forced a fumble and we recovered the ball on our own 11-yard line. It likely would be our last possession, and a field goal wouldn't help. We had to get the ball in the end zone.

We tried three straight midrange passes that all went incomplete against Byrd's prevent defense, which had only three linemen rushing and eight others staying back to protect against the pass. Desperate to find an answer, Tater called for a time-out, one of two remaining. He usually consulted with Coach Cadet during time-outs, but now he remained with the offense on the field and gathered us around him.

"Let me ask you something," he said to Eugene Mistrot. "Are you good enough?"

I flashed to Angie and their encounter with Curly in the park.

The rain started to pick up, and Eugene looked off at a white curtain falling sideways against the lights. "You saying I'm not, Tater?"

"I'm asking if you are."

"Doggone right I am," Eugene said.

Now Tater reached across the huddle and hooked Louie Boudreaux's face mask with a finger. "What about you, Louie? Are you good enough?"

"Hell, yeah, I'm good enough."

Tater asked the same question of seven other players before arriving at me. He stepped across the huddle and got up in my face. I could smell his breath—a cinnamon scent, just like that day in the park years ago when I first felt compelled to protect him. "And you, Rodney? Are you good enough?"

"Ask Truman," I said without hesitation. "He should be able to tell you, if he can still open his damn mouth. Now call the play already. It's time to end this thing."

Done with interrogating us, Tater calmly walked over to the head official and told him to give us our last time-out. Then he jogged over to Coach Cadet on the sideline, eyes on Angie as he went. The rest of the cheerleaders were doing a cheer, but she stood without moving and tracked his steps.

He waved. She waved back.

Tater took a squirt from the trainer's water bottle, and Coach gave him the play before pushing him back out on the field.

"He wants the Hail Mary," he said as he stepped back in the huddle. "But I'm not sure."

We stared at him, waiting for permission to speak.

"Speak up," he said. "It's now or never. What do we do?"

Everybody chimed in at once. The Bigfeet were split on what to call, but Louie and the other skill guys wanted the pass. I waited until they'd all had their say before adding my own: "I think our only chance is for you to run it."

Tater looked up.

"Everybody's expecting the Hail Mary. But the ball's slippery and the field's a giant mud pie. Truman's been rushing to my left, sprinting hard, trying to get around the corner. Let him fly by me again, then cut it upfield between Lemuel and me. You'll be in space in no time. From there it's up to you."

He still seemed unsure. I extended my hand across the huddle, blood dripping from the torn knuckles. He took it in his.

"You can do it, Tater," I said.

At the line we calculated our splits and I lowered my left hand onto the icy sod for the last time that night. The rain ticked against the back of my helmet and dripped into my earholes. Tater's voice sounded hoarse and faraway as he called for the snap. And on the second *hut* I came backpedaling out of my stance, low in my haunches for optimum punching power, showing pass to seduce Truman. He did what I'd hoped he would. He shot the gap between T-Boy and me, and I made no effort to slow him down. He flew past me with the same laugh I'd heard to start the game, and he ran himself right out of the play. *"Boo-lay,"* I said, even with my mouthpiece still in. I knew he was done.

Lemuel had the Mike linebacker tied up, and Tater raced past them into open field. He was face-to-face now with defensive players who had no one blocking them. Cutting hard from a tight pivot, he made a cornerback miss low at his shoestrings, then he stiff-armed the free safety and powered past him. Next up was the Willie linebacker, who catapulted his body in Tater's direction and would've ended the game on the spot had I not arrived in time. I picked him off in flight, ramming my helmet into the knob at his crotch. Suddenly the field was a lot less crowded. I shook off the burn in my neck and went chasing after Tater, in case he needed me. But he didn't need me.

He moved from the left side to the middle of the field, water clapping at his feet with each step. I slogged behind him as close as I could but rapidly lost ground as he began to accelerate.

He juked out yet another would-be tackler who stumbled and slid into a clutch of photographers on the sideline. He juked one more, whose bellyflop shot a geyser in the air.

"Go," I heard myself saying. "Go, Tater. Go."

But his beautiful run ended. He was crossing Byrd's 20-yard-line when his right knee buckled and he started to fall. He might've been dropping from a great height, the way he pitched backward with his arms akimbo, and the ball coming loose in the moment before his body struck the ground. Did he intentionally fumble to keep the play alive? It was a question that would come up later when Byrd's coaches argued that by purposely fumbling the ball Tater had committed a penalty that should've nullified the play and ended the game.

"Rodney," Tater called out, which suggested he knew I was trailing him and would be there to gather up the ball. *"Rodney . . ."*

The football was spinning round and round in the mud, devouring time like one of those clocks in the movies that shows how fast a life goes by. I reached down and sucked it up in stride, my weight driving me forward. I tried to hold the ball against my chest, but it fought against me. I bobbled it, nearly lost it. Bobbled it again.

I glimpsed his face as he was trying to get off the ground, and I remembered the look—it was the one from weeks before at Eunice.

What now? I thought. *Do I turn back to help him? Would he want that?*

Byrd's fastest defensive players closed on me from behind. I had only ten yards to travel but the distance seemed to build with every stride. The first of them leaped on my back, the second tomahawked the ball. I hung on somehow.

Three of them clung to my back, and then Truman Millicent made it four. He hit me as hard as I'd ever been hit, and yet I kept my feet and carried him and the others into the end zone. The ref raised his arms to signal the touchdown, and I heard the crowd above the rain. I could've dropped to the ground now, but I didn't. I could've fallen over and had them fall with me. But I didn't.

Angie was first out on the field. Then came Coach Cadet, sloshing in the mud. More and more of them ran to Tater. I saw Miss Nettie and Alma, both wearing rain ponchos, the one pushing the other, the wheelchair carving tracks. And my own parents in parkas climbing down a stadium wall, Pops running not to Tater but to Angie, trying to intercept her, to spare her.

I thought Tater would want to know we'd scored and won the game, so I went to him with the ball. Somebody had already removed his helmet. I knelt beside him as a last hard tremor racked his body and a bubbling filled his mouth.

Answering an old call, I covered his body with mine and tried to shield him from the rain.

It took days for the Caddo Parish coroner to finally issue a statement attributing the cause of death to hypertrophic cardiomyopathy. We'd never heard of it; none of us had. But apparently young athletes around the country died from it every year, stricken when they'd seemed perfectly healthy, their lives ended when moments before they'd happily been engaged in playing ball.

I didn't completely understand the term until I looked it up in a medical book that Coach Cadet kept in his office. Thickened heart muscle, arrhythmia, sudden death—these were some of the words I read. Until then I'd thought Tater had pneumonia or the flu. Coach Cadet wrote the words out on a slip of paper and added Tater's name above them. He slid the paper across the surface of his desk. I folded it in half and put it in my wallet.

There had always been those who tried to dull the glory of Tater's blaze—the white guys who objected to his existence or his beauty, and the black one, his own brother, who couldn't abide his dreams and choices. But I never doubted that he would live forever. He was too important a person in the world to do otherwise. That it was his heart's fault seemed a joke to me. His heart, of all things. God, that was the best part of him.

"Pronounce it again for me, Coach."

"I can't, Rodney. I just can't." And now more sobbing, his face in his hands, the loud protestation of his office chair as he fell back in anguish.

I've kept that slip of paper ever since, even as I've changed out wallets over the years, discarding old ones for new ones. Sometimes before big games, in locker rooms where fear had my teammates in its grip, I held the paper in my hands and spoke Tater's name into the chaos and the silence, and this comforted me.

It was the black funeral home in town that finally brought him home. Not wanting him to make the long drive alone, players for Byrd's team followed behind the hearse in their parents' cars. Adding to the procession were more than four hundred people from town who returned to Shreveport and formed a caravan like the one that had gone up for the game. There were cars and vans and pickup trucks. And there were equal numbers of whites and blacks, burning their headlights as they tracked southward from the pine forests and red clay hills to the swamps and prairie. Some of the cars were still dressed with orange-and-black crepe paper hanging from antennae, the paper bleached of color by last week's rain. Others still had windows decorated with paint: GEAUX BOYS WIN STATE, PROUD PARENTS OF #53, TIGERS FOREVER.

I didn't make that trip, having decided to stay in town with Angie in a private room at the parish clinic on Market Street. After the game, and after a long night at a Shreveport hospital where they'd rushed him to no avail, I'd returned home with the team, while she had traveled with Mama and Pops in the Comet. She'd barely said anything at all, Pops told me later, and she hadn't cried. Instead she lay under a blanket on the car's backseat, shivering against the cold even though Pops had the heater on.

They arrived at Helen Street at midmorning and she went straight to her room and put on "her record," as Pops called it. Mama was down the hall by now, and Pops was sitting alone in the living room. From Angie's room came the voices of actors delivering their lines, as the volume was louder than usual, and the music from the movie was so gloomy, Pops said, he thought about going outside to escape it. But then he looked up and there was Angie standing in the kitchen. Her cheerleader uniform had dried tight on her body, and her eyeliner stood out against her light eyes and pale, freckled skin.

"You hungry, baby?" he asked. "Can I fix you something to eat?"

His voice seemed to startle her, and before he could get up from the couch she had walked past him and reached for the Chiang Kai-shek rifle that hung on the wall.

"Angie?" he said.

The gun wasn't loaded, but Pops was on her before she could swing the end of the barrel around and press it against her chest, which seemed to have been her intention. He grabbed the rifle with both hands and pulled it away from her. Even as she fought him, he thought he should lock it in the trunk of the Comet. He was carrying it to the carport when she ran past him and went for the drawer in the kitchen where Mama kept the knives.

"No, Angie!" he yelled. "Angie. No, Angie. No, Angie."

He knocked her to the ground and wrestled the knife away before she could hurt herself, but she fought him, he told me. He'd never seen someone so determined, and he was shocked both by her strength and resolve. "She really wanted to do it," he said, weeping at the thought.

An ambulance drove her to the general hospital, where they sedated her and she spent the night, then we moved her to the clinic. She stayed under for two days. And when she finally came to, she began to scream and to fight against her constraints, and they gave her something that knocked her out again. Orderlies moved a gurney into her room and placed it flush against her bed, and I slept with her now, my arm thrown around her as I used to do. I left her only to change clothes at home and to attend Tater's funeral. I lost track of time, but I think it was exactly a week after the game that we buried him.

Coach Cadet owned some plots in a cemetery on the south end of town. And he offered one to Alma and Miss Nettie, but they wanted to put him in the little graveyard down the street from the Baptist church where they worshipped. "His sister's there," Miss Nettie explained.

Little Zion couldn't accommodate the mob that came to wish him good-bye. Hundreds mourned inside the building, and a thousand more stood outside in the damp December cold. I saw Coach Jeune from LSU. I saw another college coach who'd recruited him and who'd come all the way from Los Angeles. Inside a modest pine coffin, Tater wore his game jersey with the number 11, the ball from the title game tucked between his body and right arm. Invited to give the eulogy, Coach Cadet faced the congregation and spoke off the cuff, his voice broken by crying. The doors and windows to the church were cracked open, letting his words reach the people outside. He said he'd never known a finer young man. He also said God must've really needed a quarterback to take ours away from us.

I was one of six pallbearers, an honor I shared with the four other starters on the offensive line and Rubin Lazarus. There were also some sixty honorary pallbearers, all of them teammates who walked in double file behind the casket, each with an orange rose boutonniere pinned to his lapel. We approached the old yard crowded with aboveground cement crypts and modest headstones, and from the street in front of the church came music. I had dismissed the possibility that Smooth would show up, but suddenly he came rushing at us from the crowd. "Tater!" I heard him shout.

Dressed in a suit and tie, hair cut short, he pushed his way through the mourners and lunged at the coffin. Rubin blocked his way, using his hands to subdue him the way he did offensive linemen, and soon other teammates were providing interference. They were gentler with Robert Battier than I would've been.

"Let me . . . let me *through*. He's my brother, I tell you. He's my brother, he's my—"

Then he was weeping in Alma's arms. Years later I would tell a friend, after describing the scene, that I couldn't figure out Smooth's behavior that day, but the truth was I thought I understood it at last. Having already lost everything, for years he had given Tater his jealous cruelty, and now he had run out of even that.

When the service was over, I drove alone in the Cameo to Tater's house. A portable table, loaded with food that people from town had sent, stood outside on the porch. Schoolboys in starched white shirts picked at platters of finger sandwiches and shooed the flies away with their too-long neckties. It was so crowded inside it was hard to move, and to my surprise the mood was more festive than somber. I briefly spoke with Alma and Miss Nettie, then worked my way to the bedroom where four or five kids were sitting on the floor. I had to duck to get through the door, and one little boy nervously laughed at the sight of me. "Big, huh?" I said. I waited for his nod, then I scratched under my arms like a monkey and puffed out my lips. "Me Sasquatch. Me . . . *hungry* . . ." And I unloosed a growl like that of a monster with an empty stomach and a meal in sight.

The boy ran from the room. Then the other children followed, racing out without a sound but for their shoes on the floor.

I had the room to myself now, and I noted that it had changed little since the day I first saw it. I wondered why at seventeen he would still share the room with his auntie, when the house had space that he could've claimed as his own. The photo of Bart Starr still hung over the smaller of the two beds, and on the nightstand between his bed and Miss Nettie's was a group of framed photos, among them the picture I'd taken of Tater and Angie standing in front of her blue-ribbon painting at the Yamatorium. I studied it a moment, trying to remember what she'd called it.

"*All Kinds,*" I finally said out loud.

Next to the photo was a cigar box with his name written in colored chalk across the lid. I opened it and saw a boy's personal effects: a tarnished tie clip, a shoe buckle, three or four vintage cat's eye marbles, a report card from first grade, old stamps from foreign countries, a broken pocket watch. A packet of photos caught my attention; I removed the ink-stained rubber band that encircled it and had a look. The photos showed people I didn't know and had never met—black people, all of them. The edges were stamped with dates. The earliest, stained red from juice or something else, showed a baby in a crib, and on the back the name TATUM scrawled in pencil.

Another photo depicted a girl in a spring dress, standing in front of a clapboard house. A bolt of light fell from a chinaberry tree and illuminated her soft, poetic face. Hair in pigtails, a broad smile squeezing her eyes closed, Alma was barely a teenager when the photo was taken. ME RIGHT BEFORE YOU AND ROSALIE, the notation on back said.

I returned the photos to the box and went next to a letter, folded in half, with Angie's handwriting across the face of the envelope. Inside there was a note on stationery scented with Crepe de Chine and written in the precise script that had won her penmanship awards as a girl. Taped to the page was the key to the pool gate—old Miss Daigle's key, never returned.

I want only this time, no other. It is our time. Let them talk about us, say what they want. Will you forgive me if I don't care? It's not our problem they don't understand. For heaven's sake, Tater, what I feel for you isn't invisible like the air! It's like this key or a tree or a door. It's real, it's a hard thing. . . .

Later, as I was trying to make my way outside, Miss Nettie sidled over and asked me how Angie was doing. I hesitated, and she pulled my head down toward hers and kept a hand on my face. Word had spread about the incident with the gun and kitchen knife, and I was relieved to have the chance to tell someone that she was doing better. "We can't help who we love," Miss Nettie said in a tone that almost sounded apologetic.

I wondered if she'd caught me digging around in the bedroom.

"At night when we went to bed," she said, "we always said our prayers first, and then we talked. He asked me if it was okay to love her—not as a replacement for Rosalie, but as a girlfriend. Well, I laughed at that. Can you imagine? I told him it was the nineteen seventies, he could do anything he wanted. And you know what else?"

She seemed to be waiting for me to reply. I shook my head.

"I told him love was something he never needed to check with me or anyone else about. Love didn't need permission."

She came up on her toes and brushed her mouth against my face, and I stumbled outside where the streetlights had come on and the little boys in church clothes were playing football on the blacktop. I watched them a while, then started for where I'd left the Cameo, when the ball came bouncing in front of me. I reached down and picked it up.

"Go long," I said to no kid in particular. And all eight or nine or ten of them went running in the opposite direction.

"Me!" they were shouting. "Me. Throw it to me."

"Longer," I said, and waved them on.

You could hear their dress shoes pounding the pavement and echoing between the houses. "Longer," I yelled again.

They were still running when I cocked my arm back and let the ball fly.

I draped my suit coat over the back of the chair and loosened my tie. I rolled up my sleeves and removed my shoes. I was relieving Pops, whose shift with Angie had just ended, and whom I'd hugged out in the hallway before sending him home. Angie's gown, pressed this evening by Mama's iron, seemed to glow in the room's dim light. I sat on the gurney and swung my legs over, and my effort to get comfortable woke her. She moaned and shook her head. I moved now to get out of the bed, thinking she would need water and pills, but she reached over and grabbed my hand. I settled back in but said nothing, in case she wanted to go back to sleep. Her eyes fluttered open, then closed again.

"Was it a dream?" she asked.

I lay there, looking at her. "Which part?"

"The one at the game where he fell down?"

"No," I answered. "No, I'm sorry, but it wasn't."

"That was real?"

"Yes, it was real."

Tears moved down her face, tracking toward her ear. I wiped them away with my thumb. "What about the part where he loved me?" she asked.

"Yeah, that one, too."

"That happened?"

"Yes," I said. "It happened."

★

CHAPTER FIVE

★

I live today in Vienna, Virginia, a suburb of the city where I spent the bulk of my pro career before my retirement from football in 1995. The old town where I grew up is eighteen hours south of my front door, and each summer since I left the game I have climbed into my pickup truck (yes, I still drive one) and made the trip home. The road is long, but it beats flying, and the hours alone are good for me. I listen to old rock stations on the radio or music from the sixties and seventies that my daughter, Rachel, a senior in comparative literature at the University of Virginia, burned for me on CD. I break the trip in half and spend a night in either southern Tennessee or northern Alabama, depending on how hard I push it. I rent a room by the interstate, eat a hot meal at Shoney's, and call Regina on my cell.

"My left leg down to my toes is tingling," I tell her. "It feels like sciatica again."

"You wouldn't be feeling that if you flew back like a normal person."

"Sasquatch is too big for planes."

The last time I visited the town was especially hard on me. More than forty years had passed since Tater's death, and I stupidly surrendered to a nostalgic impulse and made a tour of all the places he and I had known together. I started on West Landry Street and the site where the Little Chef had been. The restaurant and patio were gone, replaced by a large metal storage shed and a lean-to under which someone had parked a sports car. I stepped out and had a look around. The Palace Café hadn't changed much, but the Delta Theater had morphed into something called the Delta Grand. The picture-show marquee with its burning bulbs had been removed decades ago, and the old building, barely recognizable now, served the community as a rent-a-hall for wedding receptions.

You have to be a masochist to seek out moments with losses such as these. But there I was, trembling at the reality of all that was gone.

I drove down Market Street through South City Park, which people in the town now call South Park for some reason, perhaps in an effort to distinguish it from the place where a teenager could be assaulted for being a certain race. Activity at the tennis courts was as busy as I recalled, although now it was mostly African Americans swinging rackets in the yellow sunlight. I couldn't have survived a visit to the pool, but on a whim I walked the shell drive to the baseball fields. America's favorite pastime might've dipped in popularity in other parts of the country, but by all appearances it was still much appreciated here. The players, almost all of them, were black, and I wondered where the white children had gone. I leaned against the fence at the Babe Ruth League field and waited for a familiar face to come along. None did. The calls from the players were the same as those we'd made long ago, but as I stood there watching a new generation outfitted in bright nylon uniforms that made our old ones look like burlap sacks, I wondered if any of the boys had ever even heard of Tater Henry.

Later at the assisted-living facility where he lives, I asked Pops about the situation at the park. Dementia has purged his memory of some things, but on the important subjects he never wavers. "Oh, that changed a long time ago," he said. "The whites have their own baseball park now. It's not exactly a private league, far as I know, but there aren't many blacks. I haven't been in years, not since your mother and I took T. J. that time to show him how we do it here in the country."

T. J. is Angie's son, the eldest of her three children and her only boy. He's in medical school today in New Orleans, where Angie settled after college and met Tom Robinson, the man she would marry. Tom worked as an investigative news reporter until a scandal cost him his career. Although I've heard Tom blame the Internet for making him obsolete, the reports that accused him of fabricating quotes and had his editors issuing public apologies couldn't have helped. Luckily for all concerned, Tom's parents are old Uptown money, and Angie contributes with her modest earnings as a guidance counselor at Sacred Heart, a school for Catholic girls.

I have tried to like Tom. I have made an effort. But I drank too much at a party some years ago and called him a loser in front of Angie and their kids, and since then things have been strained between my sister and me. We speak on the phone only twice a year—at Christmas and our birthday. These perfunctory chats are beneath us, but the truth is they're all we have left.

"Does Angie ever talk to you about Tater?" I asked Pops.

"About who?"

He might've been eighty-four years old, but hearing wasn't one of his problems.

"Tater Henry," I said. "You remember Tater, don't you, Pops?"

The question accomplished one thing my appearance in his room had failed to do: He got up from his chair and walked over to where I was standing. "It's been years since she mentioned him," he whispered. "You could always ask her, Rodney, but I don't know if it's wise you do that."

"Still too hard, huh?"

"Too a lot of things," he answered. "For one, I don't think Tom would appreciate the question. Would you like somebody asking your wife about her past with a colored boy?"

"Don't call him that, Pops."

"What do you propose I call him, then? African American? Those people, I tell you. They change their names so much it's impossible to keep up."

"I don't think I'd care," I said.

"You wouldn't care about what, Rodney?"

"I wouldn't care if somebody asked Regina about an old boyfriend."

"Not even a colored one?"

"No, Pops. Not even that."

The old flame came up in his face again, and I understood that nothing would ever put it out. Bent at the waist, he shuffled over to his chair and fell back into a pile of fishing magazines. "How is football?" he asked.

"Good," I said, even though I hadn't played the game in eighteen years.

Nothing's really right there anymore without Mama, but I make these annual visits as much for my benefit as for his. I need to see him, need to hear his voice in person, need to smell the talcum powder he wears under his khaki pants and western-style shirts with faux pearl buttons. I still love my father, but I don't understand him any better than I ever did.

I suspect the day is coming when he doesn't know me anymore. For now, though, we have a great old time confusing each other. I drive him by the plant and show him how little it's changed, then I take him to Wal-Mart and buy him new artificial lures even though he doesn't fish anymore. We eat hamburgers and milkshakes at the fast-food joints by the interstate, and finally, after the silences have had their effect, our long handshake leads to a tearful farewell hug.

He stands waving good-bye at the lobby door, and I keep to routine and head out for a few last stops before leaving. I bring flowers to the graveyards and say the prayers I learned as a boy. Then I run by Helen Street and the little house that burned colors in the rain. Of all the stops I make, this one is toughest.

Pops sold the house once he could no longer keep it up, but the new occupants aren't any tidier. Today there's a dented aluminum bateau resting on sawhorses on the front lawn, and a kid in a sagging diaper digs with a stick in the dirt where Mama had azaleas. I sit with the engine idling, and I halfway wait for my sister to emerge from the carport door. I want her as she was at seventeen, striding out with her sketchbook and paint box, defiant of those who would deny her and too sure of their love to back down. But in the end the only person who shows is a beefy young mother brandishing a kitchen spatula to spank her kid with.

Tater and Angie. It's a sorry confession, but I've lost them both, the one on the field that night, the other to a destiny that wasn't meant for her.

"I know you," an elderly African-American man says to me at the Exxon where I've stopped for gas. Joubert's Esso is long gone, so I pulled over at one of those places with fifty do-it-yourself pumps and a TV playing commercials in each one. Dapper in a new seersucker suit, a doctor or a lawyer or some other professional, he stands at the pump next to mine, squeezing gas into a Lexus so new it still has temporary tags.

I smile the way I always do when a fan says hi. "Rodney Boulet," I say.

"Rodney Boulet," he repeats. They usually tick off highlights from my career now: LSU and the NFL, the seven trips to Honolulu for the Pro Bowl, the bust in Canton. But this old bird isn't that easy.

"You're Angie's twin," he says.

"That's right," I tell him.

"And how is Angie?"

"She's fine, last I heard." He seems satisfied with the answer, but

I suddenly miss her and feel a need to say more. "She was never the same after Tater died. It's like she died with him. The person we knew, anyway."

It's a morbid confession to make to a stranger, but he's kind enough to offer a sympathetic nod. I put the gas cap back on and return the hose to the pump.

"How'd you know Angie?" I ask.

"I didn't—not the girl," he answers. "But we all know the legend." Then he gets into his car and drives off.

What else can I say about Tater Henry? That he never lost a game as a starting quarterback? That the town honored him with a memorial parade that turned out more people than the ones for Mardi Gras and the Yambilee combined? That a photo of him, framed in gold plate, still stands on display in the trophy case at the high school?

For a long time I wondered what he might've made of his life—what he might've become, you know? It was the same question he'd once asked about his sister, Rosalie, and I was no better at answering it than he had been. I also tried to see Tater as an adult with Angie, the two of them happy together, making their way in a world more tolerant than the one we knew. But it was so painful an exercise that I had to stop doing it.

We go on. We don't want to and sometimes don't think we can. We almost hate ourselves for trying. But we do.